King1

MW01133863

Contents

Kingmaker

Book 12 in the Anarchy Series

By

Griff Hosker

Kingmaker

Published by Sword Books Ltd 2016

SWORD
BOOKS

Thanks to Simon Walpole for the Artwork and Design for
Writers for the cover and logo. Thanks to Kent and Julie, two of
my New Zealand readers, for giving me such an enjoyable time
in Wellington.

The setting for the books

Prologue

Stockton Castle

The defeat at Oxford still rankled with me. We had been close to success and claiming the crown for Henry FitzEmpress and then, after the disaster of Winchester, we had lost it all. The civil war had dragged on for too long already and the people were weary. For the land to grow they needed peace. That defeat meant we were as far away from success as ever. I had saved the Empress but it had been at a cost. In my absence, I had lost my oldest friend, Sir Edward of Thornaby and I was surrounded by enemies. With the Empress and her brother trapped in the southwest the prospect of defeating Stephen, the Usurper seemed even more remote. The only other sparks of rebellion against Stephen the Usurper had been extinguished. The Bishop of Ely's rebellion had been quashed and the unpredictable Ranulf, Earl of Chester had, once again, sided with Stephen. I was alone.

However, I had sworn an oath and I would not be foresworn. Henry FitzEmpress, the son of the Empress, would sit on the throne of England. His mother's opportunity had come and it had gone. We both accepted that she would never be Queen of England. In our occasional, sanitized correspondence we just spoke of advancing the claim of her son. When Stephen had all but conceded defeat in Normandy I hoped that this was the beginning of a time of success. After Matilda's husband, Geoffrey of Anjou was anointed Duke of Normandy, my hopes were dashed. King Henry and

I had fought against Count Fulk for many years to prevent that very situation. It was ironic that Fulk was now King of Jerusalem and Norman knights had given the Dukedom to the Count of Anjou.

Henry was now heir to the dukedom but that brought him no closer to his crown. Between my fortress in the north and the Earl of Gloucester in the south, Stephen held all. There were many leagues of England through which I travelled at my peril. I was frustrated in my northern stronghold. Although I had agreed to allow Henry to go back to Normandy I now regretted that. I would have had him by my side so that I could guide him and advise him. I was still convinced that I had a part to play in giving the throne to Matilda's son. When I received the unwelcome news that both Miles of Gloucester and Brian Fitz Count were dead my spirits were as low as they could be. They had been both noble and skilful leaders. They had been my hope that Empress Matilda might salvage something in the south-west and might begin to make inroads into the lands held by Stephen the Usurper. As word came that many other supporters had taken the cross and gone to Crusade I turned my attention to my position. Until I could do something about regaining the throne for Henry I would make my lands even stronger. We would not sit and wait for our enemies. We would seek them and bring them to battle. I was still the Warlord of the North and the Champion of the Empress.

In the year since I had returned from Oxford, I had not been idle. Alice, along with John, my steward, chastised me, albeit gently, for not resting more. My housekeeper was like a fretful mother hen. Perhaps she was right for I was in the saddle every day. I was not a lord who went hunting, hawking and enjoying the life of a noble. I was a warrior. I had been one since I had left Constantinople. Now, by my reckoning, I was forty-three years old. There were few in my position who lived that long. Battle and disease often took knights and warriors younger than that. Wulfric and Dick were the only two of my men who were of an age with me. The rest were the younger knights; they were the squires and the sons of the knights who had first fought for me.

3

My castle had become the equal of any in the north. The Scots had long ago learned to avoid it. I had chased away the de Brus family from their lands around Guisborough and I had a tight ring of well-defended castles around my heartland of the Tees Valley. We forayed out to snuff out signs that Stephen's supporters were encroaching on our land. There had been a time when we had just reacted to danger now we sought out the danger first.

I was no longer alone in my castle. I had taken Sir Edward's two children, Mary and James as my wards. They made it more like a home again. My two squires, Gilles and Richard, were now training James to be a knight. I had three squires. Soon I would knight both Gilles and Richard. They had proved themselves worthy more than enough. I needed the young James to be a better squire before I did so. He had still to get over the death of his father. He brooded a great deal.

I had hoped that James would replace my son who was lost to me for he lived in Normandy and now viewed Geoffrey, Duke of Normandy, as someone he would follow rather than his own father. As Henry FitzEmpress was also there that was doubly galling. My son's annual letter was so formal that I wondered if it had been dictated by his steward. I had more news from my castellan, Sir Leofric, who managed my estates in Anjou.

As I looked across the River Tees, on that summer morning I could not help but feel sorry for myself. I took myself across my bailey and out of my castle to visit the church. My wife and daughter were buried there. It had been so many years since they had been taken by the plague that I could barely remember what my daughter looked like. I knelt by their grave. The silence and the darkness helped to soothe me. As I closed my eyes I saw the face of my wife, Adela. Her voice drifted in my ears but her words were muffled. It was like listening in a fog. She was trying to speak with me but I heard nothing.

"I am sorry, Adela, I will clear my mind and then, mayhap, your words will come to me."

4

Kingmaker

The other place I found solace was Norton. That had been my father's manor. He had died and was buried there. Erre, one of the Varangian Guard who served me, was lord there now. One fresh morning, taking James only, I rode the few miles to Norton. As I rode my spirits began to ride. There had been a time when there had only been farms close by the two manors. Now the fertile valley was tilled by many farmers who felt safe and secure in my northern enclave. The farmers knuckled their heads and bowed as we rode past.

James broke the silence, "The people seem happy, lord."

"Aye, they are. A farmer is always happy if he can grow his crops and raise his animals without being raided and having them stolen." I smiled. It was the first in some time. "The fact that I do not overtax them helps."

"Why not tax them more?"

"I pay no taxes. I do not pay to Stephen and I do not pay to the church. We have many expenses. I maintain an army and that must be paid for. That is the only reason I tax. I take just what I have to from my people and augment it with coin from my enemies. We are lucky that we can trade with Denmark. There is conflict there too and their most powerful leader, Valdemar the Great, is grateful for both our iron and our weapons. Alf the Smith produces weapons that are much sought after. Their civil war means profit for us and we can use that to hire men."

He nodded, "John, the steward, tells me that he seeks out old, wounded warriors who once served you and he encourages them to come here. Why, my lord?"

"Our system is based on men serving a lord and a lord serving a king. It works both ways. If they serve us then we have a duty to protect them. Besides what better farmer than one who was once a warrior? It means we have farmers who can fight!"

Norton was just a large hall and church surrounded by a strong wooden wall and ditch. The motte was small but it was the river and the swamp to the north which protected the village. My manor to the south was close enough for a refuge. Erre and the last of his Varangians had little to do save provide reassurance for the farmers that there were

warriors close by who could fight. When I arrived, their
steward, Ralph, told me that they had gone hunting. I smiled
for it would be on foot. They would have gone to the woods
of Wulfestun.

"Thank you, Ralph, I came here to visit the church.
James, water the horses. Have a look around the manor. This
is the oldest one. Stockton is bigger but younger."

I entered the small stone-built church. It had been the first
building that William the mason had built. I could not see
the priest, Father Osbert. It did not matter. I had no need to
be shriven. It was not just my father who was buried here but
the men who had followed him from the east. Most had died
during an attack by the Scots. The ones who had died
thereafter had been buried in the churchyard.

I knelt and laid my sword across the tomb. The blue stone
set in the pommel of the sword had come from the sword of
the last Saxon king of England, Harold. My father had saved
it and bequeathed it to me. It was a connection both to the
past, my father and my namesake.

I spoke to my father as though he was still alive. I know
that there were priests who would frown on such things but I
was in a church and my father had died close by. "Father,
have I failed? I have tried to do that which I thought you
would have wished and that which I thought was right but I
have not managed to do anything I intended. What should I
do? Is it better to be the willow and bend with the breeze?"

There was silence. I listened for a voice in my head but
none came. The candles, burning above the altar, flickered a
little but that was not a sign; that was just the movement of
air. I stood, disappointed, and sheathed my sword. I still had
no answers. I stepped into the light. It was so bright it almost
blinded me.

"My lord, it is good to see you."

I looked down and saw Tom Lame Leg bowing before
me. He looked five years younger than the last time I had
seen him close to Lincoln. Then he had been close to death.
Now he looked hale and hearty. Two years of life in the
north had improved him. He now had a second chance of
life. A shy woman behind him also bowed.

"Good to see you, Tom. Life is good?"

He grinned, "Aye lord. This is Morag. She is to be my bride. I am here to see Father Osbert to arrange it."

I looked at Morag. She was not young and she was homely but her arm through Lame Tom's and the look she gave him showed me that they were both happy. "Congratulations. The priest is not here." I reached into my purse and handed him a silver crown. "This is for you and your bride."

He shook his head, "My lord, you have given me all, already! I have a farm, a horse and a sword all from you."

"And now you shall have a coin." I handed it to Morag, "Here Morag, you are not stubborn like this old warrior here! Take it!"

She took it and kissed my hand, "Thank you, my lord, and thank you for saving this man. He told me what you did for him and for me."

I frowned. I had never seen the woman before. "When did I help you, Morag?"

"When you and your warriors rescued us from the Scots. We lived at Hexham and served Sir Hugh. Had you and your men not come I would be a slave now. You fetched us to Stockton and I found work. When Tom here came to the market it was as though it was meant to be. You have given two of us a life, sir."

I nodded, "Then I am happy. I pray God grants you a happy and peaceful life."

Tom grinned, "Aye sir and children! I may be old but I can still sire warriors to fight for you."

Morag blushed and nudged him, "Tom! Whatever will the Earl think?"

I smiled, "He will think that he is grateful to have the two of you in my lands. God speed!"

I mounted my horse as Father Osbert came through the gate carrying bunches of fresh herbs he had collected. I waved and headed back to my home. I had had my sign. Until Henry became a man, I would just make sure that my land was still a haven for those such as Tom. I would build up my army and my finances so that I could afford to support

Henry when he was old enough to wrest the throne from Stephen. I would make alliances with those who could help me and make sure that any who were my enemies would fear.

Chapter 1

My ship, *'Adela'*, was the way I kept in touch with the world. The Empress sent letters to La Flèche. They would be picked up and brought home to me by her captain, William of Kingston. I would send letters the other way. If there was a letter from my son then it would come back the same way. It was Sir Leofric who was the most conscientious when it came to writing. He dictated to his clerk so that there was a full letter each time *'Adela'* docked. That way I knew exactly what was going on in Anjou and the wider world. It was how I heard of the deaths of those leaders in whom the Empress could trust. We were becoming fewer in number.

My cargo ship had a good crew who shared in the profits from our voyages. They also had a keen eye for new markets. It was they who told me of the civil war in Denmark and their need for both iron and weapons. With De Brus out of the way we now controlled the iron mines in the Eston hills. Sir Gilles of Normanby kept a close watch on those and he was supported by Wulfric of Thornaby. The bends in the River Tees meant that my sentries in the east tower could see her masts as she made her tortuous way from the sea. It ensured that John, my steward, and I were there at the quay to welcome him.

John was in good spirits. "More profit sailing down the river, my lord. Perhaps we should think of building or buying another cog?"

"Commerce is your business, John. You handle the purse strings. So long as I have enough coin to pay my soldiers then I am happy."

"Then I will have the shipwrights begin work." He rubbed his hands as though the money was in our purse already. "Ethelred has said he wishes to go into business with us and he is keen for his own ship. We can enter a partnership with him."

In the last few years, we had found skilled men seeking work in our valley. The lack of taxes and relative peace and stability were both important. The river, apart from Ethelred's ferry, had been underused. When Ethelred found the five shipwrights seeking work he saw an opportunity. He built them a yard just downstream from his ferry and had huts built for them by our eastern walls. With more men wishing to fish both in the river and out to sea then it became a thriving business. So far they had not built a cog but John was confident that they could build one.

"We need to take advantage of the lack of order further south, lord. The uncertainty of this anarchy prevents growth. These opportunities only come once."

I liked John but I did not enjoy speaking with him. All was about coin and profit. I preferred speaking with my knights like Sir Harold and Sir John who were both riding my lands and their borders to keep them safe. I listened to John but I spoke with the others. That was the difference.

Richard, Gilles and James joined me. They were dishevelled for they had been practising. James was a raw talent. He had his father's build and natural ability but he needed his skills to improve. He could ride and he could fight, after a fashion. What he could not do was fight on the back of a horse. He needed to do so well and so my two squires spent every waking moment with him.

"Do you think the war is really over in Normandy, lord?" Gilles's father had been Norman and I had taken him, the only survivor from his whole family, under my wing.

"Count Geoffrey is now Duke of Normandy so it is no longer our concern. Perhaps Sir Leofric will enlighten us."

The letter from my castellan was as important to me as the cargo the cog carried.

James was excited. I could see it as he leaned on the wooden rail eager to catch the first view of the merchant ship. His father had not spent as long with his youngest as he had with his elder brother, John. Now James was receiving more attention and it showed. He had not forgotten his father and his brother, no man did that, but he was realising that he had a life and he had a future. Instead of falling into a pit of despair, he had risen to a world of hope.

Richard said, "I expect Gilles will be hoping that the cog brings some of those oils from the east so that he can smell better."

I turned and looked at my squires. Gilles had reddened, "What is this?"

"Nothing, lord! I shall box Richard's ears later."

James laughed. He was the youngest of the three and his laugh was still that of a child, "It is my sister. Gilles is sweet on Mary."

I saw, from Gilles' face, that this was true. It was to be expected. They were close in years and both attractive. "You two behave as my squires ought or get yourself hence."

"Yes, lord!" They both looked down the river.

I winked at Gilles who gave me a wan smile. I would speak with him later.

John rubbed his hands. "She is well-laden! I asked him for as much wine as William could manage to carry. We sent more barrels over to Anjou when he set sail this time."

"Barrels?"

"Yes, my lord, there were too many breakages when we used jugs. If we use barrels then we can put them in jugs ourselves. Despite the fact that York is closed to us we do a brisk trade in wine with them. The loss of Normandy and Anjou means that the Norman who dwell there are desperate for wine."

He had more ways of making money than I could even contemplate. He was good for the manor, however, for I had the best armed, armoured, supplied and trained men at arms and archers in the land. My archers were the elite in a land where the bow was still the deadliest weapon on the battlefield. It had won me a battle more times than enough.

"It is good to be home, my lord!" William of Kingston shouted when the cog was still forty paces from the shore.

John said quietly, "He took a wife a year since, lord. Harold the rope maker's daughter. They live on this side of the ox bridge where they have a rope walk. She is heavy with child."

"Thank you, John." I had missed much in my town. It was no wonder that William made such swift journeys. He was eager to be with his wife. I began to feel guilty for sending him on such errands.

My sentries caught the thrown lines and tied the ship to the stone quay. William leapt ashore and gave a slight bow, "A good trip, my lord and I have letters for you."

I resisted the temptation to ask if any were from my son or the Empress. "Thank you, William."

He hesitated and then asked, "Am I likely to be needed to sail soon, my lord?"

I smiled, "Not for me. I am happy for you to be with your wife but John here holds the purse strings."

John gave a wry smile, "I am sure we can manage seven nights for you!"

"I would have given you fourteen!"

John said, "Let us split the difference, my lord, ten!"

Although I was desperate to read the letters, bound in an oilskin, which William handed me, I also needed to get his news. He was our eyes and ears on the world.

"There is unrest in the counties north of Normandy, lord. The counts of Holland, Brabant and Hainaut are in dispute with the Count of Flanders. They each seek cities to take from the other. The alliances are shifting since France made peace with Normandy. If there was no civil war in Denmark then I think that whoever was king would take advantage of the situation."

"How goes the civil war in Denmark?"

"There are four contenders. King Erik the Lamb is still the king but it is in name only. Sweyn, Canute and Valdemar are all more powerful. You were wise to trade with

Valdemar for I think that he will win and besides he is the most honourable."

We had almost reached my gates. "And to whom do we sell our iron and weapons?"

William looked at John and then back to me, "We just sell them to merchants in Edjberg. It is on the west coast of Denmark and is easy to get to. It is a good port and well protected. Their king lives on the east coast at Hedeby. It would take many days to reach it."

We reached my inner bailey and I could tell that he was uncomfortable. I put his mind at ease. "I meant no criticism. It is not our civil war and we are right not to be involved. As Christians, we do not like to profit from war but we must survive."

He looked relieved, "The profits are great, lord, although I think the merchants we sell them to make even more. They are more than generous to us when we arrive and vie for my business."

John put his arm around my sea captain, "Then before you rush to the arms of your wife we must go through your manifests."

He rolled his eyes, "I think this must be the price I have to pay to have ten days with my wife."

I smiled, "So it would seem, William. I would have you bring her to meet with me. John, invite the captain and his good lady to my table." He nodded and I added, "But not tonight eh?"

Once in my hall, I waved a servant over, "Roger, have Alice send me some wine, cheese and bread. I will be in my solar."

"Aye lord."

As I turned I saw my three squires, "And I have no need of you three but I fear you have need of water, soap and a comb. Go!"

My solar faced south and west. It afforded me a fine view down my valley. It was a place of calm. I was about to enter when I saw Mary approach. In the corridor, I could hear the bantering voices of my three squires. She looked wistfully at them, "What is amiss, Mary?"

She brightened a little, "Oh nothing, my lord. Save... nothing."

I put my sealskin package on my table and beckoned her over. Putting my hands on her shoulders I said, "When your father died and you became my ward I told you then that I would be your mother and father. Tell me what troubles you?"

She buried her head in my shoulder and began to weep. Between sobs she spoke, "I am grateful that you have brought me here and I want for nothing but..." She looked up. "James has the other squires and I am left alone. When you are busy then I rattle around this castle. I miss my mother. Alice is kind and she does all that she can, however, your household demands much of her time. I sew and I try to keep myself occupied but... "

"But you need a companion." I nodded. "I have been remiss and I apologise. I am a gruff old soldier who is used to the ways of war and not the ways of women." I pointed up. "My wife, Adela, would have chided me."

"Oh no, lord!"

"She would and I will address the matter. Now promise me that you will not hide your pain beneath your brow. You will tell me all. I am not such an ogre am I?"

"Oh no, lord, you are the kindest of men and I am being foolish."

"You are not. You are a young woman who is now orphaned." Alice appeared with a servant and a tray. "Now go and wash your face. You should smile and not weep." She curtsied and hurried from my hall.

Alice followed me into my solar and when the servant had laid down the tray dismissed him. "Is there anything I could do, my lord? I have seen her lonely but she is a lady and I am but a servant."

"You are more than that, Alice, and we both know it. My wife would have known what to do." I tried to think back to the times before she had died and before we had had William. "I will try to get some of the girls of the town to come and spend time with her."

"Girls of the town, lord?" Alice sounded outraged.

I smiled, "John of Stockton married Alf's daughter did he not? Besides, I think it would be good for all of them. I will visit with my burghers and invite a selected few."

Alice nodded and then brightened, "I have an idea, lord. I am handy with a needle and I know that the Maid Mary is too. Perhaps we could make a tapestry?"

"That is a most excellent idea. Have you the materials?"

"We have a bolt of cloth and some thread but, perhaps William could trade for more. I know that the women of Holland and Hainault are renowned for their needlework."

"Where did you hear that?"

"John, your Steward, and William of Kingston were speaking of it as I passed."

"Then we will do that. It will be good to have the sounds of women's voices here once more."

As I sat down I reflected that since Harold had gone back to his home in Hartburn and John had taken over the manor of Elton the castle had been empty. Tristan now lived in Yarm and the three families had brightened my life. Perhaps that was why I was in such a sour mood of late.

I laid the three letters before me and took a sip from the wine. It was not the new wine. That would need time to settle after the long journey. This was the last of the wine we had brought back when last I had been to Normandy. That seemed like a lifetime ago.

I recognised Leofric's hand and that of the Empress but the third I did not. Its strokes were larger. I turned it over and saw it bore the seal of Henry FitzEmpress. He had not written to me before. I opened it and read that first.

Rouen,

My Lord Cleveland,

As you must know by now my father is now Duke of Normandy. I wished you were there when he was anointed but there was no time. As the war in England is at a standstill I would beg of you to visit with me. You have yet to finish my training as a knight. I pray that you can come. Your son is now at

court and I am certain that he would like to see his father. He often speaks of you.
   Your former squire,
   Henry FitzEmpress
   Marquess of Caen

I put the letter down. It was ironic that the son I could never acknowledge was the go-between for my lawful son and myself. I re-read the letter. Should I go?

I laid it down and took the one from Leofric. I was not yet ready for the Empress' words.

La Flèche
My lord,
I hope this letter finds you well.
Your manor prospers and we have had both good crops and large numbers of animals being born. Your tenants prosper and the manor grows. I have sent my steward's accounts to John so that he may approve them.
I now have another son. God has granted us a healthy baby. I gave money to the church to have a new altar built in celebration. Our land is prosperous now that peace is here and it is right that we give thanks to God.
Now that the war is over in Normandy there are many warriors seeking employment. I have twenty such here now. We cannot afford to keep them all nor do we have need of them but I will send the better ones to you should you need them.
How goes the war in England? We hear little in Anjou. The little I do know suggests that you are the

*rock in the north while the Empress has her lands in
the south-west. Will this anarchy ever end?*
   Your servant and castellan,
Leofric of Stockton

An idea began to form in my mind. I was lucky to have
such a loyal knight as Leofric watching out for my interests
in Anjou.

The last letter had the most familiar hand of all, Matilda,
Empress and now Duchess of Normandy.

Devizes
My Lord,
   **The news that my husband is now Duke of Normandy
gives me hope that, perhaps, our fortune is changing. The
loss of Sir Miles and Sir Brian has cut us deeply and you
are now the rock in the north.**
   **My brother and I have the lands hereabouts secure but I
have heard disturbing news that the Earl of Chester is
contemplating siding with the King once more. If he were
to do so then it would put us in a difficult position. Since
the defeat of the Bishop of Ely and Geoffrey de Mandeville,
we have not had a victory.**
   **I am being put under pressure by the Pope to relinquish
this castle of Devizes. The Bishop of Salisbury supports my
cousin and he has entreated the Pope to have it returned to
him. If I had to leave here I would be in a very difficult
position. I am not certain that I could remain in England.
My brother is a comforting presence.**
   **I am just grateful that I have such a loyal friend and
knight as you. You are ever my champion and so long as
you live then there is hope that my son may one day
become king but I think that is in your hands rather than
mine.**
   Your friend,
Maud

Was I being asked to visit with her? I did not know.
Ranulf, Earl of Chester was a snake but I dared not

intervene. He had yet to change sides, and any move from me might drive him into the court of the Usurper. The invitation from Henry was tempting. My lands were safe, for the moment, and there appeared to be little to threaten us. I knew, from my conversations with Stephen the Usurper, that he respected me. Perhaps he even feared me. The last thing he would do while I was quiet would be to poke me. A roused warlord would hurt his control of the north. The taxes he took from the lands around York allowed him to be generous. As I sipped my wine I began to formulate plans. For the first time since the flight from Oxford, I saw some light in this dark tunnel of intrigue and politics. Henry was the future not only for me but also for England. It hurt me to think the thoughts that trickled through my mind but the Empress could do no more. Once the people of London had rejected her then she was a lost cause. By her own admission, she might leave England soon. That would be a mistake in my view.

After I had reread the letters and finished the jug of wine I went to my chamber to secure the letters in my chest. I had had Alf make me a lock for it. I trusted my own people but we had visitors and some of the letters contained delicate information. Alice met me in the corridor. "Alice, I have invited Captain William and his wife, Morag, for a meal. It will not be tonight but it will be tomorrow."

She smiled, "Good. The table is a little bare with just the five of you around it. We need company. Poor Mary has to endure the talk of men. It is all about war."

"Just so. See to it." I left my hall and headed for the town. It was a bustling and thriving place now. The industry was to the east of the town, closer to the sea. The winds normally came from the west and it took the smell away. On the odd days that it came from the east and we had to endure it the older folk said it was a punishment from God for some misdemeanour. Poor Father Henry had spoken to them but they still clung on to their superstitions. Many still kept the remnants of paganism in their hearts.

I first visited Alf to tell him that his weapons were highly prized in Denmark. As I passed his hall, now a grand two-storied manor house which put Harold's to shame, I realised I had no need to do so. Alf had put his profits to good use. His smithy had grown from a single forge and anvil to a veritable hive of workshops. He had his two sons working as well as five other smiths whom he had taken on. One was a smith who worked in gold and silver. That was a clear sign of our prosperity. It was no wonder that so many people flocked here. In a land riven by strife and disorder, my manors were a haven of peace and security.

"Alf, I see you are enjoying the fruits of your labours."

My smith was sitting and watching his sons work. He stood, "It is why we have sons, my lord, so that we can enjoy the rewards of their work."

I laughed. "Your weapons and farm implements sell well. We are all rewarded."

"It is thanks to you, lord. Before you came here this was a huddle of mean huts now it is the most important place between York and Durham. Some would say more important."

I went closer. "I may be going away again but this will not be a long trip."

"You are entitled to go to the outside world, my lord. Since you returned from Oxford you have not ceased in your labours and we all appreciate it."

I nodded, absent-mindedly, "Tell me, Alf, your daughter has now left to live with Sir John at Elton but are there other young women of the town who are of a similar temperament?"

"If you mean ladies, my lord, then I pray you to speak plain."

I smiled, "I do."

"There are one or two. All the women and the girls have good hearts but they can be a little..."

"Unrefined?"

He picked up a piece of rough silver ore. "A little like this. Of great value but hiding its true qualities until it is changed. Aye, there are some. Why do you ask, my lord?"

19

"The Maid Mary of Thornaby has few companions. I would have one or two spend time with her at the castle. It will help her and, I daresay, they will enjoy the experience."

He nodded, "I have three in mind, my lord. I will present them to you after church on Sunday."

"Thank you. I would not offend any."

"Nor will I! I have been married long enough to know the pitfalls of speaking too plainly to women!"

As I approached my main gate I saw Leopold of Durstein. He was planting four heads on the spikes we kept there for just such a purpose. Sir William and his archers were walking their horses through my gates.

"Where did you find them, Dick?"

"They were north of Thorpe, my lord. William of Wulfestun alerted us to their presence. Aiden and his scouts found them for us. I would have brought them back for trial but they fought. You do not try to capture a dangerous animal. You kill it."

"Are they Scots?"

"No lord, from their tongue they were English. Brigands and bandits I think."

"Good." Brigands were a nuisance and not a serious threat. Had they been Scots I would not have dreamed of leaving. I beckoned him closer. "I may take a trip to Normandy on the *'Adela'*. I will not be away for long. What say you?"

"The land is as safe as it had been for some time and we will not make the same mistakes that were made before."

"You mean Sir Edward?"

"It does not do to speak ill of the dead but aye." He handed his reins to Aelric. "And who would you take?"

"Just my squires. Sir Leofric has some new men at arms and with the war over I do not need protection. It is my valley which does."

"Will your son be returning with you?"

Dick had been with me since before William was born. He knew my son well, "I think not. He has chosen to be a Norman knight just as I chose to be an English one."

"I miss him, lord."

"As do I, Dick, as do I."

I looked at the sun. It was getting late and I headed into my hall. When I reached it I saw Gilles sitting there along with Mary. They were not speaking but I could see, in both their faces that they wanted to. They just did not know how. I decided to be the bridge.

"Mary, Alice, and I have arranged for some of the young women of the town to come here on Monday next. I have a mind for a tapestry and Alice said she would help you to sew it. I know you are skilled with the needle. What say you?"

She beamed, "That would be good, my lord. What would be the subject of the tapestry?"

I confess I had not thought of that. My heart said it should be something which showed the courage of my father and the housecarls who had fought for King Harold but I knew that was a politically sensitive matter. Then it came to me, "How about St. George and the dragon?"

"St. George and the dragon, lord?"

"Yes, Mary. It is a legend from the east where I grew up how a knight rescued a maiden from a dragon and slew it. He became a saint."

Her face lit up. "I would like that. A dragon would be exciting to sew but the thread would be expensive."

"Do not worry about the cost."

"And the knight, would that be based on you, my lord?"

I laughed and shook my head, "No that would not be right. You need a young knight for this." I pointed to Gilles, "Use Gilles as your model."

They both brightened at that. "I will use some charcoal to try out some ideas. Would you help me, Gilles?"

"Of course. With your permission, my lord?"

"Of course." For the first time in a long time, I felt that Adela would have been proud of me.

The next morning, I was up early with my squires. I told them about the possibility of a journey to Normandy. Although they were all excited Gilles was the least excited. While Richard worked with James I spoke with Gilles.

"I said nothing yesterday, Gilles, for it was not the right time but your interest in Mary..."

"My lord, that was Richard! He and James were just
being foolish."

I looked at him and he averted his gaze. "Do not lie to
your lord, Gilles. It is not what I expect of you. I saw you
and Mary yesterday and I know the truth of it."

"Yes, my lord, I am sorry. You are right."

"I do not object but she is my ward. I have to ask you
what your intentions are for Mary is a maid."

"I know, lord and... I know not." He shook his head, "I
like her and yet I fear to speak to her for compared to her I
feel like a barbarian. She is a lady."

"Aye, she is but her father was as lowly born as were
you. You are now a squire and a gentleman. In time I will
knight you. So I ask you again, what are your intentions?"

He took a deep breath, "I would court her."

I smiled, "Good. I think that this is right. Try to speak to
her. She is of your age and there will be much you have in
common."

"May I tell her we are going away?"

"After I have announced it to others, of course."

That evening both Mary and Gilles went to great lengths
to look their best. When Captain William and his wife,
Morag, arrived, they too had made sure that they were
wearing their finery. Morag was lucky. Her husband's travels
meant she had better clothes than the other women of the
town. It was the first time I had met her and she was pretty.
She was also of an age with Mary, which surprised me for
William of Kingston was in his thirties.

Morag bobbed a curtsy, "I am honoured, my lord. That
the daughter of a rope maker should be invited here, to your
table, is beyond my wildest dreams."

"You are welcome for where would my captain and his
ship be without your ropes? And where would the town be
without the trade he brings?"

I had invited John the steward as well and it was a merry
company. Morag chattered like a magpie and I saw William
of Kingston becoming embarrassed, "My love, you do not
need to speak all the time."

She looked around and realised that she had been the only
one talking, "I am sorry. It is just that all of this is so
exciting! All of this…" she swept her hand across the table.

Richard said, "But we are just eating venison! What is
exciting about that? There is nothing special about it."

Mary admonished my squire, "Richard, sometimes you
ought to think before you open your mouth. Do you not
know that venison is reserved for lords? Men can lose their
hands or eyes for poaching."

"But not here, Maid Mary. My lord allows some men to
hunt for he wants none to starve."

I nodded, "Gilles is right but few men have the skill to
hunt deer. Do you enjoy the taste?"

Morag was not put out by the comments, "I did not mean
the meat, my lord, I meant the room, the linen, the knives,
the goblets. It is like a palace."

I saw both Mary and Gilles smile. Morag was without
guile. I nodded to Mary who began, "I do not know what
your skills are with a needle, Morag, but while your husband
is away the Earl has asked me to sew a tapestry for his walls.
If you could help me I would be grateful."

Her hand went to her mouth and I thought she would
burst into tears, "Me, help you, my lady? Of course and you
need not worry about my skills. When you make ropes for a
living you have nimble fingers. Oh, how exciting is this?"
She patted her rounded belly, "Of course, the baby will
inconvenience me for a short time but..."

Mary was shocked, "Do not worry, Morag! The baby is
more important!"

Morag tucked into her venison, "My sisters have babies,
my lady. So long as they are fed then they sleep most of the
time. I will still be able to work!"

I smiled at William, "Your wife is a force of nature,
William."

"It is why I married her, lord. It is now a joy to come
back from the sea. I am a happy man."

"Good. On your next voyage, you will have four
passengers. I take my squires to Normandy and Anjou." I
looked over to John, "We will go to Anjou first and then

Rouen. I am invited to the court. I will keep William and the ship with me so that we can sail home. I do not wish to be stranded in Normandy."

"I will arrange the cargoes accordingly."

William said, "There is a new port where we might trade, lord. North of the port of Brugge is the County of Hainaut. They have a new port there, Antwerpen. It is small but growing. It serves the County of Hainaut. When I was in Denmark I met a captain from there. He said it might be worth our while to trade with them. Their Count is Baldwin and he is keen to enlarge his territories and to steal trade from the Flemish."

"We have fought the men of Flanders before. Perhaps we will. You had better make sure that Alf has plenty of trade goods. We do not want to disappoint them." John would be happy about the trade. I was happy for the alliance. Who knew when an ally to the north of Flanders might not be useful?

I glanced over and saw that Mary and Morag were busy in their own conversation. The smile on Mary's face was more than welcome.

The evening was a great success. Not only did Morag and Mary become great friends but Gilles managed to speak with Mary. They both looked happy. I felt content. It was not war and it did nothing to regain the land for the Empress but I had begun to make two young people happy. I knew that Adela would be happy.

Chapter 2

We left twelve days after the feast which had filled me with such hope for the future. The delay was my doing. I had to visit with all of my knights and tell them my plans and my news. The last time I had left I had almost lost my lands. I had learned my lesson and I gave clear instructions to each of them. There would be no repetition of the disaster which had almost destroyed my land the last time I had been away. This time I appointed Wulfric to watch the east and south and Harold and Hugh of Gainford to watch the west and north. Sir Edward had let me down and paid for that with his life. My knights had also appreciated the potential danger of laxity and would be vigilant.

Mary now had three women to help her to sew my tapestry. Alice acted as a sort of mother figure, organising the young woman, and Mary seemed much happier when I left. She and Gilles were closer for he had had to pose while she made drawings of him on the canvas. The two girls from the burgh giggled at Gilles' embarrassment until Morag shut them up. As we left the River Tees on the tortuous journey to the river I joined him at the stern. He was staring west as though he could still see Mary.

"She will forget me, lord! When I come back she will not know me!"

"We will be away a month, perhaps two. I am sure she will not. Besides, when you are a knight you will not have a choice. If your lord tells you to campaign then you will do so."

"Is that how all armies work, lord?"

"No. Your father, for instance, left my service to go back to Normandy and he hired out as a mercenary. Some men like that life. Sir Edward and Sir Wulfric were hired swords for many years. You can choose a leader and if he is successful then you stay with him. If not, you leave and go to another. Your father decided that his family was more important and he left his paymaster."

It took many hours to reach the sea. When we reached the seal colonies I knew that the sea was not far away. As we passed the Nab of Eston the wind took us and we headed into bigger waves. Gilles and Richard laughed at poor James who had never been to sea. He had a gruelling day and a night until the winds lightened and our motion became easier. He was green and had nothing left in his stomach to bring up. "Is it always like this, lord?"

"Just the first voyage and then you will find your legs. Keep watching the horizon and when they bring around food eat some."

"I could not!"

I laughed, "Then I will order you to do so."

William kept us to the middle of the German Sea. There was danger from ships loyal to Stephen along the English coast and there were still raiders who came from Norway and Denmark. There were fewer of them but Vikings still existed and would race out with their longships to snatch unwary travellers. We kept a good watch. William had plenty of bows and arrows aboard as well as hatchets and short swords. His crew were warriors all. They could handle themselves in a fight.

As we neared Dover I took to wearing my mail and coif while carrying my sword. If my enemies knew I was abroad then they would risk dashing out to take me. Without my archers and men at arms, I was vulnerable. As we cleared the narrow straits I breathed a sigh of relief. We still had dangerous waters to navigate but we had sea room to escape any danger. Opposite Dover lay Calais, and Thierry of Alsace, the Count of Flanders, was no friend of mine either. The relief of passing his coast was offset by the seas we encountered. The waters off Ushant were rougher than I had known them for some time. We all had to bail as huge seas threatened to swamp us. We were lucky that we had such a well-constructed ship. I wondered if Ethelred's men would make the equal in my new shipyard. It would be safer to have two ships sailing in close company.

The mouth of the Loire was a sight that brought conflicting emotions; there was joy at knowing we were close to our destination and, at the time, misery for it would take days to work our way upstream tacking back and forth up the island infested river. For James, it was all a joy for he had never been here before. Richard and Gilles pointed out castles and familiar features. They had done this journey many times. When we struck the Main I knew we were tantalisingly close to home. I prepared myself for landing and when Henry the Breton shouted, "La Flèche!" then we knew we had but a short time left aboard.

Leofric and his wife and eldest son awaited me as we docked. I saw that she was with child again. They had three children already. Leofric now looked older. I could see that his hair was thinning and he had the slightest of paunches. He had had little fighting in the last few years and it showed. I remembered him still as a young boy keen to serve. It would not be long before he was thirty.

His wife was always pleased to see me and after kissing my hand she threw her arms around me. I did not mind. I have never stood on ceremony. "Elise, you grow more beautiful each time I see you!"

"You are a flatterer, my lord, but I am always happy to see you and I see you have a new squire."

"This is James of Thornaby. His father was Sir Edward Lord of Thornaby."

I saw a look of sadness flicker across her face and then she smiled, "And you are welcome to our home, young sir. Come, Gilles and Richard, let us show your new companion our castle." She took her eldest son's hand, "Alfraed, leave your father to speak with the Earl."

As she led the three of them up to the castle I said, "You are a lucky man, Leofric."

"I know, lord. Each morning I wake and count my blessings." His smile left his face as he said, "I was sorry to hear about Sir Edward. He taught me much. I shall miss him. His son is a good squire?"

"Do not fish for compliments, Leofric! You know how much I valued you and John when you were my squires. James is young and has much to learn but he is improving. He progresses much as you did. This will be good for him." As we passed through the gatehouse I saw men practising. "They are the new men of which you wrote?"

"They are. They are good men all of them. Have you need of them all?"

"I will take the ones you think are the best trained for if there is peace here then idle hands look for mischief."

"Is there trouble in the valley, lord?"

"No, but it has been quiet for some months and it is only a matter of time before trouble flares once more. As long as we can pay for the arms and armour of my men that is all that I am concerned about. I leave my steward to balance the books! And before you ask he was pleased with your accounts. Do not forget to improve your castle and the lot of your family. You have done me great service and more than repaid me for your position."

"I am happy to serve and I like it here. I feel more like an Angevin now than an Englishman."

"And I dare say my son is of the same opinion?"

"I believe, lord, without speaking out of turn, that he is more of a Norman than many who were born here."

"Well, I shall see him soon. I leave in two days' time. I have been invited to court by Henry FitzEmpress."

"My wife will be pleased that you will spend those days with us. She enjoys your company, my lord."

"With the land peaceful you should take her to England. She might enjoy Stockton and at the moment it is safe there too." He raised an eyebrow. "No, Leofric, it will not last. The Scots are up to something but I cannot work out what. King David is supposed to be an ally of the Empress but he has done nothing to regain her lands in the south. He just seems eager to take land around the borders." I smiled, "At least he did until we stopped him. It is thanks to the steel that is my men at arms and the ash which is my archers that keep him at bay. No matter what the size of army he brings we can send him packing."

We had reached his hall and the servants had laid out olives, cheese, bread and wine, "But you cannot attack him?"

"No. My army can keep him at bay but we lack the numbers to make a decisive victory."

"Then the end of the war is no closer."

"It is not but I think my task is now to prepare Henry to become King of England. His father is Duke of Normandy and Henry is young. Young men sometimes do foolish things."

"Is it not his father's job to make him fit for kingship?"

"His father has enough to do with neighbours like Flanders and France." I changed the subject for Henry was my son and I would be the one to prepare him to be king. "This is good cheese."

"It is a local goat's cheese. I am partial to it myself but some of the English archers do not like it."

"They like what they know."

I met the new men the next day. Some had fought for Stephen and some had fought for the Count of Anjou. Leofric knew his warriors and along with Griff of Gwent and James the Short they had culled the numbers. The three of them assured me that the ones I would take were trustworthy. Leofric's men wore the same livery as mine so that, although they did not all have the same mail and helmet, they all had the same surcoat and shield. That would do until we reached our home.

Richard and James were disappointed to be leaving so soon. Elise had made a great fuss of them and Leofric's young daughter had liked the attention they gave her. William was eager to be at sea. Morag was due to give birth in two months' time. He chivvied the servants loading the cog for he was eager to complete this mission.

The journey to the sea was much quicker than the one upstream and we almost flew down the Main and then the Loire. James had his sea legs and when we struck the sea he did not blanch at all. Some of the Angevin warriors did for they had never been to sea. That helped James more than anything. He now knew that his weakness was common. We did not head for Caen but Le Havre. The journey to Rouen would be tortuous and Le Havre was easier to reach. William was happy for it meant he could go home quicker. We did not have to navigate a river. Gilles helped me to make sure that my new men were well presented. We were going to court and I knew that they would be judged.

We had not warned any that we were arriving. I just had a letter from Henry. At Le Havre, we hired thirty horses to carry us and our baggage to the castle. William would use the time we were away to trade.

As we rode along the road which ran next to the river James asked, innocently, "Why did we not sail to Rouen?"

"It is sixty miles upriver. We can ride that in half a day, perhaps a little longer. The ship would have taken at least a day." I held my finger up to the air. "See how the wind is against us. This is better. We can see something of the land. I have not been here since King Henry was on the throne or at least not in peace. I was usually looking for an ambush. I shall enjoy this ride."

And the journey was pleasant. We were so well armed and in such numbers that I think we could have travelled with enemies about us but we were greeted with warmth from the Normans. My son's surcoat was similar enough to mine for us to be welcomed. Here it was my son who was the hero and not me. We still had twenty miles to go and I turned in my saddle to look at the men who followed my squires.

Every group of men at arms had their own informal leader. With mine, it had been Edward and then Wulfric. Now Edgar led the men at arms back in Stockton. I waved forward Ralph of Nottingham; he had been the one to organize the men. He was a tall man and younger than some of the other men at arms who now bowed to his authority. They spoke well of him. "Tell me, Ralph of Nottingham, how you ended up with Sir Leofric."

"Sir William of Burton was fighting for the Earl of Gloucester. When the Earl returned to England we stayed here. I think that Sir William hoped for a manor. When the peace came there was none." He looked a little uncomfortable and shifted in his saddle.

"You will learn, Sir Ralph, that I prefer openness and honesty from my men at arms. I do not berate for honesty."

"Sir William was a little too fond of local women. Not the ones who are happy for such attention you understand, my lord, but ladies. The Duke was not satisfied with his behaviour. He did not reward him. Sir William could not afford to pay us and he and his squire disappeared one day when we were in Rouen. We heard a rumour he took a ship to the Holy Land. He owed us money."

"Us?"

"There were six of us left, my lord; all from Nottingham. We tried to get work but there was none. It was your son, Sir William, who sent us to La Flèche. He gave us coin and food. He was good to us, my lord. As soon as we met Sir Leofric I knew him for an honest knight and your name sir, well it is well respected. I am just grateful for a chance to serve a noble knight once more."

"Your lord should not have abandoned you. I fear that, unless he changes, then his nature will destroy him. The Holy Land, from what I have heard, is a treacherous enough place at the best of times."

"Aye, sir. I would not fancy it myself; too hot and full of the Musselmen. Nasty they are, or so I have heard."

I nodded. Many English called Muslims, Musselmen, and they feared their cruel nature. They could never understand a religion that forbade drinking. There were many English, Norman and Angevin knights there now. It was seen as a quick way to make much money and live well.

We saw the walled town of Rouen ahead of us. The greatest town in Normandy, I had yet to visit it. I had fought in many other parts of the County but never here. My banner must have been spied from afar for, when we were a mile from its walls riders galloped out to meet us. I saw, from the

31

banner, that it was my son, his squire and the leader of his men at arms.

I could not keep the grin from my face. I had missed my son. He was now a man grown and he had filled out. He too looked happy to see me and clasped my arm. "I am glad to see you, father! We did not expect this!"

As he turned his horse to ride next to me I said, "Henry FitzEmpress invited me over. It was quiet on the border and I wished to see you again. I was anxious to see my grandchildren."

"Ah well in that you will be disappointed. They are with my wife at my estate in Ouistreham."

"I thought that, with the war over, you would have been there with them."

He waved an airy hand around the land through which we travelled, "This is a great land for hunting and the Duke keeps a fine table. The court is here now and celebrates our great victory. Do you know that we have peace with France? King Louis acknowledges the Duke as the rightful ruler of Normandy. Perhaps his new Crusade shows a change of heart."

"We have no victory in England and the Empress is beleaguered. It would be over if we had half the knights who hunt and enjoy the Duke's fine table."

He lowered his voice, "Do not speak like that when we are in the presence of the Duke. He will not like it."

I smiled, "You should have learned by now, William, that your father cares not whom he offends so long as he speaks the truth and does what is right."

He shook his head and laughed, "You never change. Aye, I know. You might have been born in the east but you are English oak." He shrugged, "The Duke holds you in high esteem. Perhaps he will forgive you your bluntness for you are, along with the Earl of Gloucester, the two rocks on which he can depend. How long do you stay?"

"Not long. I am anxious to return to my valley. It is quiet now but it will not stay that way for long."

He turned in his saddle. "I see you found the men I sent to your manor."

"I am grateful for that. We need a large army."

"How do you afford it? We hear that Stephen controls the north."

"He thinks he does but there is a valley which resists both him and the Scots. Both enemies fear to take on the Warlord of the North."

He looked thoughtful, "Perhaps I should bring my men there. Life will become dull here soon enough."

"You would be more than welcome. You could bring your family too!"

He said, rather too quickly, "They are happy in Ouistreham. I would not disturb them." He turned to Robert of St. Michel, his sergeant at arms. "Take my father's men to my hall. There is room enough for them there and we will go to the castle."

"Aye, my lord!"

As we rode through the gates our men at arms left us and we wound our way through the busy streets. I noticed sour faces amongst some of those we passed, "I take it not all those who live here were happy that Geoffrey of Anjou captured their capital."

"You are right. Some feel that Count Fulk has achieved that which he planned and Anjou has captured Normandy through the blood of Normans. It does not sit well. I am certain the presence of young Henry will change their minds. He is popular." We dismounted as we approached the gate to the castle. My son suddenly turned, "You did know that the Duke's father, King Fulk, died last year."

I shook my head, "I had not heard."

"Aye, a hunting accident. Baldwin is now king there. I thought I should mention it. The Duke was much affected by the death. His father never saw what he achieved."

It was not Geoffrey, Duke of Normandy, who greeted us but Henry FitzEmpress. He had grown. The last time I had seen him he had been the same age as James. Now he was almost thirteen. He looked like someone on the threshold of manhood. I saw that he was the raw clay that could be moulded into a king. I hoped his father was taking on that responsibility.

"Earl! I am pleased you answered my letter. Gilles! Richard! You are men grown!"

They both bowed. They had helped to train Henry when he had been, briefly, my squire. "And you have grown too, my lord," Gilles spoke for them both.

"Come, when you were seen I had rooms prepared for you. The last time I shared rooms with you two did I not? Here we want for nothing!" he turned to me, "How is my mother, Earl?"

"She is in Devizes, and your uncle keeps the enemy at bay. I have seen neither for some time but I believe they are well."

"Your rescue of her across the frozen river is spoken of and sung by our troubadours. It is the stuff of legend. I wish I had been there with you!"

"It was a hard and dangerous ride. We were lucky."

"No, my lord. The Good Lord favours you."

"Where is your father? I am anxious to speak to him." I needed to persuade the Duke to help his wife by bringing soldiers to England.

Henry looked embarrassed. "He is somewhere. Robert, take the earl and his squires to their rooms. We will hold a feast for you. I will see the steward." He turned to me and his face showed neither deceit nor dishonesty as he said, "I am pleased you are here. I feel safer already and when time allows I would speak with you alone."

"Of course. I am your servant."

I was intrigued. What was going on?

William nodded, "And I will see you later, father. I have a little business to conduct. Until the feast!"

I was given my own room and my squires the antechamber. The castle had been built in the time of the Conqueror and they always built well. When I had washed and changed from my mail into one of my silken tunics I decided to take a walk around this castle which had held out for so long against Geoffrey of Anjou. I was always interested in the way castles were constructed. I was not so vain as to think that my castle was perfect. There were always ways to make it better. "Gilles, you and the others can amuse yourselves before the feast. Do not let James get into any trouble!"

"Aye lord."

The castle was partly stone; there was a round keep but most of the buildings were made of wood surrounded by a stone wall. Caen had a more substantial castle but this was built for comfort. There were nooks and crannies everywhere. I heard giggling as I approached the southern bailey. There were some fruit trees that had been planted to give some shade. As I turned the corner I saw the Duke of Normandy. He was with a woman and they were kissing beneath a medlar tree.

He stood when he saw me and waved the woman away. Holding out his hand he said, "It is good to see you, Earl! Is this not great news! I am now Duke and we have peace with France! The rebellion is over! I am grateful for the part you and your son played in this. You will not be forgotten."

He seemed to be ignoring the woman who was now sitting by a stone watering trough casually running her hands through the water.

"It is not over in England, my lord, and Stephen has a son."

"His son is a shadow of his father and I do not fear him." He shrugged. "Perhaps I will take your son and an army and conquer it but I would have some pleasure from my victory first."

There were many things I objected to in his words not least '*conquer*'. If he tried to do that then I would fight him. I decided to let the matter lie for nothing good would come of it.

I waved a hand around the bailey, "You have a fine castle."

He shook his head, "This needs work! It is not fit for a Duke! When time allows I will rebuild it in stone to become the finest of palaces. So, tell me, what brings you here?"

"Your son invited me. He was keen to show me his father's new Dukedom."

"He is fond of you, Earl. He seems distant to me. Perhaps our sons were switched at birth eh?" I kept an impassive face. "We must hunt while you are here."

"Perforce my visit will be brief, my lord, but I would go hunting."

He looked over at the woman, "Excellent. I believe your son is within."

I knew I was being dismissed and I bowed. I headed for the hall where I knew I would find William. I needed words with him. As I entered I heard laughter. William was at the centre of a group of knights and squires. He was regaling them with some tale. I would have to find a quieter time to speak to him. I went to the table with the jugs of wine and poured myself a goblet. There were seats around the outside of the room while the table dominated the centre. I sat on a seat in a darkened corner of the hall. No one had noticed my arrival and I sat quietly reflecting on what I had learned. If I was honest with myself then none of it was a surprise. Geoffrey's ambitions had always been known to me. It was just that I did not know they extended to the throne. I suppose I had always suspected that he would have women; he was fourteen years younger than Matilda and she had lived in England almost since her father had died. Yet the deception did not sit well with me.

"You are quiet, Earl." I turned and saw that Henry FitzEmpress had joined me. He had a goblet of wine in his hand. "Is there aught amiss?"

There was but I did not want to discuss it. I did not like to do it but sometimes it saved further questions, "It has been a long journey and I am no longer a young man."

"The nobles all say that you never age. You are the same now as when you were young."

"Is that a good thing I wonder? Why did you invite me here? It was not just to show me the castle. We both know that."

He lowered his voice and moved closer to me. "I thought that my father fought to regain the Dukedom for me or my mother but it seems he wanted it for himself."

"You will inherit the title and the land when he dies. Are you so eager to rule? You are still young and have room to grow."

"It is not for me but my mother. It was you who saved her and now she is cornered again. My father should be preparing to sail to England and regain my mother's inheritance instead of..." he looked beyond the wall. He knew of his father's infidelity.

I could see the dilemma for Geoffrey. If he regained the crown for Matilda then she would be his liege. I now knew Geoffrey's true intentions, "He has just won back Normandy. He should be allowed some time to enjoy it."

"You would not."

I did not answer, "What would you have of me?"

"Do as you did once before. Take me to England and teach me how to be more like you."

"What about your father?"

He shook his head, "He does not need me. I sent for you because I know the next few years will see me become a man. Every knight who has been your squire has achieved great things. Your son is the greatest knight in Normandy and by his own admission, he was made by you. Sir Leofric is admired in Anjou. He has the best-managed manor and is well-loved. I have seen how the knights in England fare under your tutelage. Before I can be a king I need to be a knight and you will make me one."

"If your father allows then so be it but I will not cause a rift. Your mother will need his help sooner rather than later and we have few enough friends at the moment."

"Then I will seek his permission."

I was unable to talk with my son at the feast. There were too many around us. We spoke but not about what concerned me most. My squires enjoyed the company and young Henry bombarded me with questions about our escape from Oxford Castle. My son had a room close to mine and as we ascended the stair I found that we were alone. As we reached my chamber I said, "The Duke has dalliances with women?" I phrased it as a question so that he could deny it.

He smiled, "Of course he does. He is a man and he has needs. His wife is in England! Surely you understand."

I shook my head, "No I do not." A chilling thought struck me. "You do not have such needs, do you?"

His face told me all that I needed to know. I was not drunk. I had barely had a quarter of the wine the others had consumed but it made my tongue marginally less guarded. "How could you? You have a wife and children!"

"Do not lecture me. I am a lord and I answer only to the Duke."

I shook my head, "No, my son. There are others you answer to and if you do not see that then I have failed as a father."

I turned and went into my chamber. My son had changed and I had lost him.

I rose early and left the castle on my hired horse as soon as the gate was opened. I headed out into the country. I needed to ride to clear my head and my thoughts. I recognised that there was something of the hypocrite in me. I had lain with the Empress. It had been once and was not a dalliance. It was more and we both knew it. It was a sin and I had paid for that sin with the death of my wife. From what my son had said he was fulfilling an animal need and that was not Christian. I regretted ever bringing my son to Anjou all those years ago.

By the time I returned my horse was lathered but I had exorcised my demons. I could not blame my son and I could not blame the Duke. By the same token, they were both lesser men in my eyes because they had given in to their carnal needs. A true knight did not do that. He dedicated himself to being a warrior who defended his people and that included his family. I had put the desire for the Empress from my mind after my one fall.

The Duke was eating in the Great Hall when I arrived. William was there as well as Henry. They turned as I entered.

"Your squires said you had risen early, my lord."

"A good ride clears a man's head and gives him an appetite, my lord." I sliced a large chunk from the ham and put it on a platter with some runny cheese and I took half a loaf of bread. Eating meant I did not need to speak.

"Henry here says that he wishes to travel with you again." I nodded. "I confess I had grown used to his company but, at the same time, I noticed he came back better for the time he spent with you and those who teach him weaponry said his skills were excellent." He smiled at Henry. "You are a great leader and you taught me well when I was a callow youth such as he."

I swallowed the bread and washed it down with some watered wine. "He is a good learner and my men are the best of teachers."

"Then I give him to you for a year. Besides he can see his mother if he is in England. This time, however, I give him four men at arms to watch him. He is now the heir to the Dukedom!"

I said, quietly, "He is still the heir to England."

The Duke laughed, "That is a lifetime away! Stephen shows no signs of dying. Besides, I may follow my father and get my own kingdom in the Holy Land. That would be something would it not? Duke of Normandy, Count of Anjou and King of Jerusalem! Tell me, will you need horses?"

"We have horses in England but if the Marquess has one he wishes to take then I can take it. I have my ship waiting in Le Havre." I knew that William would be anxious to leave and any joy I had had at meeting my son again had turned to ashes. I too wanted to go home. I needed to be with honourable men once more; my men.

The Duke nodded, "Then I will hold another feast this night and you may leave in the morning."

Chapter 3

Henry's horse was called Bucephalus. I hoped he knew what he was doing, for naming a horse after such a famous one was inviting trouble. I persuaded him to leave the horse at home. "The voyage may discomfit him and besides we have fine horses in my stable."

Reluctantly he left the horse at Rouen but I was pleased he had his bodyguards. His four men at arms seemed to know their business. Ralph of Nottingham knew them from the campaigns against the rebels and he vouched for them. "They are four hard men, my lord. Not that clever but tell them to hold a bridge and they will. If they are asked to protect the young lord they will die before anything happens to him."

"Good."

We headed for Antwerpen. I regretted agreeing to this for we would have to sail close to Flanders. The peace which had been brokered was not yet fully in place. A captain could decide to raid an English ship and claim that they thought we were still at war. When we headed into the estuary which led to the port I became happier. Antwerpen was a new port. I could see that the Count of Hainaut had spent a great deal of coin to build quays of stone and warehouses not to mention a large open market. Hainaut was a small county and, like my valley, could only raise a large army by making money through trade.

We were the largest ship in the port and the harbour master came aboard and made a great deal of fuss moving two smaller vessels to remote berths to enable us to have a prime position. I saw more ships moored further along the river. They were closer to the noisier part of the port. We were in a quieter berth which was closer to the sea and closer to the warehouses. For some reason, we had been accorded favour.

The harbour master did not recognise me but knew that I was a lord and he was deferential, "My lord, welcome to our port. The Count is keen for ships such as yours to visit us. You are English are you not?"

"We are, from the north of England. My captain here has many goods he wishes to trade."

"Excellent. Will you stay ashore this night?"

"Perhaps."

"I would advise it, my lord, for the tides here can be tricky and it is difficult to leave at night."

"Then we will stay. Come, we will walk ashore while the captain discusses business. Ralph, I would have you accompany us. Five men should be enough to protect us, eh?"

"Aye lord. I will choose the best."

We went ashore with swords but without helmets and shields. There were still a few traders selling their goods. As we passed one I saw that it sold threads and I remembered Mary. I haggled for some gold, silver and red coloured threads and then asked for needles. When he told me the price Ralph could not keep his feelings to himself, "Lord, that is as expensive as a good sword! A fortune for a couple of dozen needles!"

I smiled, "Nonetheless I will buy them. Gilles and I know some women who will appreciate them more than a sword." Gilles grinned.

Henry, Richard and James went off to spend some coins themselves. The bodyguards were close to them. They would be safe enough. There was a merchant selling weapons. He had some fine daggers, stilettos and short swords. The bodyguards glared at any who approached their charge and I turned my attention to the ships in the harbour. We were the only English ship in port. I saw one French and two Flemish ships as well as a Norwegian knarr, a Swedish knarr and two Danish knarr. It was the two Flemish ships that interested me. They were not as tubby as the other merchant ships. They looked almost lean by comparison. I wondered if they doubled as warships. Their crews were also well armed but the biggest difference was in the attitude of the crews. The other sailors all spoke pleasantly and waved to us as we passed. The men of Flanders scowled. Perhaps they did not approve of the peace.

When the squires and Henry had made their purchases we found a tavern. I paid for a jug of their golden ale. The men at arms approved although the squires and Henry were not certain if they liked the taste. By the time we headed back to our ship, the traders had all gone home and one of the Flemish ships had left port. They must have had a good pilot for the tide had turned.

William looked happy when we reached the ship. "We made excellent trades, my lord! They paid my first price and we did not need to haggle. Next time I will ask for more! The harbour master sent some food over. He is keen for more business."

I wondered if our luck was changing. When I woke I saw that we were the only ship left in the harbour. The others had left on the rising tide. William explained that we had had to delay our departure as our cargo had not been unloaded the previous night and we were waiting for our bolts of cloth to arrive. I was glad that we did wait when the mailed horsemen rode in from the east.

They reined up next to the warehouses. My men at arms looked worried. "Keep your hands from your swords. We are guests in this county." I walked down the gangplank. Their leader dismounted and approached me. He was about the same age as me but he was a veritable bear of a man.

"I am pleased you have not left. I am Baldwin, the Count of Hainaut. They call me Baldwin the Builder!" He laughed, "You can see why!"

"And I am the Earl of Cleveland."

"I know. It is why I hurried here! I have heard of you. You are the Empress' champion!" I nodded. He put a huge paw around my shoulder, "Come let us talk in private." He led me to a quiet part of the quay. "When I heard you were here I came as soon as I could. This is a propitious day. I would like an alliance with England."

The turn of events took me by surprise. "But the Empress does not rule it yet! Stephen is still the King."

He shook his head, "He will soon lose control. Now that Normandy has fallen England will follow and I would like to be friends. We are a small county with many enemies. I am gambling that the Empress will win; especially with you as her leader. I keep abreast of events outside my small county. An alliance with England could help us."

"And how would that help us?"

He smiled, "I was told that you were clever. The port of Bruges, in Flanders, is silting up. Soon it will not be the major port on this coast. It will be us. Already they are improving Dunkerque and Calais but they are nothing compared with us and we have access to the interior of France. We have strong links with Denmark and we can have free trade between our countries."

I nodded, "Perhaps we can. There is someone to whom you should speak." I waved Henry over.

"A squire?"

I smiled, "No, my lord, this is Henry FitzEmpress. He will be the next king of England." I saw the Count's eyes widen. I gave a slight bow to Henry, "This, my liege, is the Count of Hainault. He would have an alliance with you and your mother."

Henry was quick-witted, "And what do we gain from such an alliance?"

"Free trade and an ally which is north of Flanders."

"We are at peace with Flanders."

The Count smiled, "There is a difference between words of intent and actions. The Flemish have lost the support of the French that is all. It is temporary. My spies tell me that they plot against your mother. Queen Matilda has the support of the Flemish people. Besides, my young prince, the men of Flanders have peace with King Stephen. I offer an alliance to the house of William of Normandy. There is a difference."

Henry said, "Then I will ask my mother when next I see her but, for myself, I see no reason why we cannot be friends."

He was learning fast for he had not said allies, he had said friends. There was a clear distinction.

"Thank you and as a sign of the friendship we will send our ships to trade with you at Stockton." He looked at me, "If that is acceptable to you, Earl?"

"It is."

"My lord, the tide."

William's anxious voice made us turn. "We must leave."

"Before you go, be wary of the ships from Flanders. Trust them not. The two ships which were berthed here were not welcomed by me but I cannot afford to offend Flanders. We have a peace of sorts but I know that it cannot last."

"Thank you for your warning."

As our cog made its way to the sea I said, "Ralph, have the men armed and prepared for danger."

"Is there trouble, lord?"

"There may be. The Count warned us of Flemish ships."

"If it is the two which left before us, lord, they were both smaller than we are."

"But there are two of them. It costs nothing to be vigilant. Let us regard this as a test for the new men. Distribute the bows to those that can use them and have the men disperse themselves about the deck. Stay hidden. They may not know the numbers we have. We only took five ashore."

"Aye lord."

"William of le Havre, you and the other bodyguards stay close to the Marquess. Your bodies will be the best armour he can have."

"Aye lord."

"Gilles, bring hatchets and short swords on the deck and place them by the mast."

"Aye lord."

William of Kingston shouted to the ship's boy, "Tom, up the mast and see what is ahead."

I joined William at the rudder. He had armed himself already. "Did you see the ships when they left?"

He smiled, "We watch every ship, lord. We need to be able to spy out danger quickly when we are at sea. Those two ships were the only ones whose captains did not speak when I went ashore. The others warned me of shoals, mudflats and other dangers. It is what we do. We are a fraternity of the sea. The two Flanders ships kept to themselves. You may be right. They were smaller and rode lower in the water but they did not appear to be laden. We are. I think they have large crews."

I was happy now that Henry had not chosen to bring a horse with him. If there were to be rapid movements then the last thing we needed was a skittish horse.

"Come, my lord, we will stand by the stern rail with Henri the Breton, the helmsman."

Henry FitzEmpress said, "You think they would attack us?"

I pointed to my swallow-tailed standard which flew from the mast, "This marks my ship. I fear that the Count was right and they wish me harm. This may not be the doing of Stephen but we know that the Queen and William of Ypres are both from Flanders. If they could rid the world of the warlord of the north then a thorn would be removed from their side. I think it is better to be cautious."

I had begun to think that all the portents were wrong when Tom shouted, "Ship to starboard, captain!"

"What is she?"

There was a pause. "Flemish! She is the one which left on the morning tide, captain!" The ship's boy had sharp eyes.

"Then let us see if we can put some distance between us. We are favoured by the winds." He turned to Henri the Breton. "A couple of points to larboard, Henri."

"Aye captain."

I looked astern and saw the sail of the Flemish ship as it began to close with us. It was moving quickly. "William, this wind, it aids the other ship too does it not?"

"Aye, my lord but it will take a long time for him to reach us and it may well be dark by then. We can lose him at night."

"But where is the other ship? We were warned of two. I see only one."

"Aye and this is the one which left on the morning tide."

I turned to Henry, "I have learned long ago that a battle at sea is much like a battle on the land. You use strategy. You force your opponent to do something which you want. I fear they want us to sail this course and the wind and their presence has ensured that we do. One ship left before the other. What if that second ship left early to be in a position to ambush us?"

"But how could it know our course..." Henry suddenly looked aft. "They are driving us to their waiting ship!"

William looked around, "You are right!" For the first time, my captain did not look confident.

"Captain, if we headed a little more to starboard what would be the result?"

"They would begin to catch us. The course would take us closer to Denmark." I could see that I had puzzled him. A captain never wasted wind and I was asking him to do just that.

"And if we made a larger move to starboard?"

"Then they would catch us rapidly."

"You said you wished to trade with Denmark, head for Edjberg. It might be logical if we headed there. We will see what this ship of Flanders does."

"But we have nothing left to trade!"

I smiled, "When we see what the enemy intends we can draw them close and if you then went to larboard...."

William grinned, "We would fly for we would have the wind! If there was an enemy ahead of us we might catch them unawares. The sea is emptier than you think. They will be waiting for two sails to approach. When they do not if the captain is nervous he might move! Henri, give me the rudder. Prepare to come about!"

We had been heading west by north and, as his crew ran to the lines to adjust the sail, William of Kingston changed

46

the course to north by east. Although smoothly done Alain of Navarre, one of the bodyguards, lost his footing and fell over. Henry and my squires laughed. It eased the tension. I stared astern. The Flemish ship was taken by surprise and they tried to turn before their sails were properly set. I saw them in disarray and they fell back a little as they lost way.

William grinned, "Now we have a race. Let us see who the better captain is!"

On this course, the ship from Flanders did not catch us as quickly. We had created a gap and William exploited it. When we saw the coast of Denmark ahead, William turned to me, "Do we put in to port?"

I shook my head, "As you say we have nothing to lose. We have eaten into the day and confused the men of Flanders. Let us go home!"

"Stand by to come about!" He began to turn the rudder, "Come about!"

This time the bodyguards grabbed anything that they could to maintain their balance and it proved wise for, as we turned, the full force of the wind caught us. The sail billowed and we leapt forward. Once again our move caught the enemy by surprise and we saw them recede into the distance.

"They will catch us, my lord, but by then it will be dark."

The fates sometimes hear our words, or so the older, more superstitious sailors say. We had fooled the ship astern but what we did not know was where the second ship waited for us. The fact that it had no idea where we were did not matter for, not long after we had made our turn, the second ship of Flanders loomed up ahead. It was sailing a course from southwest to northeast. Their captain had gambled and won.

"To arms! Ralph, keep the men hidden below the gunwale." I turned to William. "What will he do?"

"If he has no hostile intentions he will keep to his course. If he wishes to attack us then he must change course and get to windward."

"What can we do?"

"If I turn a little south then, if he does make a turn, we can use the wind and return to our east by north course."

"Then let us do that."

It soon became clear that their intentions were hostile for he made a turn to the east too. With the wind behind her, the Flemish ship began to pull ahead and then she made a turn to larboard. She would be alongside us soon. I looked aft. The second ship of Flanders was closing but not quickly enough.

William looked at me and I nodded, "Come about!" He put the rudder over and we were on a converging course with the enemy. I could see that his decks were filled with warriors.

"Ralph, have the archers thin their ranks a little as we close. Keep the rest hidden!"

"He means to put his ship across our bows." William was just keeping me informed. Here he was the general. He knew the sea and he would make the decisions. He put the rudder over to starboard just as my six men at arms with bows began to loose at the enemy. One enemy fell with an arrow in his arm. Our move took them by surprise. They turned too and we would meet larboard to starboard.

Drawing my sword I said, "Come let us greet these pirates!"

My squires, Henry and his bodyguards headed towards the larboard side. I saw my archer's arrows hit men waiting to leap aboard and they pitched into the sea. I saw warriors with grappling hooks ready to bind us together. I picked up a hatchet and held it in my left hand. Gilles saw me and copied my actions. Even though my archers hit many, as we closed their hooks struck our deck and began to draw us together. I began to hack at the rope holding one as they pulled closer.

"Ralph! Now!"

Ralph and the rest of my men rose as one. I severed the rope by me but enough of the others had caught and we were tied. My archers put down their bows and took up their swords as thirty-odd Flemish soldiers and sailors threw themselves aboard.

I threw the hatchet at a Flemish warrior who was about to swing over. It caught him a glancing blow on his helmet and he fell into the sea between the two ships. He screamed as his body was crushed between the two hulls. I held up my sword and one impaled himself as he leapt across the narrowing gap. He hit my sword with such force that I was able to let my sword slip behind me and his momentum carried his body from my sword. A Flemish man at arms balanced precariously on the rail as he raised a spear to strike at Gilles. I brought my sword down on his foot, half severing it. He fell screaming between the hulls. His body was held as he bled to death.

Gilles, my squires and Ralph, had kept them from the vicinity of the mast but Henry and his bodyguards were beleaguered at the bow. "Ralph, clear them here. Squires, with me!" I drew my dagger.

I ran down the deck, dimly aware that the Flemish ship had lowered his sail and the *'Adela'* was pushing the two ships further north and west. I brought my sword around in a sweep to take the head of a sailor who had just pushed a pike into the side of Alain of Navarre. I sensed a weapon to my left and I lifted my dagger to block the axe which struck down. It slowed it down but the blade still struck my mail. I stabbed forward with my sword and it came out of the man's back. I pushed his body from the blade. Henry and his remaining three guards were fighting bravely but even as I watched Stephen of Chinon die as two men struck him at once.

James had not fought in a battle before but he saw Henry in danger and, racing forward, he stabbed one of those who had killed Stephen and stood back to back with Henry. I shouted, "James, use your dagger too!" My new squire did as I ordered.

Two men were standing on the rail ready to join the others. I ran at them. I swung my sword at their knees as I threw the dagger at them. My sword hacked into the knee of one. The dagger caught a glancing blow to the second. He lost his balance. Both tumbled between the ships. The two hulls ground together making their bodies pulp.

"Richard, cut their lines!"

Gilles was showing that he was ready to be a knight for he fought with a sword and short sword. The men at arms and sailors who fought him did not have his skills. As I stabbed one through the side he and Henry finished off those who were around him.

"James, help Richard cut the lines! Gilles, guard Henry!"

I turned and ran down the cog. I could see the second ship heading for us. Half a mile away she would soon be upon us. William and his crew were defending the rudder. I ran to the clay pot where we kept coals to light our lanterns at night. Sheathing my sword I unhooked it from its sconce. "Ralph, clear a path for me!"

Ralph and two of my men at arms laid about them recklessly driving the Flemish back. There was a gap to the side and I ran and hurled the pot at the mainmast of the Flemish ship. As the flames suddenly leapt up the mast the men of Flanders gave a wail. The last two ropes were severed and, as the fire took hold, a gap appeared. I ran to the rudder and used my sword to despatch two whose backs were to me. I saw that the wind was bringing the second Flemish ship closer but the first one was now ablaze. Aboard the fiery ship, all thoughts of aggression were gone as they tried to fight the fire. There were screams as the last of those aboard us was killed and then we were clear. William moved the rudder a little and we caught the wind. The smoke from the burning ship told us that it was now astern of us. The second ship would not catch us now. They had to sail around their consort and I did not think they would risk that. We had beaten off their attack but at a cost. I saw two of my new men at arms who were dead while others were wounded. With two of Henry's guards gone we had paid a price.

I went to the stern and watched as the second Flemish ship went to the aid of the other. They might save her but the sail had gone on the burning vessel. While my men went around dispatching the enemy wounded I went to see our wounded. Ralph was there already, binding wounds.

"We were lucky, lord. The wounds are not serious although Roger of Doncaster might well now be Roger Three Fingers. He lost two fingers from his left hand."

"He was lucky then. He can still hold a shield."

"Aye, he can, lord."

"Take any weapons you find. They might be poor quality but those we cannot use Alf, my blacksmith, can melt down. We waste nothing."

"And the bodies?"

"Feed the Flemish to the fishes. Wrap our dead in their cloaks and we will bury them in my churchyard."

I went over to a shaken Henry. He was looking at the bodies of the two dead bodyguards. Alain of Navarre's wound had been a bad one and he had died while we fought. William of Le Havre said, "Do not mourn them, my lord. They died doing that for which they were paid. When we took this job from your father, we accepted a high price and knew that the one we would pay would be higher. It is our lot."

I noticed them searching the bodies of their two comrades. I said nothing but they were aware of me watching them.

William of Le Havre smiled and said, "Do not think us thieves, my lord. We are not. If I lay there then they would be doing the same. The four of us have made a pact. We share all the coins that we receive and earn." He held up the purse he had taken from Alain of Navarre. "This takes me one step closer to a farm in Normandy."

James looked wide-eyed at them, "So you profit by the deaths of your comrades?"

"Someone always profits when a warrior dies, is not that so, lord?"

"It is. The men of Flanders had little but we shall take it and we shall share it. What is the alternative? Let the fishes have it? This is a cruel world in which we live, James."

"I can see that. I suppose I must get used to it if I am to be a warrior and a knight like my father. I will have to learn to be stronger."

William of Le Havre smiled at James, "And thank you, young squire, you are inexperienced but have courage beyond your years."

Henry nodded, "Aye James. I would have such a squire as you when I am knighted."

I saw the happy smile on James' face. "If James would be your squire then I will train him for you. The squire of a king is better than the squire of an earl."

Gilles said, "With due respect to the future king of England I would rather serve you, my lord!"

Henry nodded, "As would I."

By the time we reached the mouth of the Tees the ship had been cleared of the Flemish dead and cleaned. It took us a day and a night to do so. We then began the tortuous twisting journey upstream. It was almost dark when we saw the lights of my castle and detected the smell of tanning and ironwork. We were home.

Chapter 4

I saw, as I disembarked, that my steward and castellan were eager to speak with me and they looked as though the news they had was not good. I needed to speak with them quickly and I sent my squires to familiarise Henry and his bodyguards with his new home. He had lived here before but we had made changes. They would also need to see the captain of the guard for the new passwords. I arrived in my hall alone and told William and Alice of our new guests and men at arms. Alice had a frown when she realised that we had royal guests. She liked a warning. Mary showed her new confidence by putting her arm around my housekeeper and saying, "Come, Alice, Sir John's quarters have only recently been cleaned, it will not take us long to make them presentable for a future king. Ladies, we will help."

I saw that Morag was not with her ladies, "Where is Morag?"

Alice smiled, "Her husband has returned at the right time, lord. She is about to give birth."

John of Craven and John, my steward, awaited my attention patiently. John of Craven was an old campaigner and he came directly to the point. "Lord, Sir Wulfric and Sir Tristan have reported scouts in the south. They both suspect that there is some malice afoot. These are neither brigands nor bandits. Your knights have men at arms and scouts out. They patrol the land between Chop Gate and Piercebridge and Sir Wulfric has warned the fyrd they may need to be called out."

Sir Wulfric had shown good judgement. "Good. Have
Aiden come to me." Aiden would discover the danger faster
than any other scout. John of Craven left us, briefly, to send
a guard for my scout and I turned my attention to my
steward.

"I took the liberty of ordering more arrowheads and
spears from Alf, my lord. It seemed a judicious move."

"You did right. How goes Ethelred's new ship?"

"We have the keel laid, my lord, why?"

"We now have a new trading partner; Hainault. They will
be sending ships soon. They trade along the Scheldt and with
the Danes."

That brought a smile to John's face, "I will go and tell
him the good news. It will encourage his workers."

John of Craven re-entered, "Aiden is out with his scouts,
lord. He will be back soon."

Left alone with John of Craven I said, "Good. We have
new men at arms. Take four of them for the garrison and the
rest will need mounts, mail and helmets."

John of Craven laughed, "You waited until the steward
had gone before you mentioned the expense."

"Of course. Why spoil his good humour? This way he
will be more likely to find the coin."

After my words with the Count of Hainaut, I was not
surprised by the news. Queen Matilda had ever been my
enemy. She was from the house of Flanders and she was a
wily campaigner. The north was a thorn in her side and if I
could be vanquished then that would leave the enclave in the
south-west as the only part of the kingdom which was free
from Stephen's control. She would have instigated this
movement from York. I had not arrived back a moment too
soon. When John left, Gilles and my squires returned with
Henry.

"James, show our new guests their chambers. They will
be using Sir John's old quarters."

I finally had the chance to take off my cloak and drink
some of the wine Alice had sent to me. I stared into the fire
as though I could divine the future. Scouts from the south
meant York. The Queen might have begun this but another

54

would be leading it. Who? It would not be William of Ypres. His task was to take the lands to the south and west. It would be another and that gave me hope for the earls and lords of the north had been defeated by me on many occasions. They had seen my skill at the battle of the standard and they would be wary. Aiden would need to find out exactly who led them and their intentions. Until then I was in the dark. I saw this as a chance to begin Henry's training. I would involve him in the planning of the campaign. I doubted that Geoffrey of Anjou had done that.

Gilles and Henry returned with my other squires. I gestured to the wine and they helped themselves. I outlined the problem and they listened. "You think it is a threat from Flanders, Earl?" Henry was learning to think.

"After the attack on our ship and our news from Hainaut, it would be prudent to assume so. If it is the northern barons then we have little to fear. They are neither bold nor swift. However, it is all speculation until we can discover the truth. That requires Aiden's skills." I was about to send for another jug of wine when I heard my sentries. My scout had returned.

Aiden arrived and I took him and my squires to my solar. I smiled at the lean hunter. He was not a man who was at home within stone walls. He was a man of the woods and the animals. I smiled, "Aiden, did you have a good hunt?"

"Aye lord. There is a fine hind for you."

"Good but your skills will be needed for a different kind of hunt. I want you to hunt men. We have enemies to the south. Sir Tristan and Sir Wulfric's scouts have seen signs. I need you to take Edward and Edgar to discover any that they have missed and to discover the intentions of those who sent them. They will be coming from York. There may be foreigners. Watch out for warriors from Flanders."

"Aye lord." He turned to leave and then stopped, "While you were away we found two more young lads who are good with animals. I took them on." He smiled, "John the Steward questioned their value."

"And you, quite rightly, ignored him."

"Of course, my lord. This way we can train them and eventually you will have five scouts. None of us is getting any younger. I will leave before dawn."

After he had left us I said, "James, go and tell Alice that we are ready for food." He nodded and left. "Gilles, I want you to lead the new men at arms until we know their worth."

"What of Edgar, your sergeant at arms?"

"He will lead them eventually but I want you to become used to leading men. If I am to make you a knight I need to give you the experience of leading men in battle. It seems we may be testing our mettle sooner rather than later. Ralph of Nottingham impressed me. Let us see if he can impress you. I will make do with Richard and James as my squires. Richard, you will give the standard to James. It might teach him caution. He was a little reckless on the ship. He is brave but you must balance that with some caution when you are young. You may go now. I will have no need of you until the morrow."

"Aye lord."

"And Henry, you need to warn your two bodyguards that they will be needed. Go and choose three horses for yourselves. Let us see if you are a good judge of horseflesh."

Gilles remained behind after Richard and Henry had gone.

"Lord?"

"Yes, Gilles."

"I have thought about what you said before we left for Normandy. I would like your permission to court the maid, Mary. It might be she laughs at me and rejects my courtship but at least I will know and can get on with my life."

"Wise. It is a sign of your increasing maturity. You have my permission. And if you would like a little advice, I would give her a gift. It should be nothing which is too valuable but something which shows that your intentions are honourable."

He smiled, "I bought this in Antwerpen." He took out a beautifully decorated comb. It was made from ivory and was most delicate. It looked like the kind of work that came from the lands of the Norse.

"That looks expensive."

He smiled, "I could have bought many needles, my lord, but I thought this better."

"She will love it."

I heard one of my sentries shout, "Patrol from the west!"

I left my hall and went to the outer bailey. The patrol would be Dick. He, Sir Tristan and Sir Harold rotated the patrols amongst them. It stopped the horses from becoming fatigued and kept the men on patrol sharp.

Dick and his archers rode in. My archers were unique. All of them were superb archers. That could have been said of many English archers. They all had a well-deserved reputation. However, Dick and his archers also fought as men at arms and the only ones who were superior to them were my own. They fought in short mail shirts that did not impede their archery. They also wore helmets and carried, not the usual short sword of most archers, but a long one. They used them well.

He smiled as he dismounted, "Back from your travels, my lord! And not before time."

"The south?" He nodded. "And I have news that Flanders is become involved too."

"They are mercenaries without honour. We do not fear them."

"No, but they can cause mischief. Did you see aught on your travels?"

"We hung a few brigands and cattle thieves close by Piercebridge. Sir Phillip had had trouble with brigands too but he and Sir Hugh scoured the land of them."

"But no Scots?"

He shook his head, "No Scots. I believe that King David has finally decided that we are too big a mouthful."

"He is supposed to be an ally of the Empress but I have seen precious little evidence of that. We had better be ready to ride at short notice. I have brought more men at arms from Anjou. The garrison will be bigger."

"And we have six more trained archers. It has taken since the Battle of the Standards to do so but it is worth it. They have fitted in immediately. God willing there will be another six next year."

"You still use the ones training as horse holders?"

Nodding he said, "It works. They see how the archers fight and they can copy them. The fact that they are desperate to join them helps too."

We walked back towards my hall. Dick knew me almost as well as any. "How is your son?"

I felt a pain in my chest as he spoke the words. I had lost my son. I knew that. "He is well thought of and he is a leader at the court."

"But he does not come home?"

"No, Dick, I fear that he is now Norman. He will never sit in my castle." I shrugged, "It was not meant to be."

"I have no children." He chuckled, "At least none whom I remember but if I did I would want to see them. I would want my grandchildren to know me. You are a mighty noble. You have the ear of kings, queens and empresses yet you do not have your family around you." He put his hand out to touch my shoulder. He was one of the few who knew me well enough for such an intimate gesture. "I share your pain, Warlord."

His words made me realise what I did not have. I had no family and I was alone. His words did not bring comfort. That was not his fault but his simple statement brought my isolation into focus. We walked into my hall in silence for no words were necessary. That was the beauty of old friends. They could say what they felt and not worry about the ramifications.

That night as we ate I felt as though I had lost one family but gained another. Mary, my squires, Henry, Dick and John of Craven were a disparate group but they all got on. I could not help notice that Mary and Gilles' heads were together for much of the evening. I had no idea if he had given her the comb yet but their bobbing heads spoke volumes. James and Richard were busy talking to Henry which allowed me and John of Craven and Dick to talk of military matters. It was in our blood and as natural as talking about the weather.

"The new men are excellent, Earl. They are well trained and prepared for work. We could do with more like that." John of Craven was an old soldier and an excellent judge of men.

"Sir Leofric will get them for us but he is careful to choose those who are trustworthy. There are many out there who are not."

"Your wisdom in acquiring good breeding stock has paid off, lord. The fields of Hartburn are filled with colts and fillies. Sir Harold is becoming a good horse master."

I nodded as I sipped the new wine from Anjou. It was rich and heavy, just the way I liked it. "With Alf producing such good mail the world would be perfect but for the fact that Stephen is King of England!"

Dick leaned back and smiled, "I think the tide is turning, lord. It may not seem it to you but Normandy is just the beginning. If Stephen does not have the revenue from his manors in Normandy he cannot be so generous to his men in England. Some of the brigands we hanged told us that they had fled from masters who could no longer keep them. They had lost the patronage of the King. It will cause unrest."

John of Craven nodded, "It is true, lord. I came from the west of the land. There the lords like to live well and keep the people poor. You do not do that. When first I came here I found it hard to comprehend. When times are good you share with your people and when times are hard they do not suffer. If the wolf was at the gates then the people would stand behind you. Each time I walk through Stockton I am welcomed. Why? Because I serve you and protect them." He sat up in his seat, "I hope I am not speaking out of turn, lord, but we worry about you. You seem to bear so much on your shoulders."

"I do not complain. My father taught me to take responsibility. I try to do that."

"But what of you, lord? Where is your gain? Your treasure?"

I looked at Dick. "My family!"

He nodded and lifted his goblet, "And that brings me back to our earlier words. Warlord, I admire you more than you can know. Warlord!"

John toasted me too. The others had been busy in their own conversations but they heard the toast and all of them stood and said, "Warlord!"

For some reason, that simple act brought tears to my eyes. I felt foolish and I left my hall. I was the Earl of Cleveland! I should be above such emotion. I went to my solar and stared out across the Tees. I could never have the Empress. I could never acknowledge Henry as my son. My legitimate son would never live in England again. What was I fighting for? Why did I go on? I ascended to the tower and the crenulated battlements. I looked out over the dark waters of the Tees. My life was not the one I had hoped for. However, it was the one I had been given. I leaned over to look down at the glowing brazier of Ethelred's ferrymen. They would not have a life but for me. It was a small thing but it gave me hope.

There was a movement behind me. The warrior in me made me whirl and I saw Mary. She looked fearful. "I am sorry, lord. My father told me never to approach a warrior unawares."

I smiled, "I am sorry, child. Forgive an old soldier."

She came over and took my hand. Her fingers were soft and gentle. "I am sorry that we upset you, lord."

"You did not. I drank unwatered wine. It was I who was foolish."

She took my arm and began to lead me back to the solar. "You are never foolish. Sometimes I wish you were for that would mean you were happy. You always seem sad."

"I am not but I have much to think about. Do not worry about me, Mary. You are young and have a life ahead of you."

"Without you, I would have no life." She squeezed my arm, "Gilles gave me the gift and spoke to me." She turned and embraced me, "Thank you for giving him the courage to speak to me."

"You are happy for him to court you?"

60

"I am."

"You know that I will be as your father. You have an inheritance as does James. When I gave the manor to Sir Wulfric I did not give him your father's treasure. John has used that wisely and it grows. When you marry you will have a fine dowry so choose the husband that you want."

We were walking through my solar. "And it is Gilles that I want." She giggled. "I will make him wait and wonder. Morag and Alice told me to do that but I will be his when time allows."

"He will be a knight next year and I will find him a manor."

"You need not. We are both happy here. You are like a father to us both."

"Then the world is well."

She kissed my hand, "One more thing, lord, and then I will leave you. Gilles and I would like this tryst to be kept secret."

"That will be difficult if he is paying you extra attention."

She smiled, "It is Richard and James. They will mock Gilles."

"I understand."

After she had gone I reflected that this was trivial, in the greater game, but nonetheless, it was important to two young people. It made me smile and made me less melancholy.

Aiden and his scouts returned two days later. Alice wrinkled her nose as she admitted them to my hall. I knew why. They had lived on the back of their horses for three days and they smelled of sweat and horse. It showed they were diligent.

"Is there danger?"

"Aye lord. Osmotherley is refortified and they have rebuilt the walls. Northallerton is filled with armed men too. There is an army preparing to move."

"Here?"

"That would be my guess, my lord. They have a line of sentries and they are to the north."

"You got by them?"

"Of course. They were soldiers and not the men of the wood. There are the nobles you might expect to see; we saw their banners. There are also mercenaries. We heard the language of the men of Flanders as well as French."

I nodded. That was what I had suspected. "And numbers?"

"That is more difficult to estimate for their camps are large and we could not gain entry to their castles for obvious reasons. No more than a thousand and no less than six hundred. We counted the gonfanon of eighty knights."

"Have you any idea who leads them?"

"The Constable of York and the other barons. We did not recognise the Flemish just their banners."

"You have done well. I will summon my knights and we will leave in three days time."

Aiden looked worried, "I would make it two, lord. They appeared almost ready to move."

"Thank you."

After they had gone I took the wax tablet I used to put down my thoughts. I tallied numbers and worked out how many I would need to leave in garrisons. I had just over two hundred knights, men at arms, archers and squires. With horse holders, servants and scouts that would rise to two hundred and fifty. At best we would be outnumbered two to one and at worst four to one. I took a piece of parchment and hurriedly wrote upon it. I sealed it with my ring.

I held the wax tablet close to the fire and smoothed out my numbers. I would keep that knowledge to myself. I shouted, "Squires!"

The three of them and Henry had been in the antechamber and they rushed in.

"Gilles, ride to Sir Philip. Tell him I need him and his archers. Then ride to Sir Hugh and give him this letter. Richard, ride to Sir Wulfric and then to Sir Gilles of Normanby. Tell them to leave a garrison and return here with the rest of their men. We go to war. James, ride to Sir Harold, and Sir John. Ask them to bring all of their archers and men at arms here."

When they had left us Henry asked, "What of Sir Hugh and Sir Tristan?"

I was aware that I was training a future king. I needed to explain my motives and strategy. "I pray you to sit and I will tell you." He sat and I poured us both a goblet of wine. "The supporters of Stephen are gathering north of York. From the intelligence, I have they could number anything between five hundred and a thousand men." I saw him nodding. "We have just over two hundred warriors. I cannot leave the north undefended. I may be wrong or there may be other enemies Aiden has not seen. I must be cautious. Sir Hugh will watch the west. Erre and John of Craven will watch the north. We will gather at Yarm. There is no need for Sir Tristan to travel north merely to return south."

"Then you will bring them to battle?"

"Eventually, yes. First, we will weaken them. Then we will annoy them and finally, we will draw them to a place I have chosen where we have a chance of defeating them."

"You know of such a place?"

"I know of many. The best they have taken. They occupy Osmotherley. Had they not done so I would have used the site. However the road north passes up a bank some twelve miles north of that. I have fought there before. We can use the reverse slope to hide our men and we can make the ground before us a death trap."

He sipped his wine and was thinking about my words. "Why not call out the fyrd? Then we would equal their numbers."

"Aye we would but it would be false equality. When King Harold fought your great grandfather at Hastings it was the fyrd who lost the battle for King Harold. They thought they had won and they charged down the hill. They were slaughtered and the finest warriors on the field all fell."

"Who were they?"

"They were the housecarls. My father had been one of them and would have been with them had he not been wounded at the battle of Stamford." I smiled, "If that had happened then I would not be here."

"Do you know how you will fight? Will you do as my father does and use your knights and men at arms to charge them?"

"If I had parity of numbers I would but they could have as many as eighty knights and I have but eight. The advantage I hold is in my archers. They are my secret weapon. Our knights and men at arms will hold the enemy while the archers slaughter them."

"That does not sound glorious!"

"It is not. It is war and if you think that war is about glory then I fear you will win little. War is about defeating those who are trained as you are, armed and dressed as you are and fight over the same ground. It is the smartest mind which prevails. When you are King of England or even while you are trying to be king, then choose your battles. If you can avoid fighting then do so. If you can choose ground which suits you then grab it with both hands. And if you can deceive your opponent then that will give you the battle."

He drank deeply. His father loved glory. He was a brave leader for he led from the front but he could be reckless. The Duke was lucky that he had the likes of my son at his side. I had trained William well. He might have forgotten me but he had not forgotten the education he had received under the eyes of me, Sir Wulfric, Sir Edward and my archer knight, Dick.

"You have planned all of this without knowing their precise plan?"

"I know the land. There are two places an army can cross the Tees; Yarm and Piercebridge. The place I have chosen, Arncliffe, is well placed to stop them no matter which crossing they choose. Aiden has told me where they are. Northallerton and Osmotherley are not far from each other. By placing myself between them I invite attack. That is why we must lessen their numbers first."

"How will you weaken them?"

"We use my scouts and my archers. Dick and his men are woodsmen all. They are skilled with knives and daggers. We go into their camp at night and we slay as many as we can while we try to either drive off or capture as many of their horses as we can."

"We? You will lead?"

I nodded, "That is my weakness. Should you ever fight me then use that weakness. I will always be where there is the most danger."

"Why?"

"My men expect it but more importantly I expect it. It is how I have always fought and I am too old to change."

"You say if I ever fight you. Why should I do that? You are my champion."

I emptied my goblet, "Because, Prince of England, there may come a time when I become an inconvenience and you have to eliminate me. Then you might fight me."

"That day would never come. You have been the most loyal of my mother's knights. When I am king you shall be elevated to sit at my right hand."

"That is kind but do not make promises which you may not be able to keep. Stephen the Usurper is reaping the whirlwind he has sown. He promised the world to his supporters and now he cannot deliver."

"I would not be as Stephen. I would be as you or my grandfather."

I stood, "Good. Come we fight one battle at a time. Let us prepare for this one."

Chapter 5

As we headed south from Yarm we did not look like an army. An army had a huge baggage train and was spread out over many miles. We took up a bare eight hundred paces. Dick, my scouts and my archers were spread out ahead of us. Sir Phillip commanded the fifty archers who remained with the main body. The rest of us were close enough for conversation. I saw Henry looking around. He appeared to be disappointed in the retinue which headed south.

"Earl, with so few men, would it not be better to sit behind our walls and make them bleed upon them? There your archers could inflict great casualties upon them. Your castle is strong."

"True, but what of the rest of my land? You have seen Yarm Castle. Sir Tristan has improved it but could it withstand an attack by five hundred men?" He shook his head. "And what of the people who live in my valley? They could not all shelter in my castle and even if they did their animals would all be taken and their crops destroyed. We would starve. This anarchy has killed more who work the land than the knights who prosecute the unrest. Remember, Henry, that when you are king you must ensure that the people prosper. They are the roots of the land. They feed the buds that grow."

He looked around at the farms we passed. These were in the borderlands but my valley was a safe haven. My men kept the predators away.

"So you go forth to fight them on their land."

"The land that they hold. There is a difference. Until Oxford, we held all of the land as far south as Pickering and Helmsley. This is our land and we know it well. The folds and fields aid us."

"The battle of Winchester cost us, dear."

"It almost cost us the war. Your mother was close to being captured. So far she has avoided that ignominy."

"My mother is not a general." I did not point out that his father and uncle were. He would know that and draw his own conclusions. We passed Appleton and he said, "If you had been general then we would not have lost at Winchester."

"I would not have fought at Winchester."

"Why not?" He looked surprised as though that battle had been inevitable. It was not. The Earl of Gloucester had chosen that battle.

"There was nothing to be gained. Your uncle was annoyed because the clergy refused to support your mother. He went to bend them to his will. You never win such support by force of arms. We had Stephen in Bristol Castle and I would have made Queen Matilda and William of Ypres come to us. We could have defeated them. We have the better knights."

"But they have more men."

"Stephen has ingratiated himself with the populace of London and the larger towns. He has bought the common man and they fight for him. What they lack in skill they make up for in numbers. However, if they had faced me and my men they would have been destroyed. London is not England, Henry, remember that. Those in the city are self-serving and greedy. They produce nothing and take all."

He said nothing and that pleased me for it showed he was thinking and reflecting. He would make his own judgements but I had planted seeds.

Our camp would be close to the villages of Harlsey and Arncliffe. There was a stream and it was sheltered. An enemy would have to be upon the camp before it could be seen. I rode with my squires to see the land where we would fight the battle. Henry and his two bodyguards accompanied us. It was just a mile or so from our camp. The road climbed a gentle but taxing incline from both the north and the south, reaching a small crest. To the left, there was flat land before the escarpment rose steeply towards the priory which stood there. The priests would continue their lives as though we were not even there. To the right, the land fell rapidly to an area of soft, spongy and swampy ground. I had fought here before and our enemies would know the terrain but that would not give them a better idea of how to defeat me.

As we viewed the land Henry said, "This is a good position. If you were attacking then what would you do?"

I pointed west. "I would send mounted men all the way around to attack our rear while our foot held their attention here."

"Suppose they try that?"

"I will have scouts watching there. If they try that then we fall back. There are a series of these inclines all the way back to Yarm. The further north they go the fewer opportunities they will have to flank us." Even as I told Henry the dangers I did not think it would come to that. They had not enough decent leaders to divide their forces and they would fear my mounted archers. "Come we have seen enough and my scouts will soon return. We can then begin the next part of my plan."

Wulfric had organised the camp. He had been a man at arms and he understood what was needed better than most. Already he had erected a palisade of stakes around the horses. There was a ditch around the camp and he had used the bushes and brambles to make a barrier behind it. Ample sentries were in place. With Aiden and my scouts discovering the whereabouts of our enemies, we could plan for our defence.

"Sir Harold and Sir John, take your men and prepare the battlefield."

"Aye lord." They took their mattocks, axes and other tools and headed for the rise. They would build a barrier half a mile wide behind which the archers and dismounted men at arms could shelter.

Henry looked around, "Where are the tents?"

Wulfric laughed, "We need no tents! We are warriors. A little rust just gives our squires something to do is that not true, Thomas?"

His squire, Thomas, son of Oswald, grinned cheerfully, "My lord, cleaning rust from your mail is what I live for!"

Wulfric threw a rock at him, "Cheeky young villain!" Thomas ducked out of the way.

Henry looked confused, "When my father goes to war we have tents, servants and we have cooks for our food."

Sir Tristan had campaigned with us since he had been a squire and he explained to the future King of England the way we fought. "We travel faster this way. If we have to flee it is easier to do so with fewer servants to worry about."

I pointed to the south-west, "At the battle of the standards Prince Henry attacked the Archbishop's baggage and it meant only my battle was able to pursue the Scots. We could have defeated them once and for all had we not had a baggage train. I rarely take baggage. We are not far from home. We will not be here overlong. It will take just three days for us to achieve our aims."

Tristan nodded, "When we do return home then the comforts there are all the sweeter for the hardship we endure."

Wulfric tapped the ground with the haft of his spear. "Not to mention that sleeping on the hard ground makes for light sleep and that is always a good thing."

Our men at arms had food cooking by the time my archers returned. As Dick dismounted I said, "Aiden?"

"He was heading for the rear of their lines. He and his scouts had sharpened knives."

I nodded, "Even though it might alert the enemy to our presence if Aiden and his men could slit a few throats on the York side of the enemy camps then they might start looking over their shoulders. That will work in our favour. I want them to worry where we are." I pointed to the fire, "Come, sit, eat and tell me what you found."

With some ale in his hand and a hunk of cooked, salted ham in the other he began, "They have their two castles and they are well defended but betwixt and between they have

camps. There are four of them. The nearest is just five miles
down the road nestling on the east side of the road by a
spring." He drank.

"They have sentries?"

"Aye."

"Have they dug a ditch and erected stakes?"

Dick grinned, "Oh no, my lord. These are confident
fellows. They have their horses tied to a line with one sentry
only."

Wulfric laughed, "Then we have them. We use the trick
we used at Berwick. That time it was the Scots who were ill-
prepared."

"You are right. While Dick and his archers cut the horse
lines we will ride through the camp causing as much damage
as we can." My men nodded. It had worked well the last time
we had tried it. "And the next camp, how far away is that?"

"A half-mile to the west in the next dell."

"Then while you drive their horses back we can swing
around and attack that camp from the south. They will not be
expecting that. Horses from the south might mean
reinforcements."

Henry spoke, "But it is a risk, Earl. They might anticipate
that you might try something like this."

"True but as Dick said they have no defences and they
will be confused. We attack at night and sound pays tricks in
the dark. Sir Phillip, Sir Gilles and Sir Tristan. I leave you to
guard the camp. Henry you and your bodyguards will stay
here too as will James."

Both were disappointed, "Why lord?"

"Neither of you has charged into battle in daylight. At
night it is ten times more difficult. We cannot be watching
out for two novices. Besides, our camp needs eyes upon it. I
charge you to give my knights all the assistance you can."

Wulfric mused, "What I cannot understand is why they
are attacking now?"

"I think this was put in place while I was in Normandy.
This shows planning. The two Flemish ships were there to
take me. They have failed but their leaders on land have not
had the news yet. I think they believe me dead or captured.

They hope to repeat the trick which worked last time. They strike while I am absent. They must have spies and allies in Rouen. We made no secret of the fact that we would travel to Hainaut. The Count of Hainaut told me that the two Flemish ships did no trade. Their sole purpose was to capture or kill me."

Wulfric growled, "They caught me out once, lord. A second opportunity will not occur!"

As dusk approached we prepared for our raid. We would not need helmets for we would need our eyes and ears. The helmets would hang from our cantles but we would need a spare spear. I knew that I would lose my lance at some point in the first charge. The spare fitted beneath my left leg and shield.

We were about to leave when the two newest scouts rode in on their ponies. Hal and Osbert were little more than twelve summers old. I had seen more meat on a sparrow yet they were bright-eyed and knew their business, "Lord, Aiden sent us. He said we were not yet ready to cut throats. They are at the last camp; the one closest to Northallerton. They will cause mayhem there."

"Good you two can help my men guard the camp!" We headed off down the road. There were eighty-four men at arms and archers as well as four knights in my small battle. We were led by Dick. We followed his instructions and did as his signals commanded. After half a mile, we left the road and our movements became quieter as we walked our horses along the grass which lay adjacent to the road. After a mile he left us leaving his archer, Richard of Middleham, to guide us to the camp.

We smelled it before we saw it. There was a strong breeze from the south and it wafted the smell of the camp towards us; wood smoke and cooking mutton. The local farmers were paying the price for this attack. Richard used hand signals to slow us down and then to warn us of the precise location of their camp. Wulfric brought up the rear. I was at the fore with Sir Harold, Sir John and Gilles. Their squires and Richard were behind us as was the archer, Richard of Middleham. His bow would come in handy.

I waved the column forward and we walked. We moved to the trot and then the canter. Our hooves could now be heard but I knew that the enemy would be confused over the direction of the sound. Night did that. Men would be eating, talking, drinking; they would not be ready for a sudden savage attack. They would look to the skies to see if this was thunder preceding rain. They would turn to each other and question the noise. They would seek the direction from whence it came and all the time we would be drawing closer with death in our hands.

I had my lance held overhand. It made for a better strike. I rested it across the cantle of my saddle. I saw shadows ahead and the shadows moved. There were five sentries. They turned as we hurtled towards them. I stabbed down at one and my lance entered his back. The others were either trampled or speared too.

As his body slid from the lance's head I shouted, "Left and right!"

We went from a column to a wide, loose line. We needed to cause maximum casualties whilst sowing confusion. We did not ride knee to knee, we just rampaged through their camp each rider choosing his own course. I saw a mailed warrior grab his shield and turn to face us. I couched my lance and rammed it hard into his open side. His shield was not quick enough nor was his mail strong enough and my lance tore deep into his body. This time I could not save the lance and I released it. I drew my sword, to save time, and I swung it at head height. My arm jarred as it struck the back and spine of a warrior running from me. He gave a primaeval scream as my blade grated along his backbone. The enemy were fleeing. I saw two of them tumble over fires and others were pitched to the ground by the ropes holding their tents. Our weapons were not the only ones to cause wounds and death. It seemed to last but a heartbeat or two and then we were through their camp and into the dark once more.

I reined in and turned to look at my men; most seemed to have safely arrived. When a gleeful Wulfric, the last of my men, reined in I said, "Richard of Middleham, lead us to the next camp." I sheathed my sword and drew my second spear. Shorter than the lance it was slightly less unwieldy.

We headed through the dark. I trusted my archer completely. He had been trained by Dick and he would lead us safely to the place from which we could launch our second attack. I hoped that Dick had managed to capture the horses. That would be a double help. It would deprive the enemy of horses whilst adding to our own herds.

We covered the mile quicker than I had expected we would. We had walked our horses for they would need to charge again soon. This time we were upwind of the camp and did not smell it. They might smell us although I doubted it. We relied on Richard. He signalled and we formed our column again. I spurred my mount. This time there were just two sentries. The turf on which we rode did not make as much noise and the two died without knowing who we were. From the direction, we approached we might have been reinforcements. The camp was awake and alerted because of our attack on the neighbouring camp. There had been noise, screams and the sound of battle. They were, however, looking in the wrong direction; to the north and when we burst into their camp, in three long lines, it caused confusion as they panicked.

It was like hunting deer. The enemy were confused and disorganised. Many had no mail and died quickly. I struck three fleeing warriors before my spear broke and I was forced to draw my sword. I had to lean forward to strike men as they threw themselves to the ground. It availed them nought for they were trampled by horses that could not avoid them. I saw two of my new men at arms ride ahead of me. They grabbed the ropes of a tent as they passed and dragged it across the fire. It was an inspired move for the canvas ignited and, as they dragged it towards the horse lines, it made the horses panic too and they tore the stakes holding the lines out of the ground. They thundered north. Our attack was so quick that we were through before they could take a breath and, once we were in the dark, I turned to watch for Wulfric and the rest of my men.

I recognised my new men; the ones who had used the tent as a weapon. "That was well done, Ralph of Nottingham. You think on your feet. I like that!"

"It is a shame we have no treasure from this, lord!"

"We have horses and they are as good as treasure."

Wulfric arrived. "We lost but two men at arms, lord, and we have destroyed two camps!" He sheathed his sword and rubbed his stomach. "I have an appetite!"

"We will drive the horse which fled the camp towards our men."

Once the danger had passed the horses stopped and looked to return to their masters. We stopped them by driving them north. As we neared the road our sentries guided them to our own horse lines. Dick was waiting there.

"A rich haul, lord. We captured twenty-five mounts. Some are war horses." He pointed. "We found another twenty-one which fled north."

"Then the raid has been worthwhile. Now we prepare our defences. Sir Wulfric, I want you and Sir John to use your men to guard the archers."

"After we have eaten, lord!"

"Of course. The rest of you ride to the main camp and let your horses rest. We may need them tomorrow."

As we walked our mounts down to the dell I heard James and Henry asking Gilles and Richard about the attack. Envy oozed from their words. Richard shrugged, "It all happened so quickly, my lord. The enemy loomed up out of the dark and you barely had time to think let alone bring back your arm to strike them."

Henry nodded, "So you struck none?"

"I killed three and there are another three who will not fight on the morrow. Gilles killed more."

Gilles said, "I was lucky. I am bigger than Richard. Do not forget that my father was an archer. I have naturally broad shoulders."

Henry looked puzzled, "Your father was an archer? Yet you would be a knight."

"Mine was a man at arms who served the Earl." James knew his father's story well and was proud of it.

74

I saw Henry taking that information in. He was used to nobles and the sons of nobles. This was a different world. As they sat around my fire I realised that this was part of his training to be a king. He was seeing the real people he would rule and not the fawning courtiers who sought his favour. Their language was rough as were they but they were the rock upon which a good king built his kingdom. As Ranulf, the Earl of Chester had shown, nobility was nothing to do with birth. He was as far from being a noble as a swineherd for he did not do the honourable thing. My father would have called him a nithing. My men fell upon the food as though they had not eaten for a week. Battle did that. I was not hungry and so I slept. The older I became the less I ate. I remembered that my father had been the same.

When I awoke it was not yet dawn. Gilles was shaking my arm, "Lord, it is Aiden, Edgar and Edward, they have returned."

I was awake in an instant and I pulled myself to my feet with the aid of Gilles' arm, "I fear I am getting old, Gilles."

"Never, lord."

Aiden and his two scouts were each eating some stale bread and ham. Aiden laid down his ham as he spoke to me and pointed south. "We went around each of their camps, lord. We had just left the second one you attacked just before you arrived. That was why there were just two sentries. We were late as we went to Northallerton and used our bows to slay four of the sentries on watch." He laughed. "They will have little sleep. On the way back we found eight horses. We brought them back. They are much discomfited by the attack, lord."

"Have Hal and Osbert along with Edward here drive the horses back to Stockton. They can be shared out later."

He nodded, "As for me, I shall sleep!"

"Thank you, Aiden. Gilles, you may return to your bed too."

I was awake. I would not be able to sleep anymore and I walked the five hundred paces to Wulfric's camp. Dick was awake along with Sir John. Wulfric's snores made me smile.

He could sleep through anything. "Do you think they will come, my lord?"

"I think they will come but I know not if they will fight. I want them to believe that the archers and the two conroi are our only warriors. I want to tempt them into attacking. If they do then I will lead our horsemen around their flanks to destroy them. However, it may be that they just come to inspect us. I will live with that too. If they do not attack, then we try another tactic. We use the archers to infiltrate their camp and cause mayhem with their knives."

Sir John pointed towards the camp, "Young Henry, will he fight today?"

"He might, why?"

"My men know not what to call him. Is he prince or lord? What do they call him? They do not wish to cause offence."

"Tell them to call him, sir, for he is noble-born. We knights can call him Henry. His title is Marquess but I do not think he likes the title. It reminds him that his father took the title, Duke."

When I saw dawn begin to break over the hills to the east Sir John ordered his men to stand to. Dick had already been around to rouse his men and the archers had made water and eaten by the time we saw the sun.

I nodded towards Wulfric. "Best wake the bear, eh John? He will be annoyed if he misses anything."

I turned as Gilles, Richard and James appeared. "Where is Henry?"

Gilles smiled. "He sleeps. He complained about the ground but he slept like a baby. We did not disturb him, lord. We only came to receive our orders."

"James, stay here with me in case I need you for messages. You two go and water and feed our horses. Prepare them for battle."

They left. James stood just behind me and we waited. I saw nothing but one of my archers did for I saw an arrow soar followed by a cry.

Will Red Legs hurried towards me, "My lord, Dick says to tell you they have their scouts out."

Even as he spoke I saw more arrows arc into the sky and heard more shouts. My sentries were woodsmen and were well hidden. These enemy scouts were not as good as my men.

I walked towards the road. We had made a barrier there made of brushwood and brambles. It would not stop a horse but it would slow them down. On both sides of the road, we had embedded stakes. If an enemy attacked us we were forcing them up the slope into a narrow trap. There, forty of my men at arms would stop them, no matter how many came. At the moment the men rested. It was the archers who would watch. There were over eighty of them. My ten sentries, who were ahead of the others, could not be seen but the rest were spread out to the east and west of the road. The banners of Sir Wulfric and Sir Phillip told our enemies that knights were here.

I had begun to think that they would not come. It was late morning and, after the first visit by their scouts, we had seen nothing. I did not need my sentries to report to me. I saw the banners as their army headed north towards us. I saw them as they appeared up the road. The road had a dip about a mile away and they rose, like a metal wave over the top.

"James, go and tell Sir Harold to prepare the men. The enemy comes."

Wulfric, John, Dick and Phillip hurried to my side. "You all know what to do?"

Wulfric nodded, "Aye lord. We commit them to the attack and when they close we sound the horn three times."

"Do not be too heroic, Wulfric! Just make sure that they press to the centre. Give us plenty of time eh?"

"Of course."

"Then God be with you." I waited while I watched the men at arms get into position. They each had a spear and Wulfric organized them into an old fashioned shield wall in the centre. With the front spears braced on the road, the spears behind would be presented over the shoulders of the ones at the front to make a hedgehog of steel. Although their shields hung loosely from their left shoulders they could be presented to an enemy attack in an instant.

Beyond them, I saw that they had a solid phalanx of
horsemen approaching down the centre of the road. To their
sides marched men on foot. Whoever commanded this army
had put all of his mounted men in the centre. He hoped to
break through the men in the road and then spread out once
they had passed the stakes. I could not be too accurate with
their numbers for the horsemen stretched into the distance
and the foot walked without too much order. I counted their
banners and gonfanon. I estimated fifty mounted knights.
There did not appear to be large numbers of mounted men at
arms. I recognized the banner of William of Aumale. He was
the most powerful of Stephen's supporters here in the north
and was the Constable of York. I also saw the red and white
striped banner. The men of Flanders were here. The banner
was that of Charles of Bruges. I had seen enough and I left
the rise to descend to my waiting horsemen.

James stood holding the reins of Rolf, my horse. He had
been groomed. I had not used him the night before. I did not
need a battle-hardened horse then. I did now.

After I had mounted and James had handed me my lance
I said, "They come. Sir Harold, you take your men and Sir
Gilles to the west of the road. Sir Tristan, bring yours with
me. Listen for the signal and when we hit them, hit them
hard. They outnumber us. We cannot afford to be dainty." I
turned to William of Le Havre. "Make sure this young
cockerel stays in the second rank! I would not risk the wrath
of his father if he should be lost under my care!"

William grinned, "And we might not be paid either! We
will keep him safe, lord."

I saw a scowl on Henry's face. I did not mind. Better a
scowl than an extra mouth below his chin because I had been
careless.

Leaving the archer's horse holders to guard the camp I
led my forty men at arms to the east. The rise hid us. No
enemy would know of our movements. We rode for half a
mile. I heard the thunder of hooves up the road and, as we
turned to face the south, I saw the arrows as they rose in the
sky. My eighty-odd archers could keep up a rain of arrows as
long as it was necessary. I knew that battle had been joined

when I heard a cheer and then the clash of metal on metal. Shouts and cries told me that men were dying.

We had two ranks. I rode between Sir Tristan and Gilles. Edgar was to Gilles' right. Behind me rode my two squires with the banner and next to them, Henry and his bodyguards. I knew that the strength of the centre of our attack lay with Edgar, Sir Tristan and myself. We would have to penetrate deep into the enemy ranks.

As time passed I wondered if Wulfric was delaying too long. Then I heard the horn sound. "Forward, for God, England, the Empress and Henry FitzEmpress!" My men cheered and I led them south.

As we crested the rise it looked to be confusion before us. The enemy foot soldiers were trying to get through the barrier of stakes and pits my archers had dug. Sir Wulfric and his men had not yet had to break sweat thanks to the endeavours of the archers. While half of Sir Phillip's men loosed their arrows at the horsemen which were massed in the centre the other half were slaying men at arms and with a flat trajectory were causing terrible wounds. As we appeared in their eye line there was a collective wail. I headed for the rear of the men on foot and I lowered my lance.

We rode boot to boot and we came at a steady pace. The men on foot were not all mailed. As they saw us I saw a sergeant at arms trying to organize them. Even as he pointed at us an arrow blossomed from his neck. A shield cannot protect a whole body. The shields that had been carried at Hastings were bigger than the ones we used now. A man on a horse with a lance has a choice of targets. Most men try to protect their heads. The first man I struck did so. His thigh was exposed and my lancehead tore into the muscles of his leg. He fell screaming in agony as blood spurted from the severed artery. I allowed my right hand to slip backwards as his body fell from the tip. I brought it back to the couched position. In that fleeting moment of death, the men on foot had begun to flee. They did not see forty knights and men at arms; they saw a wall of metal and horseflesh. Even as they ran my archers reaped a harvest.

Ignoring the men on foot, we could catch them after we had destroyed the mounted threat, I wheeled to charge the right flank of the knights and men at arms on horses who were attacking my centre. Their shields were on the opposite arm and we rode up the slope to the road ready to cause mayhem.

I glanced to left and right. My men were still in a long line. Rolf was a powerful horse and he had edged slightly ahead. I allowed that for it meant I would be the tip of the arrow. I saw a red and white striped surcoat. It was a knight of Flanders. I rode Rolf directly at him. He was not at the fore and he turned his horse as he became aware of our attack. The knight next to him tried to do the same but an arrow plummeted down and struck him in the neck. As the knight of Flanders tried to turn I stood in my stirrups and punched forward. He could not bring his shield around in time. He tried to fence with his own spear but my thrust brushed it aside and my lance tore deep into his middle. The tip ripped through the mail and into his gambeson. I saw his face contort as the metal head delved deep into his body. The forward momentum of his horse drove him from his saddle and dragged my lance down. I let go and drew my sword.

The archer's arrow meant that Gilles had no opponent in the front rank and even as we hit their line his lance drove deep into the side of an unsuspecting knight. I swung my sword and hacked into the arm of the knight behind. The blow was so powerful that it almost tore my sword from my hand. I pulled back a little on Rolf's reins to slow him. It had the effect of making him rear and his hooves smashed onto the thigh of the next knight. I brought my sword over to strike down on his shoulder and he tumbled from his horse. Our attack on their weak side was causing mayhem.

I saw, ahead of me, Sir Harold approaching from the west of the road, we had almost severed their line. He had brought his men from the other flank. They had not expected us to attack for they outnumbered us. Now was the time for the second part of my plan. Their leaders were between us and Wulfric. Leaving my dismounted knights to finish those off I wheeled Rolf and shouted, "On! South!"

Sir Tristan, who was next to me, still had his lance and as he punched into the helmet of one of William of Aumale's men at arms I stabbed under the arm of the man at arms next to him. All order had gone from our lines now but it mattered not. We were amongst men who had lost their leaders. Where they had been following their knights and leaders they were now faced with their enemy. Our archers were still sending arrows over our heads into the massed ranks of horsemen before them. Inevitably they broke.

When the ones before us turned to flee through their comrades it caused confusion. Horses reared and men were thrown as the men at arms, many of them mercenaries, tried to save their lives by fleeing the field. In many cases, it was in vain for we were in hot pursuit and an unprotected back is an easy target. There were knights before us and they were frustrated in their attempts to rally their fleeing men at arms. Soon I heard the familiar cries of, "I yield!"

One knight and his four men at arms continued to stand and, seeing my banner he yelled, "I will kill you, Earl of Cleveland!" Swinging his war axe the knight with the yellow and green checked shield rode at me.

His men at arms guarded his flanks and I ignored them. Gilles, Edgar and Tristan could deal with them. The knight was a more dangerous opponent. He rode at my sword side. His axe was more powerful than my sword and I had just a shield to protect me. There was no one to my left now. I watched as he pulled back his arm to swing at my chest. Jerking Rolf to my left I pulled my shield up. I would form a barrier across my chest. At the same time, I swung my sword at head height. This was not a time for the faint heart. His axe smashed into my shield and the blow was so powerful that I reeled. Only my cantle held me. When my sword connected with his neck he died but the force of the blow threw me backwards over the rear of Rolf's rump. Even as I fell I tucked my head into my chest. There were horses charging behind me. It would be ironic to have my head caved in by one of my own men. I hit the ground hard. It knocked the wind from me and I saw stars.

I felt something clatter into my head and then all went black.

"My lord! I am sorry! My lord, awake!" It was Henry FitzEmpress' voice I heard. I opened my eyes and saw him and Gilles standing over me. There was relief on their face when they saw I lived. "I could not reach you in time! I thought you dead!"

"We have sent for a healer." Gilles smiled but I saw concern in his eyes.

I held out my arm for Gilles. As he pulled me up I said, "I need no healer. I was knocked from my horse is all." I nodded at Henry. "The same thing happened to your great grandfather at Hastings I believe."

Richard rode up with Rolf, "We have the field, my lord. We have a great victory! The enemy soldiers are fled and their knights yield!"

I sheathed my sword and holding Rolf's reins said, into his ear, "Well done, my steed. That was my fault and not yours." Once on his back, I could see men at arms running down the fleeing men on foot. Other men at arms were dispatching the enemy men at arms who were badly wounded. I saw the body of the knight whose axe had almost done for me. My shield had been almost cut in two and I would need another. The body and the head of the knight lay ten paces apart. He would have known nothing of his death. He would have been alive one moment contemplating his victory over the Earl of Cleveland and in the next ... oblivion. Such were the narrow margins in a battle.

I saw Edgar grinning, "A spectacular fall, my lord! At our age, it is not the best thing to do." He was always the same. No matter how many times we fought Edgar was always there like a rock.

I nodded, "Aye Edgar! I am slipping. Did we lose many?"

"Jean of Angers and Guillaume of La Flèche have served you for the last time. Others are wounded. Sir Tristan lost a couple of men too. He is leading the others in the chase."

Any loss was sad but these men had fought with me for some time. The two dead men at arms had both joined me years ago when I had been given the manor of La Flèche. Both Angevin, they had become Englishmen by choice.

"Make sure their families receive their share of the treasure."

Henry, who had been silently listening to this, said, "But they are dead!"

"And they served me. They deserve a share of the spoils of war. This is a lesson for you. Keep loyal men around you." He nodded but, as we discovered later, he was not listening and he paid the price of that temporary deafness.

Fifteen knights had been captured although, sadly, William of Aumale was not amongst them. We sent the three squires who had yielded for ransom and then, after dismantling our defences, we headed back up the road to Yarm. Our dead were buried in a large grave by the side of the road. We marked it with a single cross. When we passed it as we rode the road we would remember them. On the other side, we made a pile of the enemy dead we had fought and, using the stakes which had kept them from us, we burned them on a pyre. The blackened earth remained for the rest of the year. It was a reminder to the enemy of the dangers of taking on the Warlord of the North.

Chapter 6

I kept the knights waiting for ransom at my castle. Gone were the days when I would have asked for reasonable amounts. Now we asked for all that we knew they could pay. It was another lesson to teach. Knights would think twice before joining a venture to attack us. Amongst the knights, we had captured was Diederik of Brugge. He was one of the Flemish knights. He was a surly man. The knights who yielded had given their word and were allowed the freedom of the inner bailey. Most accepted their imprisonment with good grace. The only knight who was deliberately unpleasant was the Flemish knight. The rest behaved civilly towards my people.

John of Craven came to me on the third day. He was angry. "Lord, that foreigner is upsetting my men. He is disrespectful about you and the women of the house. It is all that I can do to stop them from laying hands upon him. The other knights are all gentlemen; they are English!"

I smiled. John had the typical attitude of most of my men when it came to anyone not born in England. They were foreigners! "I will have a word with him." I waved over Henry, "Come, you can have another lesson in leadership. This one is called diplomacy."

I approached the knight who was alone. He was shunned by the other knights. That told me a great deal. "Sir Diederik, a word."

His lip turned into a sneer, "What words of yours would you think I would hear, barbarian?"

My men had to take that but I did not. I backhanded him across the face with a blow so hard that he reeled.

His hand went to the sword he had already surrendered. "I will kill you for that!"

"Watch your tongue or you shall spend the rest of your time confined to a cell. You are my prisoner and you lose all rights if you choose to behave in such a dishonourable fashion."

He looked surprised, "What have I done?"

"You have insulted my men, my ladies and my name!"

"Your men are peasants!"

I had had enough, "John, fetch two men and confine this man in a cell!"

As they pinioned his arms he struggled in vain. "My cousin William of Ypres will hear of the manner in which you have treated me!"

"Good! Perhaps he will challenge me. Each time he has had the opportunity he has declined. Perhaps every man of Flanders is a coward."

"I am insulted!"

"If you wish I can have your sword brought and you can try to redeem your honour here and now. What say you?"

As with all bullies he backed down. I saw fear in his eyes as he shook his head, "Fight King Henry's champion in his own castle? You must think me a fool."

I smiled, "Yes I do." His head bowed, "Take him away and report any more insults to me. This has increased his ransom. Each insult from now on increases the amount!"

Henry smiled, "What lesson was I to learn, lord? How to use my hands as well as my sword?"

"That you must face up to bullies wherever they are and in whatever form they present themselves." Each day was a new lesson for Henry. I did not spend my time with courtiers; I was a warlord whose every move, action and word had a purpose.

With the new horses, we had acquired we had to build more stables. The inner and outer baileys did not have enough room and so we built them to the west of the western wall of my castle. Although beyond the ditch and moat they could be watched from my walls. We built a hut and Hal and Osbert lived there. It suited them and they were able to act as stable guards. The mail and weapons we had taken were as valuable as the coins we took from the purses of the dead men at arms. Those that we did not reuse we would sell to the Danes and others who wished to buy weapons from us. My steward was happy.

Summer was drawing to a close and I had not visited my western borders. Taking Ralph of Nottingham and the new men as well as Dick and his archers we headed west. This was partly to show my new men at arms our land and also to let Henry know the value of our valley. The fields we passed were filled with farmers and their families gathering in crops and collecting animals from summer pastures. They were prosperous. It had been many years since we had been threatened from the north and even a couple of summers without a raid brought great wealth to my people. They waved to us as we passed. My banner was recognised as were my men. It was a sign that they were safe and secure. There might be anarchy beyond my borders but within all was peaceful and prosperity reigned.

Sir Phillip was now prosperous. As the nephew of Archbishop Thurston, he had come to me as a captain of archers. Now he had men at arms guarding his castle which improved year on year. When he received his share of the ransom he would be even richer. I saw that there were more people living close by and he had improved the defences of this vital river crossing. We did not stay long for I was anxious to get to Barnard Castle. Sir Hugh's former home at Gainford now had a small garrison. There might be a time when it became Sir Hugh's once more but it was still a useful refuge when enemies threatened. It had a ditch and a wall around the hall. In contrast with the simple castle at Gainford, Barnard Castle was a redoubtable fortress. The mighty castle had an impressive position. Perched on a rock high above the river it protected my valley from the west. Sir Hugh had cleared much of the woods to the east to afford a fine view as we headed towards it. That also allowed the garrison to see us and we were spotted a mile away. Sir

Hugh awaited us as we entered the gates and went into the outer bailey.

He bowed, "Good to see you, my lord and you too, Henry FitzEmpress." He stood back to appraise the future king. He was impressed. "You will be a knight soon."

They were the right words and pleased my charge. "And this castle, Sir Hugh, is truly impressive." He looked at me. "The Scots claim it, do they not?"

"They claim all of the land north of the River Tees. They lost it to your great grandfather and now seek to reclaim it through stealth."

As we walked towards the inner bailey he said, "My mother has a treaty with her uncle, the King of Scotland."

"She does and that is why we do not do as my men and I wish and that is to invade Scotland and take back the castles they stole from us."

"Stole is a strong word, my lord." Henry had not lived close to the Scots and he believed the stories they had spread.

"Not strong enough. I lost knights who were loyal to England. I have a long memory and I will pay them back. Until your mother gives me permission then the Scots are safe... so long as they do not try to take a single blade of grass from that which I hold!"

Henry laughed and I saw his bodyguards smiling. "You make a hard enemy!"

"And there is another lesson for a future king. Make your enemies fear you." I turned to Sir Hugh, "They fear you, do they not, Sir Hugh?"

"That they do. I ride abroad at least once a month. I ride as far as their first castles. Any Scots I find I hang. Any brigand I find I hang."

Henry asked, "When did you hang your last Scot?"

Sir Hugh smiled, "A year since; they have learned." He turned to me. "I take it you were victorious against the men of York, my lord."

"I was. We were outnumbered but they had too many mercenaries. They fled the field when we attacked them.

They left only fifty dead upon the field but there will be many more cripples begging in York's streets."

We stayed three days and travelled north and east so that Henry could see that which had been lost to the Scots since the civil war had begun. As we headed back home I saw that it had been a worthwhile journey. Henry spoke of making our castles stronger and building more. "The Romans looked to have the best idea. Build a wall." We had travelled as far north as the Roman wall and, like me, he had been impressed. "If we could build castles closer to the wall then we could stop any incursions."

"We could but it is hard to have knights who wish manors here. The land is poor. You cannot grow wheat. In winter it is cold and harsh. Sir Leofric in Anjou noticed the difference. For a knight to live up here he has to be as hard as the land around him."

"Sir Hugh seems to manage."

"He comes from Gainford and his wife is the brother of Sir Tristan. The land is in their blood."

"Yet you came from a country even hotter and you live here."

"My father was born and bred just south of the Tees. I am no Greek. If you are to be King of England then remember your blood. Your father was Angevin but your mother was born in England. Your great grandfather chose this country in which to live; think about that."

When we reached home all of the ransoms save the one for the Flemish knight had been paid. I went to see him, "Perhaps the fact that your countrymen do not seem willing to pay your ransom speaks much about you, eh?"

He smirked, "Beware, Warlord, William of Ypres may be coming here to defeat you as he did with the Earl of Gloucester."

It was my turn to smile, "I have only faced William of Ypres once and that was at the battle of Lincoln. We captured a king and your master fled the field. He is welcome to come and I will see that he does not run away this time; he will crawl on the stumps of his legs!"

A week later there was great excitement as Ethelred's cog was launched. His wife named her after herself, *'Mary of Stockton'*. The name seemed to suit her and she floated on the river easily. It would take until autumn to fit her out and have her ready for sea. On that same day, William of Kingston went to sea. He had goods for Antwerpen and Edjberg. His wife, son in arms, came to see him off. Soon we would have two such ships and my people would be even richer.

Mary and Gilles escorted Morag back to the castle. From the looks Mary was giving the babe I knew what was in her mind. I would need to think about knighting Gilles soon. All Saints Day would be a propitious time. I would speak with Father Henry and Alice about it. It would need a feast. The last knight I had dubbed had been Sir Gilles of Normanby and that had been when Sir Edward was still alive.

I had had no letters since I had returned from Normandy. Perhaps there were some waiting for me in Anjou. I found it hard to be isolated in my valley, not knowing what was going on in the wider world. I penned one to the Empress telling her of the battle, her son and our new alliance. I did not tell her of her husband's infidelity. Nothing could be gained from that. Then I wrote to my son. I knew that bridges needed to be rebuilt and I was getting no younger. I would have to make the first move if I wanted to see my grandchildren.

I was halfway through it when I heard a cry from the battlements, "Riders approaching from the south. They bear the livery of Flanders."

I knew that this would be the ransom for Diederik. I went to the outer bailey. "John, have our guest and his baggage brought here. He may be leaving but have two men to watch him."

The gates were opened to admit six riders. They had with them a magnificent warhorse as well as two palfreys with a chest between them. The leader dismounted and bowed, "I am here to pay the ransom for Sir Diederik of Bruges."

"He is coming but he proved an unpleasant guest and I have increased the ransom."

The knight looked nonplussed, "But that is unheard of."

"As is a knight insulting his host."

"But we brought no extra coin!"

I nodded, "Then I will take the warhorse as compensation." I turned to my men, "Remove the saddle and put it on the palfrey. That is good enough for him." The knight looked as though he was ready to object. I spoke coldly and quietly, "You know that I am the Warlord of the North and I answer to no man. Do not try my patience or I will keep your Sir Diederik as a permanent prisoner."

The knight was beaten and he nodded. His men had just removed the chest and put the saddle on one of them when Sir Diederik appeared. He grinned as he passed me, "I will not forget you, Earl. One day I will have my vengeance!"

He turned and strode towards the warhorse I said, "John, have your men take my new horse to my stable!"

The Flemish knight turned and his face was filled with fury, "This is an outrage!"

"I told you that you would pay for your insults. Choose your words a little more carefully next time!"

He mounted the palfrey and spurred it out of my castle. The knight who had delivered the ransom nodded, "I see that you live up to your reputation, Earl. You fear no man alive and live by your own rules."

"That is why I have the title Warlord. Safe journey and I pity you the company of that man."

He shrugged, "He is my half brother. I have little choice."

My new horse was magnificent. He was golden and reminded me of Scout, my first horse. I had named Rolf after a brother knight who had fought alongside me and I did the same for my new mount. I called him Edward. When I used the name he seemed to like it. It lifted my spirits. I was rid of an unpleasant guest and the payment for his visit was a magnificent horse. Life was good.

I felt so pleased that I summoned Gilles. "Yes, lord?"

"I have a mind to dub you on All Saints Day. What say you?"

"My lord, it will be an honour. Am I ready?"

"That we shall see. There are oaths you must learn and you must hold a vigil on All Hallows Eve. I have no doubt you will pass the tests but I have known others who have failed. And then you will need to decide what to do about Mary eh?"

"We would be wed, lord."

"Good, then when you both come to me with a date we shall see about the feast and the dowry. I know not how much longer Henry FitzEmpress will be with us. I think it would do you good if he were here when you married."

"Lord?"

"When he is king and I am no longer here you might need a friend who can give you favours."

"But where are you going, lord?"

"I am going nowhere but I grow older and life becomes neither safer nor easier."

I am not certain he understood me but he hurried to speak with Mary. I went first to see Alice and John and then Father Henry. All were delighted but Alice was the most pleased. She was very fond of the young couple. It would be like her own children getting married. Her husband had died in my service and she had dedicated her life to the castle, the manor and to me.

When autumn came to our valley it came with wild and wet winds and the days suddenly felt short indeed. I rode with my men at arms and squires as often as possible. It was interesting to see Henry develop. He became a much better rider. My squires knew horses. Henry was from Anjou and could ride. Gilles, however, came from Normandy and he could do things with a horse which were hard to understand for they showed an ability to almost talk to the horse. Unlike me, Gilles had never been knocked from his saddle. Despite the fact that when he had been younger he had been a stripling he had always managed to hold his own. He passed those skills on to Henry. Richard showed him how to use a sword on horseback. Time passed quickly and Henry became a potential knight. Each night we would play chess and talk of war. All of my squires became better warriors as a result.

The three of them became more than had I just trained one. They fed from each other.

By the time *'Adela'* nudged her way into port, there was little to distinguish between my squires save that Gilles now carried himself with more confidence. There was just Henry and me at the quay watching the *'Adela'* tacking along the river. Gilles and Richard were with Father Henry preparing for the ceremonies. Richard would be a knight before too long and he was anxious to learn what was needed.

"Earl, will you give Gilles a manor?"

"I may. He has not asked for one."

"That should be the gift of the king should it not?"

I laughed, "It should but do you think that Stephen would allow me to do so?"

"What happens when he is gone?"

"Then you will be king." I could see where he was going with this. "I am the Earl of Cleveland. You may well wish to give my manors to other knights. That would be your choice for all of them have been appointed by me, as Earl of Cleveland." He nodded, "Of course, the reason I had to do so was because they died trying to save England from your mother's enemies."

"I was not saying I would take them from you. I like all of your knights and know that they are noble even if not noble-born. I asked you because when I am king there will be knights who supported Stephen. I need to know what to do about them."

The *'Adela'* was almost at the quay, "When you are king I would spend time learning who you command. There may be some of those who supported Stephen who are worthy knights. There may be others who support your mother who are not."

"You mean like the Earl of Chester?"

"Exactly like the Earl of Chester."

As the ropes were thrown we moved out of the way of them. William of Kingston shouted, "You have a visitor, lord, from the Count of Hainaut."

As the ship was secured and the gangplank was lowered two young men stepped ashore, "I am Lothair son of the

Count of Hainaut, Earl. My father has entrusted me with a most serious mission. I must speak with you alone."

I shook my head, "Whatever you say to me you can say to this young man. He will be my lord one day but you are right. This is not the place to speak. For one thing, the wind has chilled me to the bone. Come to my hall."

He turned, "Dik, fetch my bags."

"Aye lord."

I examined Lothair as we walked to my hall. He was slight. His hands were smooth and his arms were not muscled. I did not think he had been trained as a knight. He looked to me like a priest and yet he did not wear the robes of a priest. Alice had anticipated us and was waiting in my hall with wine and food. She had Seara, one of the house servants, poking the fire to make the hall homelier.

"Thank you, Alice. There will be a young man with bags. Have him taken to a room. There will be two guests. See that we are not disturbed."

"Yes, my lord." She shooed Seara out and then shut the doors behind her.

"Sit and tell me this mission."

"My father thanks you for the weapons, lord. They are most useful and he would like some more." I saw Henry frown. This was not something that needed secrecy. I waited for I could tell that the young man had not finished. "And the men to use them." He sipped his wine. "I have coin with me."

"Let me understand this. Your father wants to hire my men to fight for him?"

"Yes lord. We are being threatened from the south. The men of Flanders seek to destroy our prosperity. We have taken much trade from them. Our allies in Holland are also being threatened but we bear the brunt."

"Your father could have sent this request in a letter."

"He feared interception. I was a safer option."

"Yet you are not a knight."

"No lord. I am the youngest of my father's three sons. I was sickly as a child and was not trained. My father thought

I might join the church but it was not for me." He shrugged, "I am expendable but I am happy to serve my father."

I liked Lothair. He made the best of what he had. "And so you use your head where your brothers use their arms."

"Yes, lord. It was my idea to ask for your men. We all heard how you defeated two ships and your reputation on land is known across the whole of the lands of the Empire. You are the Empress' champion and have never tasted defeat. I thought that with you at our side we could not lose."

"I am flattered. However, we have our own civil war here and your country lies many leagues across the ocean. If I were to relax my watch then who knows what might happen. Tell me of this threat."

"The Count of Flanders sends bands of men raiding the country. We do not have castles as strong as this and the Flemish raiders take all from our people. We live by our industry. We make fine cloth and if we cannot feed those workers then we are lost."

The door opened and Alice said, "The young man has unpacked. Shall he join you, lord?"

"Send him in."

I had not noticed him before for he had been collecting the bags but Dik was the opposite of Lothair. He was broad and he was strong. He carried a sword and looked as though he knew how to use it.

"Come and join your master. There is wine as well as food and a fire to warm you."

"Thank you, lord."

I turned back to Lothair. "I cannot help you with the men, not directly anyway but I have some ideas. Would you care to hear them?"

"I am disappointed but any help would be welcome."

"I will be sending my ship back in the next month or so. She can take you home and deliver the next shipment of weapons. It will also carry Henry back to his father." Henry looked surprised. "The winter storms will soon make the journey both difficult and dangerous and I believe you have learned much already eh, Henry?"

"I have but there is more to learn."

I nodded, "And those lessons will continue but for the moment let us address the problems of Hainaut for there may be a lesson here for you too." He smiled and sat back. He was learning and he was growing. His father had been more volatile when he had been the same age. Blood would out; Henry was more like me than Geoffrey of Anjou.

"I would suggest, Lothair, that after you have spoken to your father you go with Henry here to Rouen. There they have warriors who have just fought in the Norman wars. There are many there, my son amongst them, who would be warriors that you could use. I will also send a letter to my manor in Anjou. My castellan trains men for me there. I could allow your father to hire those until this threat is over. What say you to that?"

"It is not perfect but it gives us hope. Thank you."

"And then I will take you around my castle for if you build castles such as this then the men of Flanders will not be able to suck the lifeblood from you."

"This would take too long to build. We need help now."

"This was not the work of one day. But if you wish what can be achieved in a short time then Henry here will take you to my smaller manors and show you the castles they have built there. We have a ring of them around my land protecting us."

With the delicate business out of the way, I sent for Gilles, Richard and James. "Tomorrow you will be preparing for your vigil, Gilles, and then your wedding. Richard and James, I want you to go with Henry and show this young man the castles of Yarm, Hartburn, Elton and Norton. I want him to see how a small number of men can defend a large area."

"Aye lord."

"And I will leave you now for I must see my steward and my smith if we are to fulfil this order from Hainaut."

Lothair rose and bowed, "Thank you, Earl. I hoped for help and although this is not what I wished for I see that is the best that you can do. I thank you."

After they had left us I spoke with Henry. "I need to speak directly with your mother. If I travel to Devizes there are many risks, especially if you travel with me. That is the main reason I am sending you home. Only you know of my plan. I trust Lothair but who knows what he might say."

"But I would come with you and speak with my mother."

"You need to put into practice that which I have shown you. Begin to build up your own army." I had given him a share of the spoils of war and he now had coin. "You know what men you ought to choose. Choose wisely."

"I will and I understand. Thank you, Warlord. I had thought that I would learn all that you knew but I have spoken with Gilles and the others. It is a long road we travel."

"And the slower the journey the more chance we have of reaching the end!"

The next days were a blur. This was not war but it was the work of a lord. Hainaut was now my ally and I was obliged to help them. I was thinking a little of myself too. The men whom Hainaut used could become warriors who would fight for Henry and for me. Lothair's voyage home would be delayed until after Gilles' wedding and that would follow his vigil. Henry and Richard joined him for his vigil and it helped them both. I saw them both change when they emerged in the dawn. The whole experience was the most powerful one for a young man. The wedding which followed was a celebration for the whole valley. All of my knights and their families attended. They were honouring Sir Edward and his memory just as much as the wedding of two young people. After the wedding, as my whole town celebrated, I sat alone with Henry.

"I am not done teaching you, Henry, but I have set you on a path. You are like the apprentice. I have shown you how I make a sword and now I let you go to make a dagger. When the dagger is perfect I will take you under my wing again and improve your skills. Lothair's visit was timely for it showed me that you need to be in your father's land. Ask him if you can run the County of Anjou while he is busy in Normandy. Learn how to organise men and to prepare them for war. There may be some of your Angevin knights who wish to serve Lothair's father and it will put him in your debt. Who knows when you may need to call in that debt?"

"Have you done this, Earl?"

"No, for I fight only for you and your mother and I am no king but if I had to then I would. You should lead your own warriors. Your father did at your age. Sir Leofric is close by and he can offer you advice as well as helping you choose good men."

"I can see the lessons you have given me and I have heeded them. This, too, seems like good advice but what of my mother and the war? Are we any closer to ending this war?"

I could not lie to him. I shook my head, "At the moment the answer would be no. We lack men and we lack leaders. I need to visit your mother to decide how best we should proceed. Your Uncle needs to be consulted too. Going to the southwest means travelling through a hostile country where men will try to capture me. If you were with me that would increase the risk. I have not come this far to take such a risk. There will be a time when you and I can ride abroad. That time is not yet come. When you have gathered men about you and you have learned to lead them then send for me once more and I will continue with the lessons."

Chapter 7

The castle seemed emptier without Henry. Part of that was the fact that Gilles and his new bride were often closeted together and that left me with just James and Richard for company. It was also the fact that the nights had drawn in and winter arrived like a wolf from the north. Winter in England was always hard. We had a merry time at Christmas and my knights all came for the celebrations but when they left I rattled around again inside my castle. I spent many hours alone planning. With our two ships tied to our quay for the winter, we had little news from the outside world. The plans I had put in place were now beyond my control. I hoped that Lothair was able to hire men from Normandy and I prayed that Henry would choose good men to lead but I could nothing about either. I planned, instead, how I could reach the Empress safely. I needed to persuade her and her brother that we had to go on the offensive. We now had an ally. The County was only a small one but it was a start.

One piece of news I did receive was that Ranulf, Earl of Chester, had been imprisoned by Stephen the Usurper. This was after he had helped Stephen to capture Bedford from Miles Beauchamp. A merchant heading for Durham from York stayed in my castle and paid for his lodgings with news from the outside world. There were things I did not fully comprehend. Stephen and Ranulf were playing a game by rules which were unknown to me. I still did not understand the man but it made my journey south even more imperative. By the time Easter approached I was ready to leave for the court of the Empress. I summoned Sir Gilles of Stockton, Sir Harold, Sir Dick, Sir John and Sir Wulfric to my hall.

"I intend to leave at the end of the week and travel to Devizes to speak with the Empress and the Earl of Gloucester. Wulfric, I leave you to command the valley in my absence. Sir Gilles, I leave you to command my castle and I give you James as your squire." I saw the disappointment on James' face. He had wanted to come with me. "I will take all of my men at arms and Dick's archers. Now that we have two ships sailing to Anjou we can expect more men. Sir Gilles, you can have the first choice of those men. Perhaps you might spend some of your wife's dowry eh?"

He grinned, "Aye lord and then I will have to start to earn coin myself."

"You might do that with the patrols that Wulfric will organize. We learned our lesson last year. We need to keep warriors on all of our borders."

Wulfric asked, "How long will you be away, lord?"

"Half a year? Who knows? I will not be able to keep in touch directly but use our ships and Sir Leofric. The seas between Bristol and Angers are safe."

Wulfric asked me, "Lord, do you need to take such risks? We are safe here. We are prosperous. We could sit here and become even more powerful. Who dares to attack us? There are none!"

I nodded, "That has crossed my mind but I swore an oath. What is a man if his word means nothing? Besides it is just myself that I risk."

Wulfric shook his head, "No, lord, for you are the Tees Valley. Without you, we would be easy prey for an enemy. None of us is arrogant enough to believe other. We are warriors but you are the leader. You have shown that time and time again. I am just happy that it is Dick and his archers who protect you."

We took spare horses and we took a handful of armed servants to act as horse holders along with Dick's younger archers. The night before I left Sir Gilles came to me, "I would come with you, lord! You know that."

"I do but you and Mary need time to become familiar with yourselves and your new role. Soon you will have a manor. Learn how to be lord of the manor while I am gone. Alf will help you for he is wise. You have not asked for a manor yet but you will and this will be good experience for you."

We left as dawn was breaking. The ground was growing warmer but it was still desperately cold as we headed west. I had decided to travel along my valley and then cut through Craven. Although there were some Scots there it was a quiet country and I had decided to visit with the Countess of Chester. The Earl of Gloucester's daughter was cut from a different cloth to her husband. She had steel within her and was loyal to her father and her aunt. More than that, she had more sources of information than I had. I had been away from the intrigues for too long. We spent the first night at Barnard Castle. If we rode hard, the next day we could be within half a day's march of Chester.

Richard was more attentive now. He knew that he would be a knight before the year was out. I would have to take on another squire. I was happy to be interrogated by my squire as we headed south.

Dick smiled at him, "You sound like a magpie, Master Richard. You chatter away. What is there to know? When you are a knight you tell men what to do and you lead them. It is as simple as that."

"It comes naturally to you, Sir Richard. I am not Gilles. I have much to learn."

"You are learning, Richard, and I have confidence in you." I was happy with his questions for it made the tedious journey south pass quickly. I told him all that I had told Henry and Gilles. We were lucky that the land was quiet. We were untroubled by enemies.

We woke, stiff from our bivouac, and headed south to Chester. My banner was known and the Countess was a friend. Nonetheless, we rode with helmets, lances and scouts watching for danger. Carelessness could cost a life. We were near the Mersey when riders approached us. I did not recognise the banners. There were four knights and twenty men at arms. As they approached I saw a couple of the knights couch their lances. Dick said, casually, "String your bows, lads! Just to be on the safe side."

I held up a warning hand, "We will speak first."

I waited for the leading knight to speak, "I am Roger of Wilderspool. What are you doing in the lands of the Earl of Chester?"

"You must recognise my banner. You know who I am."

"You are the Earl of Cleveland."

"Then I would like a little deference if you please."

My calm tone seemed to disquiet him. "Yes, my lord, I know you are the Earl of Cleveland but I do not know what business you have here."

"If you know my name then you know that I am Warlord of the North. I ride where I choose. Do you and your men wish to prevent me?" I nodded towards the two knights with couched lances. "It seems that two of your knights relish the opportunity of tilting with me."

The knight turned and waved an irritated hand to his two knights. They reluctantly raised them. "I merely wish to know your business, lord."

"As you ask so politely I will tell you that I intend to visit with the Earl's wife, the Lady Maud. We are old friends and I have fought alongside her father. Now does that satisfy you?" There was an awkward silence. I smiled, "Come the wind is cold and I am tired. Do we fight or travel to Chester in company? It is your choice."

He was acutely aware of the strung bows of my archers. Added to that was the fixed expressions on my men at arms. They were not worried by the men who faced us. He nodded, "We will escort you to the Countess and she can pass judgement."

"There that is better." I turned and said casually, "You may unstring your bows, archers. It seems you are not going to be plucking knights from their saddles this day."

Edgar and my men at arms sat astride their horses and waited for the knights to follow us. It was a battle of wills and Edgar won. He would watch their backs as they led us to Chester. I chatted easily with Richard and Dick as we rode the last few miles to the castle. Richard had only been on this side of the country once or twice. "This looks like good farmland, lord."

"It is. They grow wheat here. It is why the Earl was so annoyed that Stephen gave away so much of his land to King David. Perhaps that is why he is imprisoned. We will soon discover the reason. See the towers of Chester Castle." Chester was a good castle and needed to be for the Welsh lay just south of the Dee.

Maud was waiting for us as we rode through her gates. She beamed at me as I dismounted, "My favourite knight in the realm! It is good to see you, Alfraed!" She embraced me.

I kissed her cheek and then turned, "There Sir Roger; it seems I am welcome here."

She laughed, "Do not tell me that Sir Roger tried to prevent the Earl of Cleveland from visiting me."

"He was slightly unsure of my welcome and two of his knights thought that they could dispute with us."

She wagged a finger at them. "The Earl has saved your lives! This is King Henry's champion and has never been defeated." Shaking her head she said, "God spare me from unproven knights."

As she took my arm and led me to her hall she said, "The war has dimmed and faded here since my husband was imprisoned and the young warriors seek fights with any. They are like rutting stags!"

"Why was Ranulf arrested? I thought he had sided with the King... again."

"He was trapped and tricked by Gilbert de Gant and his supporters. Ranulf asked the king for his help against the Welsh. In the last year, their attacks have increased and they are bold. I would have preferred Sir Roger guarding the Dee rather than the Mersey but there is no honour in killing the Welsh apparently." She waved me to a seat and gestured for her servants to pour wine for Dick, Richard and myself. "Sir William Peverel said that he suspected treachery and that Stephen would be ambushed when he came to Wales. Stephen asked for hostages to show his good intentions. When my husband refused he was imprisoned."

"You would have been the hostage?"

She nodded, "And that would bring my father to rescue me. Stephen could draw him from his Welsh Marches and defeat him. The battle of Winchester made them believe they could defeat my father."

I said nothing but sipped my wine. These were complicated games that were being played. Gilbert de Gant and William Peverel were plotting and planning. The fact that Stephen allowed this gave me some hope.

She saw my expression and heard my silence. "And you believe that too."

I shrugged, "All men become old. I was not at the battle and I cannot judge."

"Many men say that had you been there as you were at Lincoln then the result might have been different."

"But I was not and we will never know."

"Yet Stephen has never beaten you."

"I too grow old and my power might diminish. Who knows?"

"You will never grow old." She shook her head. She knew me well and understood that I did not like flattery, even from a friend. "So what brings you here, my lord?"

"I came to see you and then I will travel to speak with your aunt in Devizes."

"Then I urge you to head east first. The Welsh attack any men who draw close to their lands. The Dee is the new border."

I shook my head, "We will use speed. If I travel too far east then I risk running into large castles with bigger garrisons. We will use speed to evade the Welsh."

"I pray you are right. Now come. Tell me all of your son and your enclave to the north!"

Maud was a vivacious and lively hostess. Dick and Richard were put at ease. We were feted and feasted well. The comfortable bed was a welcome relief after the ground which had been our bower the previous night. We left soon after dawn.

"Do not judge my husband too harshly, Alfraed. He wanted to defeat the Welsh and make us safer. He would not have fought against Matilda or her son. You have to believe me. He will do the right thing."

"I pray you are right."

As we crossed the Dee into what was now Wales I had Dick send his scouts out to warn us of danger. We were small enough in number to be able to hide but I knew that, even so, we would leave a mark on the land. So many horses meant only one thing; a conroi. The Welsh would follow us. I just hoped that we would move too quickly for them to be able to catch us. I was wrong.

My plan was to head to Gloucester. It was less than a hundred and twenty miles away. With our spare horses, I hoped we could do it in one day. It would be a long day but we were all good riders and well mounted. The first thirty miles were the ones I feared an attack for we passed close by Wrexham and Bangor. Both were Welsh strongholds.

Richard had not met many Welsh warriors yet and he was curious. "Do they have knights such as we do, lord?"

"They do but there are fewer of them. They have men at arms too but they do not have as many with mail. They use leather or padded gambesons. It is, however, their archers who are to be feared."

Dick nodded, "Aye Master Richard, they are good. Their bows are not as long as ours but they are powerful men and can send an arrow almost as far as my men. I, for one, will be happy when we have cleared their land."

"That is why I have taken us closer to Whitchurch and the lands which border the lands of the Earl of Stafford. We can swing further west when we have passed it."

We stopped to water our horses fifteen miles southwest of Whitchurch. We had passed only isolated farms and had seen no castles. We forded a narrow river and allowed our horses to drink. We ate the rations which the Countess had provided and crossed the border again into Wales. We had passed through the village of Grimpool and were travelling down narrow greenways when Ralph of Wales rode back. "Lord, the Welsh. They are waiting for us."

"Where?"

"Half a mile down the greenway. They are astride the Roman Road."

This was what I had feared. The Roman Road which ran from Holyhead to London was still the main thoroughfare. It was a well-made road and men could travel swiftly along it for it was cobbled.

"You are certain they are waiting for us?"

"Aye lord. They have their infantry ready in the centre with archers behind and horsemen to the flanks."

"And knights?"

"I saw but four banners and only ten of their men at arms are mailed but they outnumber us, lord. There are a hundred of them."

"Is there any cover?"

"There is a hedge two hundred paces from their front line."

I turned to Dick. He nodded, "We could use that. We will get in position now."

I had fought alongside my captain of archers since first I had come to England. We needed few words. He understood what we would do. As they left I turned to the servants. "We will attack the enemy. I want you to bring the spare horses along behind us. Do not gallop them just walk and then wait for us to finish with this ambush."

I could see that Richard was concerned. "But they are waiting, lord and we will be outnumbered."

"Their weakness is their centre. We will charge and punch through them. With just ten mailed men at arms, it means their centre has little mail. The danger lies in their archers. We will see, today, who is better." I turned to Edgar, "Richard will be in the third line and Ralph of Nottingham will lead the second line. Spread the new men out between the second and third lines."

"Aye lord."

I was leading thirty-four mailed men. My men at arms were the equal of knights. They thought to weaken us when we attacked and then use their knights to finish us off. We would not allow them to do so. The greenway would only allow us to have six men in each rank. It meant we would have to spread out quickly into a solid line when we neared the road. This was where our years of training would pay off. I had to hold my nerve and slow so that Edgar and the five men with him could form a line. We would have a hundred paces to cover before we struck their first line. It was a test for all of my men.

I was riding my new horse, Edward, to war for the first time. I could tell that he was eager and I had to keep him reined in. He was ready to hurl himself at any enemy. Riding on the training field was totally different to battle. This would be war and I would see what kind of horse he really was.

I saw them when we turned the bend in the greenway. There was no hill but they had formed a solid block fifteen men wide. With two knights and five men at arms on each flank that meant that they were five ranks deep. The rear two or three would be archers. We kept our lances upright. We would only lower them at the last moment. I saw the agitation when they spied us. They were not well trained. Well trained men would have stood calmly. Excitement and agitation meant nerves and that was dangerous.

I saw the hedge to the left and right. As we passed our hidden archers Dick and his men began to loose their arrows. They had the advantage of a hedge that would give them some protection and mail which would be more than good enough to stop the Welsh arrows. I held my shield before me, ready to lift it should it be necessary. Our arrows caused casualties in all five ranks and the arrows which came in reply were ragged. They were also split between the hedgerow and us. I lifted my shield and took three arrows upon it. A fourth clipped Edward's rump. He was a warhorse and he did not react.

As soon as Edgar's horse appeared next to me I shouted, "Charge!" We had a hundred and fifty paces to go. We would not hit at full speed but we would arrive together. Dick and my archers were winning the battle. Their arrows flew over in waves and the Welsh became increasingly ragged. My archers were hidden.

I lowered my lance with fifty paces to go and I spurred
Edward. He leapt and Edgar kept pace with me by spurring
his own horse. I pulled back my hand and leaned forward
into the cantle. The Welsh had a line of spears before them.
Our lances were longer. I punched forward and my spear
rammed into the throat of the Welshman in the front rank.
Edward's hooves clattered into the head of the warrior in the
second rank as I flicked my wrist and stabbed forward again.
My lance went into the stomach of a small Welshman and I
drove him into the archer behind. The archer was readying
his bow. I tried to flick my wrist again but the head of the
lance had caught in the archers' leg and it was torn from my
grasp.

While I was drawing my sword I jerked Edward to my
left and he knocked down another archer. We had broken
their line and I wheeled to the left. The archers and men at
arms who were left tried to run but my men at arms were
ruthless. They rode them down. I realised that the knights
and men at arms who had been on the Welsh left flank were
now charging towards us. Even as they closed my archers'
arrows struck home and a horse and a man at arms were
struck. Leopold of Durstein and Günter the Swabian were
with me. Neither had lances but Gunter was so strong that he
was able to wield a mighty war axe one-handed whilst
riding.

The Welsh knight who saw his chance for glory pulled
back his own lance and stood in his stirrups to stab it at my
chest. My new shield was well made and I angled it so that
the head slid along it. I did not go for his body with my
sword but his head. His shield was on the other side of his
body and he did not manage to pull it around quickly
enough. My sword bit into his coif, tearing the ventail before
ripping across his throat. His half severed head hung at a
strange angle as his body tumbled to the ground.

Günter's axe smashed through the mail and chest of the
second knight as Leopold slew the last man at arms. Two
had fled and we had the field. I reined in Edward and
wheeled him around. I saw three empty saddles. I had lost
men.

"Richard, sound the horn and bring our men back!"

The servants and spare horses had reached us and were followed by Dick and his archers. "See to our wounded and then search the dead. Collect any spare horses."

I dismounted. Edward was lathered with sweat. I took out the skin of vinegar I carried and used it to bathe the wound on his rump. He kicked his leg out. "Steady boy! This is for your own good." I examined the wound and it did not look serious.

Edgar reined in. "We have two men dead and one with a bad wound. It could have been worse."

"And the enemy?"

"One of the knights escaped and six of the men at arms on horses. They left thirty-six dead."

"If the knight escaped then they will pursue us. We will have to use the road and ride hard."

"Aye lord."

"The dead?"

"We bury our own."

Chapter 8

It was already dark when we approached Gloucester. I had thought to go to Sir William's manor. He held it for me but Gloucester was closer and we were tired. Henry of Langdale needed a healer. Miles of Gloucester had been Sherriff. I knew not who the new one was but my banner was recognised and I was welcomed.

"This is an honour for me, Earl. I am Roger, Sherriff of Gloucester. I served with you at Wallingford."

To be honest, I did not recognise him but I smiled, "That was a great day was it not? We have wounded men and we have travelled from Chester."

"In one day? That is truly a great feat. There is room for your men in the warrior hall. I will have chambers for your knights and squires in the Great Hall."

"There are only four of us. We will not take up much room." After we had stabled our horses he led us to the hall. "How goes the war here?"

"Have you not heard? I thought that was why you came."

"Heard what?"

"The Earl of Gloucester is unwell. He is in Bristol. Our forces must now wait behind our walls. Without the Earl, there is little hope of prosecuting the war here in the southwest. God, it appears, is not on our side. First Sir Miles falls while hunting and then Sir Bryan Fitz Count, the hero of Wallingford, dies. Whoever will be next?"

That was bad news. I had fallen out with the Earl but I knew that he was vital to the success of our war. If he was ill, then who would lead our armies? I was in the north and the leaders who had been here in the south-west were now dead. Sir Roger was right. It did appear as though we had been abandoned by God.

I put on a brave face. "We have had worse times. Normandy is now free. There is hope."

We left for the church at Devizes the next morning. I left Gurth and Cedric to escort Henry of Langdale to us when his wound healed. The last part would be the safest part of the journey.

Devizes was a strong castle and hope rose as we approached it. Even Dick was impressed. "This would take a good siege to destroy it."

"But we sit behind walls. We should be attacking." The news of the Earl's illness had made me melancholy once more.

If I thought to be cheered when I entered I was not. Margaret and Judith were comforting their mistress. I turned to Dick and Richard, "See to the men. Find quarters for them and have their horses fed and attended. I fear we will need them sooner rather than later."

Maud rose when she saw me and, throwing caution to the wind threw her arms around me and began to weep. "My lord, I am pleased you are here. You come at the times of the direst need." She began to sob.

I said to Margaret, over the Empress' shoulders, "What is wrong? Is it her brother?"

"No, lord, although he is still unwell. The Bishop of Salisbury has appealed to the Pope. She has been threatened with excommunication if she does not quit the castle. It seems the Bishop is working with Queen Matilda. She seeks to make the Empress homeless."

I disentangled the Empress and held her at arms' length. I looked her in the eyes. "This is not the end of the world. There are other castles. Bristol and Wallingford are both strong. We can go there."

She nodded and Judith handed her a piece of lace to wipe her eyes. "You are right. I fear this lassitude is due to my brother's illness."

"What is wrong with him?"

"I know not. His physicians are also confused. Would you and your men escort me to him? I would be at his bedside. Perhaps our presence might rouse him and do that which the doctors cannot."

"Of course." My plans to rest my men and animals were now in disarray. "We will leave tomorrow." I turned to Margaret, "Would you make the arrangements? I need to speak with the Empress." After we were left alone I led the Empress into a bower in the castle where we sat on the bench. "I have not heard from you for a while. Our son spent some time with me and we fought against the mercenaries from Flanders close by York. He did well."

She beamed, "That is good. I hope he will become king." Then she frowned, "My spies have told me that Stephen is urging the church to name his son Eustace as the next King of England."

"Then I will need to do something about that."

She suddenly seemed to see me for she smiled and stroked my hand. "You have given all for me and my family. When will you have a life, my lord?"

"This is my life. My men have asked me why I do not sit back in my valley and enjoy life. So long as our son is denied his inheritance I cannot rest."

She looked wistfully east, "My husband has his Dukedom. I have heard that many have heeded Louis' appeals for a Second Crusade and loyal knights now seek their fortune there. Waleran de Beaumont is one."

"Waleran? He is a good knight. With Gloucester and Fitz Count gone, we are losing the leaders we need."

"There is always Chester."

"His wife I trust. The Earl? He cannot be relied upon."

"Then we must hope that my brother recovers and we are able to raise an army and finally bring Stephen and his armies to battle." She held my hand. "And you and I, lord. We had one night of joy and we now pay for it with a lonely life apart."

I nodded, "It is fate but at least we have a son who can have a life for the both of us. None may ever know of his parentage. It would lose all that we have."

"I know. I must have been born under a bad sign for my life seems dogged with disasters from my brother's death to my marriage to the Emperor and then a child."

"Life is never fair, my love. We deal with what the Fates throw our way and do our best." I did not know it at the time but this was one of the last times when Maud and I were alone. Had I known I would have said more.

I was distracted on our journey to Bristol. Despite my best efforts, we were losing the war. The Empress and her brother now controlled land which was little larger than my valley. As we approached Bristol my worst fears were confirmed. The standards were flown at half-mast. Maud turned to me, tears in her eyes. "We are too late!"

We were indeed and the doctors told us that even as the Empress and I had been speaking in the bower, the Earl of Gloucester had died peacefully. He was just forty-seven years old. That was only three years older than me. It sent a chill down my spine.

The Earl was buried at St. James' Priory. He had founded it. Perhaps he had done so with the intention of being interred there. It was a pitifully small gathering. His wife and children were there but there were few lords of any note. Many had taken the cross; others had died. We had not parted well but I chose to remember those days when his father had been alive and I had ridden at his side to defeat the Welsh. The Battle of Lincoln had been the single moment in time when we had had the crown in our grasp and he had let it slip. But the glory of our victories was still undiminished.

As we headed back to Devizes I asked the Empress her intentions. She was silent and I allowed the silence to remain. It hung in the air between us like an invisible wall. She had hard decisions to make and, for once, I could not help her.

As we neared the castle she said, "My lord Cleveland, I would return home to my family. No one can say that I did not try; I did. You have done your best but with the death of my brother, added to that of Mandeville last year, and the antagonism of the clergy I cannot see how my remaining here does any good at all. I will return to Rouen."

Everyone fell silent. Judith and Margaret looked resigned and even Dick looked saddened by the words. They were like the tolling of a death knell. The slow beat of my heart filled my head. My spirits sank to a new low. I would be truly alone. My son was in Normandy. My future king was in Normandy and the woman I loved would be in Normandy. I stroked Edward's mane and remained silent. My horse moved his head closer to mine. I looked at Maud and knew that I could not blame her. She had truly done her best. I could either abandon the valley and bring my army here to the southwest or return home and try to keep an enclave there for her.

She reached out to touch my hand, "You are silent, Alfraed. Have my words distressed you?"

I turned and smiled. There could be no deceit between us. "Of course but I understand your decision. It is the right one. I just wonder at the efforts of the last ten years. Have they all been in vain?"

"We have to believe that right will prevail. You have already begun to make our son king. I beg you to escort me to Rouen and be reunited with him. He will listen to you and you are wise."

But your husband..."

"My husband is a good man but he is no Earl of Cleveland. My father recognised that as did my brother. You had your falling out but he never failed to see the hope that you brought."

"Then we will take a ship. Your men still hold Portsmouth?"

She shook her head, "No."

"In that case, we must return to Bristol and find vessels. I fear we will need to hire at least three ships for I have horses and men as do you."

"We have money to pay for them." She brightened, "Let us look on the good in all of this. At least I shall not be excommunicated."

My three men had returned from Gloucester and I gathered them and the others together in the warrior hall. "We are going to escort the Empress back to Rouen. I will not risk sending men back to the valley. We dare not lose any more men. We will all take a ship. We sail for Normandy."

They seemed undaunted by the prospect of a difficult voyage across the Bay of Biscay. My men were now my hope. I would build up an army so that when Henry returned to take the throne I would have warriors to back his claim.

It took time for us to procure the ships and to pack them with the Empress and her people's goods. They were leaving England for the last time. They had the detritus of a lifetime. If Henry was crowned they might return but that was a distant hope and, I felt an unlikely event. Margaret and Judith shed tears as we boarded the four ships in Bristol. They were no longer young and the death of the Earl had made us all realise our own mortality. We had expected him to die in battle but there were many ways for a man to die. My wife had died of the plague and others succumbed to illnesses the physicians did not understand. Judith and Margaret knew they would never see the land of their birth again.

I travelled with the Empress and her ladies along with Richard, Edgar and four of my men at arms in one ship. My servants and my horses travelled with me too. The autumn storms had begun and each dawn we woke to see our little fleet scattered. It took time to close with each other and that all added to the journey. When we saw the Seine the Empress' priest, Father Jocelyn led us all in prayers of gratitude. Maud remembered that the whole civil war had begun when her elder brother drowned aboard the White Ship making this exact voyage.

We sailed all the way to Rouen. Our tortuous voyage up the river meant that we were expected and Geoffrey of Anjou and Henry FitzEmpress awaited us on the quay. I had not expected to see Henry again so soon but perhaps this was meant to be. I had begun the work of making him king and his mother had given it her blessing. We would winter in Normandy and I would continue to work with the king in waiting.

Even as we approached the quay I noticed that many ships were being loaded. It was not cargo but knights and their horses. I quickly deduced that this was the beginning of the race to the Holy Land. The Second Crusade had begun. The war in Normandy was won but there was another in the east and there, profits could be even greater. Geoffrey of Anjou's father had won a kingdom!

Geoffrey briefly embraced his wife and then turned to clasp my arm as Henry gave a more loving welcome to his mother.

"My son has told me of your great deeds. The Count of Flanders thinks his arm has grown long. You have bloodied his nose and made him think again. It is said he now seeks his fortune in the Holy Land with this crusade of the King of France."

I nodded, "Did Henry tell you of the offer from the house of Hainaut?"

"He did and I can see him grown much already. The Count's son came here and hired some of the men at arms. The knights did not choose to go. There is more glory as well as reward fighting Islam."

"Your wife's uncle is dead, lord."

His face showed that he did not know. "It is a black day for our cause. I shall have the priests say a mass for him. Was it combat?"

I shook my head, "The doctors said it was an unknown illness. They thought that perhaps his heart gave out but he was but forty and seven."

"He was not murdered as his father was he?"

"There were no signs and his end was peaceful. It was God's will."

"So now we have lost England."

"Perhaps not. I will return to my home in the spring and we still hold out. So long as I draw breath I will fight for the Empress and her son."

"Amen to that, my lord!"

Henry joined us. "I hear, Warlord, that the Count of Hainaut is losing his war against Flanders." I nodded, noncommittally. "Now that you are here, with your warriors at the heart of our force we could join him."

Geoffrey of Anjou appraised his son, "You are the young cockerel now, eh? You wish to go to war."

It was my turn to smile, "I remember a young Count of Anjou who was little older than Henry when he went to war against Blois."

The Duke laughed, "I did, didn't I? The acorn does not fall far from the tree it seems. But the Earl has just arrived. Give him time for his men and horses to get their legs once more. Besides, I would take him hunting. The last time we had no such opportunity."

"And I would like to see my son."

"I fear he has returned to his home in Ouistreham. He received news that there was sickness."

A chill ran down my spine. "When was this?"

"A month since. We have had no word yet."

"Then when my men are rested I shall ride there." I cursed myself. I could have stopped at the port on my way here. Perhaps my son was ill too!

Although we were feted and feasted I could not enjoy myself for I was anxious about my family. The death of the Earl and Bryan Fitz Count had shown me that war and the plague were not the only killers which stalked our land. The Empress saw my concern and, leaning over, said quietly, "Perhaps no news is good news. If there was aught to be told then he would have sent word. You have a dutiful son."

I was not so sure but I hoped she was right. One thing was certain, the horses, after their stormy crossing, were in no condition to ride the seventy miles to the small port. The next day I went to the quay and asked when my ship was due to arrive.

The harbour master knew us well and William of
Kingston had given him enough gifts to ensure that he had
good berths. "Your captain thought to make one more
voyage before the autumn storms, lord. I expect him sooner
rather than later, my lord. He came with another ship last
time. I think she is slower than the *'Adela'*."

I returned to the castle disappointed. I had hoped I could
save my horses and leave sooner. The ships the Empress had
hired to bring us had now gone for there was much trade to
the Holy Land and captains made money when they could.
Richard waited for me by our chambers. "The Duke asked if
we were going hunting this morning."

I was not in the mood but my host would be offended if I
declined his offer. "Come, we will see if we can have some
diversion. What is it we hunt?"

"Deer, my lord, with spears."

That meant we would be mounted. I disliked hunting on
borrowed horses. However, I would just be cautious. There
were a large number of knights who were hunting. It did feel
good to be out of my mail. Unlike the Norman and Angevin
knights, I did not bother with a cloak. It was far warmer here
than in my valley and the weather, compared with northern
England, was clement. I also shunned a hood. I preferred to
be able to hear the smallest of noises. Richard copied me. I
would have preferred hunting deer on foot. It was always
more of a challenge. However, it was our host's choice and
we did as he did.

As I did not know the horse I rode the one the stable
master had given me towards the back of the pack of hunters.
He seemed a little lively. There were twenty knights and
squires. There were more knights than squires. Geoffrey led
and was closely followed by Sir John of Nantes one of his
oldest friends. Unlike when we hunted this was slightly more
staged. His beaters had been out since before dawn and they
would drive the deer towards us. Tired already, when they
saw us they would flee and we would easily catch our prey.
There was little joy in it. I went on the hunt to stop me
worrying about my son.

The horse they had given me was a little frisky. I took that as a compliment. The stable master must have assumed that I was a good rider. Consequently, the others left Richard and me behind a little as they hurried through the trees. I spent time mastering my wild beast. The forest had been thinned to enable hunting. This was not the forest by Preston at home. There you needed your wits about you. You used your knees as much as your hands as you wove your way through thick undergrowth and trees. This was almost a park in comparison.

"My lord, we are losing them!"

"I think, Richard, that we shall be able to find them. They are like a gaggle of geese the noise that they make."

"But they will get all the biggest deer!"

I laughed, "Come then, let us catch them."

I now had the feel of my feisty mount and I dug my heels in. Sometimes our actions are directed by other forces. As he leapt forward an arrow flew behind my back. It had come from my left. None of our hunters was using a bow. I wheeled left shouting, "Richard! 'Ware left! Treachery!" I heard a cry and saw Richard's horse fall with two arrows embedded in its head.

As I turned another pair of hurried arrows sped towards me. I lay my head against my horse's mane. It could do no good if I tried to aid Richard. I would just be making two targets easier to hit. I attacked. It was the movement of the three archers which aided me. Two were running for a better ambush site as the third aimed at me. If I had been riding Rolf or Edward I would have had more confidence in the manoeuvre I was about to try. I was wheeling left and I pulled his head to that side as though I was going to flee. As the archer's hand came back I jerked to the right and spurred him. He was fast and the arrow was released, hurriedly, when I was twenty paces from him. I felt the goose feathers scrape my cheek. I pulled back my spear and hurled it at him. It struck him in the middle of his body. I drew my sword and took off after the other two. They had split up to make pursuit harder.

Although the trees were thinner, by riding obliquely at the archer to my left I gave him no chance to have a clean sight of me. The archer kept tracking me and anticipating my movements. I slowed a little and then kicked hard. It worked for an arrow flew ahead of me. While he was pulling another arrow I wheeled right and went directly for him.

"On! On!" I urged my borrowed horse and he responded well. It was a race. Would the assassin release the arrow before my sword struck him? In the end, it was neither. He panicked and tried to run. My horse's front hooves clattered into him, knocking him to the ground. His rear hooves caved in his skull. The last assassin released a hasty arrow. It stuck in my shin. My boot prevented deep penetration. As I clattered past a branch the arrow was broken. The pain raced through my body but I ignored it. I watched the archer as he ran this way and that trying to avoid me. There was no escape. I turned my sword so that the flat of the blade was towards the man. As he jinked to the side I brought the flat of the blade against the side of his head. He went down as though struck with a poleaxe. I reined in.

I dismounted and tied the reins of my horse to a tree and went to him. I disarmed him. He had bindings on his breeks and I cut them and used them to bind his hands and his feet. I hefted him onto the back of my horse. I slung his bow and his quiver from the cantle. I headed back to where I had seen Richard's horse fall. My squire met me halfway there. Blood trickled from a head wound and he limped slightly. "Lord! Where are the others?"

"Dead! Are you hurt?"

"I bruised my knee and banged my head but you are wounded!"

The bleeding has slowed. I wiped my hand across it and said, "Come we will return to your horse and wait for us to be missed."

When we reached the dead horse I tipped the archer from the saddle. He landed heavily. I cared not. When I had questioned him he would die anyway. That was the price assassins paid. I took off my boot. It was filled with blood. The arrowhead was still embedded in my leg but there was enough of the barb showing to tell me that it would not tear a larger hole if was removed. I grabbed a handful of moss from the nearest tree.

"Richard, take your dagger and widen the wound. Do not worry if there is blood. Then pull out the arrow's head. Pull it quickly."

He nodded. He had seen my men do this before. He dried his hands and then used his knife to prise the flesh away from the wood and the metal. It sent shivers of pain racing up my leg. It would pass. He began to pull. He was helped by the fact that the arrowhead was touching the bone. It had not broken the bone but the smoothness of it meant he only had resistance on one side. He pulled and it popped out. Blood flowed and I reached up for the wineskin. I poured some over the wound. Then I jammed the moss in the hole the arrow had made.

"Tear some cloth from the archer's kyrtle and tie it tightly."

While he tied it I drank a little from the wineskin. I handed it to Richard and he drank some too. "Search him. Look for coins."

We found not just silver coins but three gold pieces. I knew that if we searched the others we would find the same. They were freshly minted and bore the image of Count Thierry. It was all the evidence I needed. Then Richard pulled out another purse. This one was hidden inside his kyrtle. This one contained freshly minted coins but these bore the face of Stephen and they were English. Here was a puzzle that needed unravelling.

"Help me to my feet." When I stood the blood rushed down my leg and I thought I was going to pass out. I gritted my teeth. I examined the bow and the quiver. I handed an arrow to Richard. "These are English arrows and this is an English bow."

I knelt again, relieved not to be standing on my wounded leg. I took out my dagger and held it close to the eye of the archer.

"Pour water on his face and wake him. Make sure he does not move. I do not want him to lose his eye until I am ready to take it."

Richard went to his dead horse and removed the water skin. He splashed water on the man's face. He moaned and then his eyes opened. He saw my face and he saw the dagger. I was using guesswork but the evidence I had led me to just one conclusion. "What did Eustace of Boulogne pay you to do?" His mouth opened and closed. "I will happily take your eye, skewer it and feed it to you. Was it just me you were to kill or my squire also?"

"Both of you! You are damned lucky! The devil must have spawned you!" he spoke in English!

"Perhaps, although as you will be seeing him soon you may well be able to ask him!"

"I will tell you nothing!"

"You are going to die. The question is how much pain you will have to suffer before that happens." He said nothing. "Richard, pull down his breeks and geld him!"

A look of absolute terror filled his face as heard the determination in my voice and as Richard tugged at his breeks. He knew that I would do it. "No! No! I will tell you and then end my life quickly!" I nodded to Richard who stopped. "He is in Bury St. Edmunds. He sent us to Bruges and the Count's man sent the four of us here to kill you. That is all I swear!"

"I believe you! Go with God."

I ripped the blade across his throat. The blood splattered the two of us. I cleaned it on his kyrtle. "So one remains at large and I think I know who he is."

"Who, lord?"

"The man in the stable who gave me this horse."

I heard hooves and looked up to see the Duke and the hunters, "Alfraed! What happened?"

"I will tell you all when we reach your castle, lord. This is not over. There are two more dead archers in the woods. They have coins about them."

We had spare horses for the game we would have caught. Richard rode one of them and we put the three bodies on the others.

The Duke looked at me; consternation was upon his face. "You are wounded, Earl."

"I will see a healer when we return to the castle."

"Are they Norman rebels?"

"No, lord, they are English."

Chapter 9

My words in the woods had stunned the Duke. We rode back in silence. As we entered the castle I headed straight for the stable. The man who had given me the horse saw his three companions on the backs of horses and made a break for freedom.

"Richard!"

Richard galloped across the bailey. He held his sword by the blade and swung the pommel into the back of the man's head. The man fell to the ground as though poleaxed.

I turned to the Duke. "He is the last of the four assassins paid for by Eustace and sent here by the Count of Flanders. There is treachery in Rouen, Duke Geoffrey."

The Duke looked at me, "How do you know?"

"This man and three others were sent here. Someone hired them. Eustace of Boulogne instigated the attack but the Count of Flanders was able to carry it off by hiring these three assassins."

"Then we will interrogate this man. Now take yourself and your squire to my healer." He held my arm, "I apologise that this happened. It should not. You were in danger while you were my guest."

I shrugged, "If I had not gone hunting then they would have found another way to get at me. It is one reason that I travel so little. I feel safer in my own land where I know where my enemies are. Here it is hard to differentiate."

"That is a harsh comment."

"But it is true. King Henry was not murdered in England but here. Think on that Duke."

Geoffrey, Duke of Normandy, had good healers. They cleaned out my wound. I did not feel the pain for they gave me a draught of something. I slept while they did it. When I awoke there was a clean smell and my leg was bandaged. The doctor held up a sliver of wood. "Your squire did a good job but if we had not found this and removed it you might have lost your leg or died. It is clean now. You need to rest for a few days. You are no longer a young man."

"And my squire?"

"A bruised knee is all he suffered. The head wound looked worse than it was. We have given him a draught of feverfew and applied a poultice. He is young and within a day or so will not even remember that he was hurt."

It was dark when I emerged. Richard met me. I saw that he limped and had a bandage around his head. He pointed to the gates. There were two heads upon it. One was the stable hand and the other was the steward. "The Duke was furious. He has sent his men to interrogate all those who work in the castle. It turned out that the steward was also in the pay of the Count of Flanders."

"With the Empress and her son here he cannot afford to have killers walking his castle."

"Dick and Edgar went into town."

I was surprised. It seemed out of character for them. "Did they say why?"

He nodded, "They said that if there were four killers inside the walls, then how many might be outside? They went to listen for gossip. I offered to go but they said that they were going in low taverns."

"Dick was an outlaw and Edgar a sword for hire. They can go into places where there is more talking done with fists than with words. Come, let us heed our physicians and take some rest. Besides, I have an appetite. Bloodletting always makes me hungry."

Henry and his mother were appalled at the attempt on my life. "I am sorry, Alfraed. If I had not asked you to escort me home this would never have happened."

"I am alive and they are dead. However, I shall be more vigilant from now on."

As we were eating I saw Dick enter the hall. He nodded and sat at the lower end of the table with the other knights. I was anxious to know his news but it would have to wait.

I noticed that Geoffrey had placed more guards close to his wife and son. "The Duke appears worried about you two."

The Empress nodded, "He has suggested that I move to the priory of Notre Dame du Pré. He felt I would be safer there."

"But you have only just got here!"

She smiled, "I understand my husband, Alfraed." Her eyes told me that she knew of his infidelity. She was moving out so that he could carry on as before. Henry's downcast look told me that he too knew of it. It was an open secret. I pushed away my platter. I had suddenly lost my appetite.

I rose to go to my chamber and Richard followed. We were halfway down the corridor when Dick appeared. "You discovered something?"

He nodded and I saw that his knuckles were grazed. "Eventually aye, lord. We met some men at arms newly arrived from England. They had fought for Stephen but the death of the Earl of Gloucester meant that there was less work for them. They were on their way to the Holy Land to seek employment there. They told us that Eustace was hiring men in England. He wished men who were willing to kill the Earl of Cleveland." He smiled, "These men thought that travelling halfway around the world and fighting infidels was safer than trying to kill the Warlord of the North!"

I nodded.

Then Dick added, "There will be desperate men, lord, who are willing to risk death for the rewards which Eustace offers. He has also hired men to kill Henry FitzEmpress. He wishes to be king when his father dies."

"Thank you for that news. It is always well to know there is danger."

"Edgar is detailing the men. While you are abroad then two of them will watch your back."

125

"And I am here too, lord."

Dick looked at my squire, "You are a good squire, Richard, but this is work for men who will strike first and worry about the justification later." He was right there. Dick and my archers were the deadliest of killers and the most implacable of enemies. Richard was the lamb and they were the wolves.

I did not sleep well that night. The pain in my leg was there all night but my mind was filled with worries about my son. How could he be protected? The departure of the Empress was also ever-present. I might never see her again. I rose before dawn and slipped from the room without disturbing Richard. It was chilly in the castle and I wrapped my cloak about me as I headed for the Great Hall. The quarters for the Duke and the Empress were above the hall. I went to the fire which had been fed, in the night, by servants. I took the poker and brought it to life. The flames danced as they flamed. I heard footsteps behind me and I saw Margaret, the Empress' lady in waiting.

"My lord, what are you doing up?"

"My leg ached and you?"

"My lady is awake too. She has sent me for some porridge."

"She is alone?"

"She is alone every night, lord." She hesitated, "I would take you to her but..."

I nodded, "It would not do. Tell her...I... tell her."

Margaret came and put her hand on mine, "She understands, lord." She shook her head, "Why is it that men need everything explained to them? There are things that do not need words. Judith and I know what you would say. Leave it there, lord, for if you voiced those words they might be overheard. Young Henry is the priority of the Empress. Use him to show her your feelings."

"I would anyway."

She smiled and it was a sad smile, "The Empress knows." She released my hand. "The Priory is a pleasant place. We have visited and the Empress has a mind to have a home built close by. But when I tire of it I may travel and visit England. If I came would I be welcome in your castle, lord?"

"Of course! You need not ask."

She had a smile like a cat which has managed to lick the cream which had spilt, "And I can bring gifts. They have fine butter and they make distilled liquor which warms." She half-turned, "Oh and I can bring news and... letters."

I nodded, "And you would be doubly welcome. I am sorry for being such a dull man. Perhaps I am losing my wits."

"Oh no lord, but you have much on your mind. None of us would change one hair on your head. To me, you are the perfect knight."

Then she was gone leaving me at the fire. I stared into the flickering flames. It was as though that was my world. It was disappearing in an inferno. My work would now be the making of a king. When my son returned I would make my peace with him and then set about Henry's training. I would keep him safe by keeping him as close to me as possible. His two bodyguards had been paid off. I would need to speak with Geoffrey and arrange for others to take their place.

Geoffrey rose late. The hall was already filled with knights and ladies partaking of the cold meats left over from the feast when Geoffrey appeared. I spent the time talking with Henry and his mother. The words I wished to say to the Empress I delivered with my eyes. Nor could I tell Henry of the danger, not until I had spoken alone with his father. Besides, I did not wish to worry his mother over much. Even so, I enjoyed the precious hour I spent with them.

He came over to speak with me after he had quaffed some wine and picked up a fowl's leg. He greeted his wife and son first, "How is the leg, Alfraed?"

"It will heal. I am a warrior. Such things happen but I needs must speak alone with you, lord."

Henry looked surprised but his mother nodded, "Come Henry. You and I can choose the horses I will be taking with me to the Priory. You are a good judge of horseflesh and I am sure the Earl will tell you if this news concerns you."

"But I am a man! I should be consulted."

I looked him in the eyes. "Your father is Duke, Henry. I promise that I will speak to you but your father must know this first. I will speak to you later. I will meet you in the stables when I have done."

Mollified he nodded and left with his mother. The Duke said, "This sounds ominous. I thought we had ended the threat but your words suggest not. What did your men discover?"

"Eustace is not only hiring men to kill me but your son too."

"Now I see why you wanted to speak to me first. I shall have to hire bodyguards again."

I shook my head, "With respect, my lord, how do we know whom you can trust? The only ones we can both trust are our households. Let me have two of my men watch over him. I guarantee they will keep him safe."

He tore meat from the bone and chewed. I waited for I could see that he was thinking. "When your son returns, you could use his men. They are of this land and are trustworthy."

"True but he is not here besides Henry's future lies n England does it not?"

"Aye and who better to watch over England's future than the English knight? Very well but I will impose checks on all warriors entering my land."

I remembered the poisoners who had managed to inveigle their way into my castle and had come within a hair's breadth of killing me. "I would watch for all assassins, lord. If I might suggest, do not hire more servants until the threat is gone or use only those that you have known for years."

He threw the bone onto the fire, "I thought when I became Duke and ended the rebellion that all of this would end."

"King Henry spent every moment looking over his shoulder and an assassin reached him in the end. I fear it comes with the title, lord."

Matilda was waiting with her son in the stables. I smiled, "You had no need to wait, my lady. I can tell Henry now."

"And you can tell me too. This concerns my son and concerns me too. Speak."

Her eyes commanded me too and I nodded. She was a strong woman and would be able to deal with the news.

"Eustace is hiring assassins to kill Henry. The Duke has allowed me to use my men to protect him. The killers we caught yesterday were not unique. Others have been paid to end my life." I smiled at Henry, "We must be doing something right if the enemy resort to this!"

The Empress nodded, "Then I am content. If you cannot watch over the future King of England then there is no hope." She hugged her son, "You wear mail beneath your surcoat from now on!" He nodded. "And I will give you twenty of my men to guard you. I shall not need above half a dozen, perhaps less, in the priory. They have all served me for years and can be trusted."

He smiled, "A generous gift." He looked at me, "So, lord, I can now begin to learn to lead my own men."

"It is a start, use it well."

We went to see my men and Edgar chose four who would now be Henry's bodyguards. "Does this mean you stay with me?"

"I had planned on staying the winter anyway and if I do leave then these four or four others will remain with you."

It was just after noon and we were heading to the hall for food when the gates opened to admit my son and his men. When he saw me he stopped, dismounted and took off his helmet. He came over to me and dropped to one knee, "My lord, forgive me! My sins have not gone unpunished."

I knew the sins of which he spoke but I knew not what he meant. I raised him up. "Speak, my son, for I see the dread in your eyes."

"My wife and my children, your grandchildren, are dead. A coughing sickness struck my home. My children died first. When I reached them my wife was dying. I spent a week trying to save her but..." He broke down and, for the first time since his own mother had died, he threw himself in my arms and cried. My men stood in a protective circle so that none other could see.

I had had a premonition of some evil but I never imagined that it was this. I held him tightly as I had when he was a bairn in swaddling clothes. If I could have taken his hurt and his pain then I would.

"They are with God now, my son."

He stood back. He spoke quietly so that only I could hear his words. "But we both know that I have sinned and they have paid the price! You were right. father and I am sorry, I am so sorry. I have to make amends. I have to do penance."

I nodded.

"I am taking a ship. I go with my men to join the crusade to the Holy Land. My life here is over. When I have done my penance I will return to England and we will get Henry's throne back for him."

"You need to think about this, my son!"

"I have thought of nothing else in the five days since I buried my wife and my children. I sat all night in my church and I had a vision of the cross. It was covered in blood. I will atone by serving those pilgrims who travel to the Holy Land." He gave me a sad smile. "I know you warned me of my actions and I would that I had heeded them. God has punished me for my sins. Do not try to dissuade me. When my guilt is gone I will return to you in England. I must go now and speak with the Duke."

I was stunned. Henry, Dick, Edgar and Richard joined me. They had heard only part of it. I told them all.

"But lord, what was his sin? How was it so great that he must leave this land?"

I looked at Henry. I could not tell him what I knew. "William, alone, knows what sins he has committed. He has had a vision during his vigil. When that happens it means God has chosen you. We must help him all that we can. He has had a terrible loss."

Dick came and put his arm around my shoulder, "My lord, you have too; your grandchildren were taken from you." His face was filled with despair. I suddenly found words stuck in my throat. I could say nothing and had I tried to speak then I would have broken down. He was right. I had barely known my grandchildren and now I never would. This was not my fault and yet I felt guilty. Was God punishing me for my sins?

I turned and left. I went to the stables and had Edward saddled. Richard and Henry followed me. "What do you do, lord?"

"I need to be alone and to ride." I dragged my injured leg over the cantle and spurred Edward out of the gate. I headed for open country.

I knew I was being followed but a glance over my shoulder told me that it was Richard, Henry, Edgar and eight of my men at arms. They would not allow my grief to put me in danger. I rode hard until my leg began to ache and Edward showed signs of fatigue. I reined in and saw that I was close to a roadside shrine. There were many of them in Normandy. I dismounted and knelt next to it.

"If my sins have caused this to happen, Lord, then I beg you to punish me and not my son. I cannot lose him too."

I kept my eyes closed as I waited for a sign or a word but all that filled my ears was the sound of Edward munching the last of the grass which sprouted around the base of the shrine. I rose and mounted Edward. The sun was dipping towards the west and, as I turned to ride back to Rouen I saw Henry and the others approaching. Henry was leading and the sun suddenly flared, making a corona around his head. He looked as though he had a crown upon it. It was the sign I sought. Henry was my son too. I would make him king. That would be my task.

Chapter 10

As soon as William left me I sent Dick and some of my archers to La Flèche for funds. William would need ships and he would need money. My money meant nothing; blood meant all. I would ensure that he had all that he needed in the Holy Land. Matilda heard from Henry of my loss and she came to see me with her ladies.

"You have had more calamity and tragedy in your life. This is unfair."

I nodded. Their sympathy was not what I needed. It would make me more upset. "We bear these events with fortitude. It is what makes us men." I gave her a sad look. "Perhaps I am being punished for my sins."

Her hand went to the cross about her neck and her eyes showed the pain. "Perhaps and it may be that I too am being punished by God." She forced a smile upon her lips. "And your son now goes on Holy Crusade?"

"He does. He now speaks with the Duke. I fear he will not return to Ouistreham."

Maud came close to me, "Should you need somewhere private I have my own chapel."

"Thank you, Empress, but I shall keep busy. We need to find a ship to take him across the Middle Sea. If *'Adela'* came into port then that would solve a problem."

"Is she due in?"

"She will be making her next voyage any time soon."

"Then perhaps God will make up for your trials by sending her in time."

I did not see William until the evening. He spent all the time closeted with the Duke. Henry, too, was involved in the discussions. It seemed I was to be excluded. The three of them emerged from the Duke's chambers. Geoffrey approached me, "I have tried to dissuade him, Earl. This is hasty and we both need him here but he is adamant."

I knew that my son was like me. Once he gave his word it was like a steel covenant. "He has sworn an oath, lord and they are always binding. We must make the best of it and besides, it is not the end of the world. Your father went there and became King. Others have served and returned home. I pray for the latter."

He nodded, "Then I will pay for his passage to the east. He deserves that for the service he has given me." The Duke turned to his son, "Come, Henry, let us leave the Earl and his son to speak."

I saw the gratitude on William's face as they left us alone and we could talk. "Now we just need ships."

"I am hoping that my ships will be here soon. I would not normally use them again but a voyage to the Holy Land might not be the trial the German Sea would present."

"And how would you get home?"

"Do not worry about that. Besides we have unfinished business with the Count of Flanders."

"I am sorry that I will not be here to aid you with that task. I would enjoy riding through Flanders with you and Henry. He will be a good king, in time."

"And you are a good knight, William. In case I do not get a chance to tell you again know that. I am as proud of you as any man is of his son. I would choose you to guard my back in any battle against any odds. I know that your mother would have been proud of you."

"Until I sinned she might. Now I think that she would disown me."

"You could not have saved your family. I was not at home when your mother and sister died."

"No, but mother chose to sacrifice herself and you were obeying the King's command. It is not the same."

I could not convince him otherwise. We spent some time discussing his vague plans. He knew he wanted to go to fight in the east but he only had a vague destination in mind. When my men returned it was with the bad news that there were no ships to be had but we had the supplies. My reputation meant that I was given time to pay for them. It was not altruism. Without ships in port, there were no other buyers.

Three days later my men rode in with the chest of coins to pay for the goods we had bought. William was loath to accept it but I smiled, "Consider it your inheritance. If you are in the Holy Land when I die how will you get it? Besides I am sure we will continue to make profits. When you are in the Holy Land, if you need any funds then send to me."

"You have done more than enough already."

"A father can never do enough for his son."

My two ships pulled in to the quay two days later. I had been distracted for those two days as the Empress had gone to live in the Priory. It was as if my world was being turned upside down. I went with William and Henry to the quay. William of Kingston beamed when he saw us, "Are you ready to come home, lord?"

I shook my head, "No and I have a commission for you and for Ethelred's ship."

He frowned, "It is getting close to the autumn storms, lord...."

"I wish you to take my son and his men to the Holy Land."

I had stunned him. I decided to put his mind at rest immediately. "Both crews will be paid. The Duke of Normandy is paying. You will also be able to trade with Constantinople. I have contacts there and you can make a fortune for yourselves."

"I need no convincing, lord. It is just that my wife will worry. She is expecting our second child and I told her I would return before she gave birth."

My son said, "Think of the gifts you can bring to her from the east. They have clothes finer than anything they have here."

My captain bowed, "I am the Earl's to command. It will take until the evening to unload. If we are to sail then I would like it to be on the morning tide. I will have to see if I can buy charts for I know not those waters."

"So be it."

Henry and my son hurried off to organize the horses and men. I told my captain why my son was going. His face fell, "My lord, I am so sorry. I would have said nothing had I known. I should have realised that there would be a good reason."

"And had I know that Morag was with child I might not have made the offer to my son. Have a swift voyage and a safe one."

The parting was hard. It was not just me who was affected. Most of my men had known William since he had been a child. The Duke had grown up with him. He was making the reverse of the journey I had made all those years ago. As my father might have said, *wyrd*! My son and I had said our goodbyes in private and while others spoke I remained silent. I did not take my eyes from my son. I wanted to remember him. I fixed every detail of his face in my head. I wished I had had an artist make a likeness of him. It was too late now. As the two merchant ships headed down the Seine towards the sea I wondered if I would ever see him again. If the war ended badly for us I might join him. The thought cheered me up.

I did not have long to brood. The next day a rider rode in from the north. I saw him throw himself from his horse and then run into the Great Hall. I was with Henry and Richard. My leg had improved and I was practising with them. They were young and agile. It kept me on my toes; quite literally. One of the Duke's guards ran from the hall a short while after the messenger had entered, "Lord, the Duke wishes conference with you and his son."

I could sense the excitement in Henry as he raced ahead, "Henry, it is unseemly for a future king to run even if it is his father who commands. He will not speak until I am there at any rate. Walk with me."

He obeyed for he still heeded my commands.

When I entered I saw that the Duke had convened a hasty
council of war. He was surrounded by his barons and earls.
He looked up when I entered, "Earl, this rider, Robert of
Mortain, is from the castle at Abbeville. Baron Guillaume
D'Aubigny has been attacked by Thierry of Flanders. We are
needed. The castle of Abbeville guards the crossing of the
Seine. If it falls then the enemy can attack us anywhere!
What is our best course of action?"

I went over to the map. "Why?"

All eyes were upon me. "What do mean, Earl? I cannot
understand the question. You mean why go to his aid?
Surely it is obvious. Flanders makes war on us."

I knew the lands in question. I had studied the maps to
occupy my mind in the days following my son's departure. I
knew the value of knowledge. I gathered it whenever I could.
"But why Abbeville? Why not Amiens where the river is
easier to ford? He chooses the place with one bridge. The
castle defends the one bridge. We would have to cross that
bridge to reach the castle. We would be packed tightly and
an easy target for an ambush."

The Duke waved his hand as though dismissing my
words. "We cannot leave the baron without aid."

"I did not suggest that. You have a good garrison in
Amiens?"

"Sir Jean de Formerie was one of my father's old
retainers. I gave him the manor as a reward for his long
service. There is no one more reliable."

"Then he will still hold it. It sits astride the Somme. You
will, perforce, have to take warriors who are afoot. I will
take my men at arms and horsemen. I have all mounted men.
We will cross the river at Amiens and travel behind the
enemy. His eye will be fixed on you. We should be able to
attack his men from the east. He will not expect it. He cannot
fight the castle, me and ambush you. It will enable you to
raise the siege."

Geoffrey of Anjou smiled, "A goodly plan but you do not
have enough men. Gilbert de Bois, your conroi is all
mounted. I wish you and Richard of Thiberville to go with

the Earl under his command. That will add forty men to his numbers."

"And I will go with my men." Henry straightened his back and faced his father.

"Your men?"

"My mother paid for twenty men at arms. They are my bodyguard." He grinned, "When the Earl's men are busy at any rate."

"But that is dangerous."

"If I am to rule England one day then I should face a little danger first. I need to know how to command men in battle is that not so, Warlord?" I nodded. "I ride with the Warlord of the North. I will be safe."

Unlike me, the Duke had more sons. He could afford to lose one and he nodded his agreement. If Henry died then Geoffrey would become the next Duke. "It did me no harm when I was your age. You have my permission. We will ride on the morrow."

"Before we do how does the castle lie?" I was not Geoffrey, I wanted as much information as I could. The maps only told me part of the story. I needed information about the castle itself.

Robert of Caen spoke, "There are two bridges and an island between. The island has trees and houses upon it. The castle has a stone keep and stands on a high piece of ground above the river."

"Good. Then I have all that I need." I could picture the land now and a plan began to permeate my head.

We had the longer journey and we left before dawn. The two knights who accompanied me were soon given a rude shock as my men rode hard. We were used to this and they were not. This was not a leisurely ride; this was a forced march. Even though we were travelling through friendly lands I had scouts out and we rode in a tight formation. It was noon when we crossed into the castle. We had been seen from afar.

Sir John reminded me of my father. He was a greybeard and his paunch showed that it had been some years since he had campaigned. I could see why the Duke had rewarded him. Amiens was a fine castle. He rubbed his hands, "I will bring my men, lord! It is time I unsheathed my sword again."

Shaking my head I said. "You can let us have twenty of your men at arms, but only if they are mounted. It would be useful to have men who know the land but the Duke needs you to hold this castle. They might well attack this one too. I would prepare for a siege."

"You are right. Count Fulk always feared fighting you for you were like a rock. I shall try to copy you." As he turned he said, "You say the Flemish are besieging the castle?"

"Aye."

"Then I wonder why the castellan did not send to me? I am but a few miles away. It will have taken his man half a day to reach you. I could have gone to his aid within the hour."

It set me to wondering too. The men of Flanders had shown themselves to be cunning. I would not take anything at face value. When we left, after watering the horses, I had my own men and sixty Normans too. I knew the Normans were not of the quality of mine but the force was large enough to be a threat to Count Thierry. We were all mounted and with my archers, I had an edge that might tip the balance of a battle.

Sir Jean gave us his sergeant at arms, Raymond, to lead his men at arms. He reminded me of Wulfric. He rode next to me and said, "You want to surprise these bandits from the north, lord?"

"I do."

"There is a road that comes from the northeast, through Saint-Riquier. It is not the road the men from Flanders would have used. There is a forest until just a mile from Abbeville. It will hide you from his sight."

"Then lead us there."

"We take that greenway ahead, lord."

We pulled off the main road and headed down a greenway with a high hedge running down both sides. I waved Dick forward. "I fancy we can teach these Flemish men to fear our archers. When we reach the forest I will take

138

half the men and attack the Flemish warriors. We will see if I can get them to pursue us back to the forest."

"It will depend, lord, on the forest. We need a clear line to our target. There are only thirty of us."

Henry said, "Dick, thirty of you are worth a garrison of others." The future king knew the value of English archers better than any.

The greenway twisted and turned. I confess I was completely lost and in the hands of the old warrior. We crossed small roads but still, we kept along the greenway. Suddenly we burst out onto a road. The sergeant at arms pointed to the south, "There is your forest, lord, and beyond it Abbeville."

"Dick, send two men ahead of us." He detailed Henry Warbow and Rafe to gallop off and scout out the road.

The old sergeant at arms was correct. We were well hidden by the forest. The road did not run straight and it was a gloomy road. It suited us.

Henry Warbow and Rafe galloped up as we saw the sky becoming lighter. "Lord, there are no siege works! The men of Flanders are not there."

Henry said, "Has my father raised the siege?"

Rafe shook his head, "I doubt it, my lord. The castle shows no sign of damage and there is no evidence of siege works. There are no counter castles, and neither ditches nor fascines."

"It is a trap."

Henry turned as I spoke and said, "What?"

I turned to the old sergeant, "Is the castle at Abbeville a strong one?"

Shaking his head he said, "A simple ditch with a lower bailey and then a stone tower for a keep. The baron has a garrison of no more than sixty men."

"Rafe, what did you see?"

"Just that, lord, a stone keep with a wooden wall around it. We could take it. If an army came then it would have fallen."

139

"Then we approach cautiously. Furl the standards. Alan of Osmotherley and Alain of Auxerre, watch Henry. Dick, keep your archers to the rear. They mark us as English."

As we left the forest I saw, ahead, the castle and around it the houses of Abbeville. There was no sign of an army attacking. The standard of Normandy still flew. We rode easily down the road. I wanted whoever was in the castle to believe that we were the men of Flanders. I hoped they would believe we were reinforcements. I now knew that the castle had fallen or had surrendered. It mattered not which. I suspected treachery. This was a border castle and I knew the temptation to change sides might be greater here. This was a trap to get the Duke and his son.

As we neared the castle I saw that the houses were still occupied. If there had been a siege they would have fled. As we rode through I raised my hand and waved. I smiled. I halted and turned to the Sergeant At Arms. "They know my surcoat. Ride ahead of us and pretend to be from Ypres. Say that I am Eustace of Ypres come to reinforce the Count."

"You wish to get into the castle?"

"I do. I would turn the tables on this Count. He thinks to trap the Duke. I intend to do the same to him."

The sergeant rode ahead of us. His men spread out making it hard for them to make out my livery. The gate was closed but the bridge was over the ditch. As we approached I heard him shouting up to the guards on the top of the gate. I thought, at first, that it was going to work but then a sharp-eyed sentry saw my archers.

"English!"

I spurred Edward on and shouted, "Dick! Clear the walls."

His men were off their horses in an instant. We distracted the sentries by galloping towards the bridge. Their crossbows clattered as they sent bolts at us. I took two on my shield. Then I saw two of the crossbowmen pitch into the ditch as my archers did their deadly work.

"Richard, Gunter, scale the walls!"

The two of them rode over the bridge and jumped up to stand on their saddles. They pulled themselves up. A spearman ran at them. It was as though a giant hand grabbed him as two arrows plunged into his chest and threw him from the wall. When my men reached the top, I saw Günter draw his sword and swing it around his head. He had a longer sword than most of my men and like all Swabians was a master with it. Richard disappeared. I had an anxious moment and then the gate opened and Richard stood there. The sergeant at arms galloped in with me. We chased after the remaining sentries. The gate into the upper bailey was open. I spurred Edward. He was the fastest horse I had owned. I was dimly aware of Henry and his guards on my right shoulder but their mounts would struggle to keep up with Edward. The enemy should have shut the gate but they held it open to allow the last couple of men through. Edward leapt in the air to clear the cowering man who had fallen before the gate and then I was through.

I whirled his head as I slashed my sword at the men at arms who were trying to unhorse me. When Alain of Auxerre burst through and joined me I knew that we had succeeded. They would not close the gate again. The two of us whirled our horses around and our swords sent the men at arms fleeing towards the keep.

Whoever commanded the keep, however, had learned their lesson and the huge door of the stronghold slammed shut. As my men galloped through the gate the men outside either surrendered or died. We were briefly troubled by a few crossbows until my archers arrived.

"Edgar, you and Dick keep them occupied. Henry, come with me and we will see what tricks the men of Flanders have prepared."

The gate did not lead directly to the bridge and we ascended the wooden wall to peer down to the south. The bridge was some three hundred paces from the castle wall. I saw men waiting. They were the ones pretending to be besieging the castle. I saw that their siege works were too flimsy. The trap became obvious. Some were turning around looking at the walls. We had made a sudden attack but there had been noise. I waved at the men. It might not have fooled them but it would make them doubt. I saw the Duke and the rest of the army as it snaked its way up the road. There was a wood to the west and I saw horsemen massing there. We could see them but the Duke could not. He had no scouts out! They intended to attack the Duke in the flank when he was on the island. He would be trapped.

I turned, "Richard, fetch the Normans. I want them on the walls, all three conroi." I saw the intention of the enemy clearly now. They would wait until the Duke was engaged with the men holding the island. The first bridge would be like a gate when the men of Flanders charged. This was a deadly trap. Had I not approached from the north then we would have known nothing.

We did not have long. I galloped Edward back through the bailey. Richard had already reached our allies and they were rushing back to man the walls. When I reached the keep I saw that Dick's archers had managed to clear the top of the stone defence.

"The Duke will be trapped. Dick, leave half a dozen archers here to keep their heads down. Edgar, leave four men to guard the archers. If they try to sortie then send for the men at arms from the walls. The rest, mount. Henry. We will need your men now."

"What do you intend, Earl?"

"We will clear the defences at the bridge before your father reaches them."

Once at the wall I found Gilbert and Richard de Thiberville waiting for me. "What do you wish us to do, lord?"

"Mount half of your men and bring them with me. I intend to clear the island. We do not have long." I shouted up, "Raymond of Amiens. I leave you to command these men at arms in my absence. If they sortie from the keep you will have to support my men."

He nodded, "We will still be here when you return! We have a fine view from up here!"

I turned, "We ride in a column of six. Sir Gilbert, Sir Robert, you will ride at the fore with my men. Richard, ride, with the banner, in the second rank with Leopold of Durstein and Günter the Swabian. Henry, I want your men at the rear.

We will push on to the second bridge and leave you to clear the island! This will be your first command."

"Aye lord. It will be like a graveyard when we are done!"

He was learning to follow orders. I could see a change in him already. I raised my lance and shouted, "Now we unfurl our banners. Now we show them that the wolf is in the sheepfold!"

We galloped through the gate and over the ditch. We wheeled right and I steadied the line to allow the others to close up. We had to hit the enemy like a steel ram. They knew we were coming. The ones at the rear had turned and seen strange faces on their walls. They hurriedly began to change their defence from the south to the north. We covered the three hundred paces quickly. The men were on the wrong side of the barriers. They had built them to stop the Duke. Now they just barred their escape. We charged the ones at the end of the second bridge. They tried to form a shield wall and to use their crossbows. Our shields took the bolts and then we were amongst them. I punched with my lance and the sergeant at arms who commanded crumpled as my lancehead tore through him. The others were dispersed leaving us the empty bridge. We galloped across and I saw the men on the island quickly trying to find a way through the barricades they had built.

Numbers were hard to estimate but I could see that there were no knights with the men who waited for us. They had crossbows and pikes. They had round helmets and they wore no mail. One or two of the braver souls tried to loose their crossbows at us when we hurtled towards them. They managed one hit on John of Norton's horse. The rest struck metal or wood. An archer can loose five arrows while a crossbowman reloads. Dick's archer's arrows were deadly. The ones who tried were slain and then we were on them. While some of my men went through the holes they had made in the barricade I jumped Edward over a low part. I was aided by the fact that the stakes pointed south. Edward's rear hooves clattered against the tops of them as we landed. Edward bundled one man over as I punched my lance into the back of a second. Our sudden appearance caused mayhem. The defenders just tried to get out of our way.

"On! To the second bridge. Leave the defenders for the Prince's men!"

The flight of those before us gave me the chance to wait for my men and to spy out the situation ahead. Already the Duke was attacking the men defending the first bridge. His men were strung out in a long line. He could not see the wave of armour that was hurtling towards his unguarded flank. As soon as we began to cross the bridge the defenders ahead heard us and knew that they were doomed. I saw men surrendering and the Duke's men cheered.

I yelled, "Ambush! Ambush! Enemy to your left! Ambush!"

My words were drowned by the cheers as the Normans thought that they had won. I could not see the column behind the Duke but I heard the noise as the Count's men struck the middle of it. It was like the sound of a hundred trees splintering in a storm. Their lances struck the shields of the Duke's knights and men at arms. The Duke turned in his saddle and looked behind him.

He was less than forty paces from me and I shouted, "It is a trap! There was no siege! This is the Count's attack!"

The Duke was no coward and he whipped his horse's head around, "Turn and let us go to the aid of our comrades!"

The Count outnumbered the Norman and Angevin force. In addition, there was no order to the attack by the Duke's men. They would lose unless we could get to their side. As we crossed the bridge I waved my hand to the left. We would try to reach the head of the enemy. The Duke led his men right and there was an empty space to the left. We poured across the open ground. I saw that the Flemish knights had begun to turn to enlarge the hole they had made in the Duke's column.

"Into line!"

I reined Edward back a little to allow Sir Gilbert and Sir Richard to bring their men next to mine. Once we were in a rough line I lowered my lance, "For God, Duke Geoffrey and Empress Matilda!"

We knew our own men. We charged into a whirling mass of steel, wood and flailing hooves. We were less than forty men but we were boot to boot and we were organized. Edgar and I both speared the knight who was about to despatch a wounded squire. I pulled my lance from his body and hurled it like a spear at the back of a knight who had stood in his stirrups to impale an Angevin man at arms. He was less than twenty feet from me and the lance hit him squarely in the back. It broke through his mail and into his body. He arched as he fell backwards. His dying hand dragged his horse backwards. Edward had to jump again and I landed without a weapon in my hand.

A Flemish knight saw his chance and he galloped at me. Rather than risk drawing my sword I held my shield before me. He saw I was weaponless and stabbed at my right shoulder. A lance is a long weapon and the tip moves. My right hand darted out and grabbed the lance behind the head. I pushed it in front of me. He was so surprised that he did not release the weapon. His own lance knocked him over the cantle. I drew my sword and checked back Edward for he was ahead of the rest of my line.

The Duke was being attacked by a conroi of knights. Even as I pointed my sword and led my men towards them I wondered if we were too late. The Duke no longer had the strong right arm of my son to protect his back. Had the fates conspired to snatch victory away from us?

The Flemish men at arms and knights who were at the rear of the line tried to turn to face us. Their lances proved an encumbrance. I saw the line ripple as confusion spread. Those of my men with lances knocked their opponents from their saddle. I brought my sword over to strike at the knight before me. He raised his shield. I hit him a mighty blow which made my arm shiver. The press of horseflesh stopped Edward and his teeth flashed around to bite the nearest horse. I stood in my saddle and brought my blade down again. I must have weakened his arm for it did not come up as high and the end cracked into his helmet. I saw the life leave his eyes.

The Duke was still beleaguered and I yelled, "Stockton! On me!"

My men heard my cry and I saw Richard with the standard leading them to me. We hurriedly formed a line five men wide and three men deep. It was but fifteen men but I had fought with these warriors more times than enough. I stood in my stirrups and raised my sword, "Charge!"

Richard waved my standard and we leapt forward. Even as we charged I saw the Duke's own banner fall. He and his oathsworn were surrounded. They had had their spears shattered and the enemy saw victory before them. With the Duke dead the Norman and Angevin forces would crumble. They had reckoned, however, without the Earl of Cleveland!

Once again Edward began to outstrip the rest and I reached the rearmost knight. He was trying to reach the Duke and only became aware of me when Edward's snorting head appeared next to him. He half-turned and I stood to deliver a blow between his head and his shoulder. He had a coif but my steel was sharp and it tore through the mail. The force was so powerful that I knew the blow had broken his collar bone even before it ripped into his flesh and bright blood spurted and arced as he fell. I held my shield before me as I swept my sword to my left. It caught a man at arms a glancing blow to his helmet and he lost his balance, tumbling beneath the hooves of Edgar and his horse.

I saw Duke Geoffrey knocked from his horse by a lance which hit his shield from the side. The head smacked into his helmet and he fell heavily to the ground. He was hurt. I pulled back on Edward's reins and spurred him. He leapt into the air crashing into the side of the knight who had unhorsed the Duke and was about to stab him. As the knight fell from his horse I leaned forward to slash sideways at the next knight. My sword struck his right hand and he dropped his lance. Richard was by me and I shouted. "Help the Duke to his feet." I could see that the Duke was merely dazed. Richard used my standard to batter his way through and he leapt from the back of his horse. It was bravely done. Edgar joined me and Leopold of Durstein. The three of us formed a protective ring around the Duke and his wounded bodyguards.

Our act seemed to enrage the remaining Flemish knights who furiously threw themselves at us. I was aided by my horse, Edward. He was a true warhorse and he whirled around in a semi-circle, flailing his hooves at the knights who tried to get at me whilst snapping and biting at the enemy horses. Even so, we were hard-pressed. A war axe ploughed into my shield. It was well made but it could not withstand such strokes. Wood splintered from it. I brought my sword from on high and, as the knight pulled back for a second strike I hacked across his forearm. My blade grated against the bone. I must have severed tendons for the axe fell from his hand. As he stared at the wound I lunged at his open mouth and he fell from his horse. Leopold of Durstein gave a cry of pain as a lance struck him in the side. I watched as Edgar was knocked from his mount by the attacks of two men at arms. He fell to the ground and lay still. Alan son of Alan leapt from his horse to stand over the body of the sergeant at arms. Günter the Swabian joined him. They would die defending their leader.

Then I heard a cry, "England and Anjou! England and Anjou!"

The thunder of hooves made the Flemish warriors turn and they saw Henry FitzEmpress leading his bodyguards and the remaining Norman knights as they hurled themselves into the enemy. It proved to be a pivotal moment in the battle. Richard helped the Duke to his horse and, clutching both the Duke's and my banner, mounted his own horse. He held both banners aloft and there was a cheer from the beleaguered Angevin forces. The enemy broke!

Chapter 11

Baron Guillaume D'Aubigny was defiant to the end. After the wounded men at arms had been despatched and the knights who had yielded secured and bound we took our battered forces into the castle bailey. Dick and his archers were sent to follow the defeated enemy and ensure that they returned home. The priests had seen to the Duke's wounds; they had been superficial. The wounded were still on the field of battle and they required more ministration than the Duke.

As we headed to the keep, the Duke showed his pride at his son's actions, "You have saved the day, my son! Had you not reached us then both the Earl and I would have perished."

Henry showed his maturity, "I think not. The enemy might have held on for longer but I do not think that the Warlord would have been in any danger. Even as we charged I saw that none dared approach him."

I was not certain that he was right but I liked his words.

The Duke pointed up at the keep from which the baron's standard flew, "And what do we do about this snake!"

"First we winkle him from his tower."

"That will be simple. We break down the door!"

"Enough of our men have died this day. We either persuade him to surrender or burn it down."

"That seems extreme."

"We can rebuild a keep but we cannot replace our valuable warriors." I saw Henry nodding in agreement. He understood the wisdom of holding on to good warriors and not wasting them.

We dismounted, safe in the knowledge that the crossbowmen inside the keep would keep their heads down and not risk incurring the wrath of my archers. I noticed that the Duke dismounted gingerly. The fall had hurt him.

"He will know that he must die."

"True, my lord, but he must have his family within. They will give us the opportunity to strike a bargain." I looked at the Duke, "With your permission?"

"Aye." He turned to his men, "And someone find me some wine!"

"Richard, find some men and have the palisade broken up. I want it placed around the door."

"Yes lord."

The keep was an older design. The door was the height of two men above the ground. It prevented a ram from breaking it down. There would be a ladder inside the keep to allow them to descend. The weakness, however, lay in fire. We could build a fire which would send first smoke under the door and, if we continued to feed the flames, would set fire to the door. It would not be swift but we were in no hurry. The men needed rest and the longer the fire took the more likely they would be to surrender.

I saw that Ralph of Nottingham had organised the men. He had been in the third rank. Those in the first two ranks all had a wound. Many still lay on the battlefield. I would have to find out what the butcher's bill had been. We waited until a large pyre had been built. Ralph had my men find kindling to lay amongst it. The taller pieces of timber almost reached the door.

Duke Geoffrey had had his wine and it must have eased his pain for he approached me. "Are we ready?"

"We are."

He turned and shouted, "Baron Guillaume D'Aubigny! Are you there?"

We were rewarded by silence, "Baron Guillaume D'Aubigny, this is your liege lord, Geoffrey Duke of

Normandy. If you do not answer me then I will order my men to fire the keep and burn all within. Do you want that?"

A disembodied voice shouted, "How do I know that you will not have one of your lackeys end my life with an arrow?"

"You have my word that I will allow you to speak unharmed."

A head appeared over the battlements, "What is it you wish to say?"

"I wish you to surrender the keep."

He laughed, "What kind of a fool do you take me for? I will be executed!"

"First we will have a trial and you can give the mitigating circumstances which made you turn traitor."

"I am no traitor. I served you but I never followed you. My heart is in Flanders. I was fighting for my country."

"And you are foresworn. You said you were under attack."

He turned his gaze to me, "It was a ruse of war. You often use such devices, Wolf of the North!"

"But I never lie. You have forgotten the oath you took when you won your spurs."

"I will not speak with a killer. I say to you, Duke Geoffrey, that I will not surrender to your justice. I will take my chance here. The Count will come with a relief force and I will be free."

"And your family? Do you wish them to die?"

"The keep is well made and we have supplies. We will trust in God."

I shook my head, "God forsook you when you lied." The Duke nodded, "May he have mercy on your soul and your family too." I turned, "Ralph, light the fire."

My men were ready. They hurled burning brands into the kindling. They were quite happy to administer justice. There was more smoke than flame at first as I had expected. As the fire took hold I saw smoke spiralling from the top of the keep as the tower acted as a sort of chimney drawing the smoke up inside. Men tried to douse the flames with water poured from the top of the keep but when two fell to my

archer's arrows then they desisted. When the fire took hold
we had to step back for the heat was great. The door began to
blister and then, more alarmingly, the mortar in the stones
began to crack.

It did not take long for the Baron to shout, "Very well.
We surrender!"

The Duke was no fool, "Unequivocally?"

"I give my word! For the love of God douse the flames!
My children can barely breathe!"

I nodded, "Ralph!"

My men ran to the fire and using pikes began to pull the
burning timbers away. The whole dissolved into smaller fires
and Henry's men poured river water on them. The fire hissed
and smoked. The keep was wreathed in smoke for a while
but it allowed those inside to open the door and allow air to
clear the smoke from within.

I turned to the Duke, "With your permission, I will return
to the battlefield and see to my men."

"Of course. My son and I will deal with these. You were
right, again. I am, once more, in your debt."

Leaving my archers to keep watch I rode with my men
back to the field of battle. It was a grim place. Already
crows, magpies and other carrion were picking over the open
wounds of the dead. Red kites flew overhead waiting for us
to leave them to their feast. The birds on the ground fled as
we passed and then descended again when we moved on.
They would gorge on the feast of flesh. Alan son of Alan
rode behind Richard. "Alan, take some men and gather as
many of the horses as you can."

"Aye lord."

"Ralph, collect armour and weapons."

It was a harsh reality that we had to look after ourselves
first. Others had fought and would claim the booty for
themselves. Richard and I rode towards the priests who had
gathered the wounded, "You did well today, Richard. That
was bravely done to carry the two banners."

"I was honoured, lord."

"Soon you will be a knight. Not this year but next."

"I am still happy to be your squire."

"I know but I need knights such as you. The war I fight will last some time."

Edgar was on his feet when we reached the improvised hospital. His arm was bandaged and I saw another around his head. There were two cloaks covering my surcoats. Two of my men had died. That was a grievous loss. Edgar saw my glance as I dismounted and said, "Henry of Langdale and Gurth."

"Gurth?" Edgar nodded. "He had served me a long time."

"He died well. They both did."

"Leopold?"

"His armour saved him but it will be some time before he can fight. The cut was deep."

"And the others?"

"Leopold's is the worst."

"We will send them back to Rouen. You will command them. I do not want to risk them more."

"Are you not finished here, lord?"

"I think that the Duke will need to punish the Count. He will need our aid."

He nodded, "The young Prince did well."

"Aye, he did. It would have been easy just to charge in but he brought the knights in solid lines."

"He will be a good king... in time."

I smiled, "You mean when I have finally defeated Stephen the Usurper?"

Edgar laughed, "That is not in doubt, lord. If you had command of all of the Empress' armies, then it would be King Henry already!" Edgar had fought alongside me longer than most and I accepted his praise.

After I had spoken to all of my men I sought out Ralph and Alan. "Have the booty placed on the horses. Edgar will escort it and the wounded back to Rouen. When William of Kingston returns it can be placed aboard the ships."

It was dark by the time we returned to the castle. The prisoners were all being guarded and the baron and his family were with the Duke. He rose when I reached him. "We will hold a trial on the morrow, Earl. I would like you to be the judge. Choose twelve knights to be the baron's jury."

I nodded.

Henry asked, "Has Dick returned?"

"Not yet. But you know Dick. He will want to make sure that the enemy has fled. He is a careful warrior."

Duke Geoffrey said, "It seems you are luckier in your knights than I. I have traitors in my midst. I cannot see any of your knights betraying you. Rather they would die for you."

"I am lucky, I know that."

Henry shook his head, "It is not luck, Earl. It is skill and I will try to acquire that too. When I am king I will surround myself with loyal knights and I will be unstoppable!"

I was woken in the middle of the night when Dick returned. He looked tired. "They took the road to Bruges, lord. They left their dead in their wake. They will not be a threat for some time."

"Good. Get some rest. Tomorrow I need you to be a member of the jury which tries Baron Guillaume D'Aubigny."

"A trial? Why not just hang the bastard?"

"You sound like Wulfric." I laughed, "Because the Duke needs to be seen as a man who abides by the law. He will still die but we will do it legally."

The Duke summoned the priest when he awoke. He had problems focussing. The priest gave him a draught of something which eased the pain. "I will have a couch brought so that I can observe the goings on."

I had never judged a trial but I had held enough assizes to know the principle. It seemed simple. I would ask for testimony and then the knights I had chosen would decide if he was guilty. My task would then be to pass sentence. I had done my best to be fair. I had chosen only those knights, like Dick, who could be trusted to be fair. That was my way. We held the trial in the outer bailey. The baron's family were present as were the rest of the knights. I was given a chair that had been rescued from the keep.

After the jury had been seated I began. "We are here to discover if Baron Guillaume D'Aubigny is guilty of treason." I pointed to the priest who held the cross and a box containing holy relics. "Each man who speaks must first put his hands upon the cross and the pyx and swear that they tell the truth. Robert of Mortain, take the oath."

After he had been sworn in I began my questions. "Did you ride to Rouen and tell Duke Geoffrey that Abbeville was under attack from the men of Flanders?"

He could not deny it as we had all heard him and he nodded.

"Speak your answer so that all men may hear."

"I did."

"Were the Flemish warriors attacking Abbeville?" He hesitated and I looked pointedly at the priest, "Your soul is at stake, Robert of Mortain."

He shook his head, "No they were not."

"Was it your decision to lie or another's?"

"It was the baron who issued my orders. He was my liege lord." He flashed a guilty look at his master.

I waved the messenger away and said, "Baron Guillaume D'Aubigny, come and take the oath."

The baron strode defiantly forward and placed his hand on the box and the cross. "The words I speak shall be the truth. I may lose my life but I will not be damned."

The man had courage. His two sons, his daughter and his wife huddled together with fearful expressions upon their faces. His words had brought home his fate.

"Did you send Robert of Mortain with false information to deceive the Duke of Normandy?"

"I did."

His answer took me by surprise. I had expected more. "Do you wish to add anything?"

He shrugged, "I could say that I prefer to be ruled by Count Thierry rather than an Angevin who is little better than a robber baron but that would avail me nothing. Let my peers make their judgement and then I will hear your sentence."

There was much to be admired in this knight despite his perfidy. I turned to the knights. "You have heard the evidence. Do you need time to deliberate?"

Gilbert de Bois shook his head, "No, lord. The baron has condemned himself. We are all agreed. He is guilty."

I suddenly realised that I would have to deliver the death sentence. There was no other way. I could, however, make it a swift end. I would not order a slow death or a dishonourable death. There were other sentences. I rose, "Baron Guillaume D'Aubigny, your peers have found you guilty of treason. Your actions caused the deaths of many noble knights and could have ended the life of a future king of England. I have little choice other than to order your death." I turned to the Duke, "Do you have an executioner, my lord?"

He waved over a huge man at arms who carried a double-handed sword. I saw that he was a Swabian, "Guiscard will carry out the sentence."

I nodded, "Then, baron, I give you a short time to take leave of your family and to confess your sins." I looked at the sky, "You will be executed at noon. May God have mercy on your soul."

The Duke had appeared ill at ease during the trial and he barely made it to the execution before he keeled over and the priest rushed to him. Henry looked terrified, "Father!"

The priest said, "It is the result of the fall. I warned him not to leave his bed."

I shouted, "Have a tent erected here in the bailey for the Duke and fetch a bed from the keep."

The baroness pointed an accusing finger at the Duke, "This is a punishment from God!" She glared at me, "And you too, Warlord, will be punished."

I smiled, "Lady, I have been punished enough. There is little that God could take from me."

By the next morning, the Duke had recovered enough to hold a council of war with his leaders. There were four of us present. "I had thought to punish Count Thierry by taking my army into Flanders and bringing him to battle but I fear we do not have the men thanks to the baron's treachery. We

need to show Flanders that we are not to be taken lightly.
Warlord, what would you suggest?"

"I agree with you, lord, that we cannot fight a major
battle but our allies in Hainaut and Holland might gain some
respite if we were to use four conroi to make raids into their
heartland and take horses and the smaller castles."

"Five."

I looked at Henry, "Five?"

"I have my own men and I can do as you suggest, Earl."

His defiant stance told me that he was ready to argue. His
father, however, made the decision for me. "Of course, you
shall lead a conroi but it will be a larger one than the twenty
men. Richard of Thiberville, you and your men will form the
conroi for my son. Let us see what the young cockerel can
do."

Sir Richard sounded less than enthusiastic when he
intoned, "Aye, lord. I am yours to command."

While Henry conferred with his father I took Sir Richard
to one side. "Henry will listen to advice. He is young but he
has a sound mind."

"Then perhaps he should lead your men, Earl!"

"Perhaps he should but I think his father thought an
Angevin should lead the men of Anjou and Normandy. After
all, he will be Duke of Normandy one day and then he will
command you. Who knows this may well advance your
position."

I could see that he had not thought this through. He
nodded, "You are right and I apologise. You have fought
alongside him I know."

"Do not forget, Sir Richard, that but for his intervention
then the Duke and I might be dead. He handled that well did
he not?"

"Aye, he did."

I left the meeting and hurried to find Dick and my men.
They had made a camp some way from the Normans and
Angevin. They were Englishmen and preferred their own
company. "We ride at dawn. We have free rein to raid
Flanders." Their faces lit up. They knew that this would be
an opportunity to make a fortune. "We will take palfreys

rather than warhorses. I do not want to risk damaging such valuable creatures. We will raid Poperinge first. It is close to Hainaut and I would help Lothair if I could. Besides, it is deep in enemy land and they will not expect us to strike there."

I looked at their faces. They were eager. "Wilfred, in the absence of Edgar I would have you lead the men at arms. Have those with slight wounds remain in camp to watch our horses. We will be raiding a second time. All will have the opportunity to become rich." That pleased them all.

Henry came to see me before I retired. "Am I ready for this?" He had offered his sword and now wondered at the wisdom of his actions. It showed he was still reckless but he had given his word and could not go back on it.

"I would have spoken up if I was in any doubt. Sir Richard is an experienced knight. Do not be afraid to seek his advice. It does not show weakness. Have you decided where you will raid?"

"Le Touquet. I wished to try Boulogne but Sir Richard told me that its defences were formidable. Le Touquet is close enough to Boulogne and is smaller."

I smiled, "You are learning. This is about hurting the Flemish and not our own men. Whatever we take from their people will hurt them and help the Normans."

"And you?"

"We go to Poperinge. It is deep enough into enemy land for them to feel safe but the land is flat. Besides, it will aid the Count of Hainaut. He is our ally."

His face fell, "I should have realised that. You think of everything, Earl."

"I have been doing this for over a quarter of a century. You will learn. You have learned much already." I was not flattering him. In the last year, he had ceased to be a youth and was becoming a man. I was proud of him.

Chapter 12

We left before dawn for we had seventy miles to travel to Poperinge. Ralph of Wales and Garth son of Gurth were the archers who scouted. Garth had pleaded with Dick to be allowed to do so. He wished to show us that his father's death had not affected him. We allowed it. He was a good archer and had many of his father's skills as a swordsman. He was a good companion for the older Ralph

As we rode Richard questioned me, "Why Poperinge, lord?"

"It is close to Hainaut but it is also a growing town which does not have a city wall. They make fine cloth and that is a valuable commodity. If we are successful then Flanders will have to draw men from the border with Hainaut to defend the land."

"Then we will need to capture wagons to carry the cloth."

"Good! You are doing as I do. You see the problems and then find solutions. Tell me what other problems will follow the capture of the cloth."

"If we have to capture wagons then we will travel back more slowly."

"And that is why I left before dawn. It will take us twice as long to get back." I swept a hand around me. "And the route I have chosen passes few places." We had travelled some thirty miles and had not seen a castle. We had barely seen anything larger than a village. We had skirted all but the most isolated farm. When we returned, we would ride down the main road but I wished to reach our destination unseen.

Garth rode back with the news that they had found the
town. "There is no river, lord and the wall is a wooden
palisade intended to keep animals out."

"Are there sentries?"

"It looks like there is a town watch."

"Good. We will give them plenty of warning of our
arrival. Dick, have ten of your men ride around the town.
When they flee allow women and children to escape. Any
wagons should be stopped. If the men resist then they will
die."

"You want them to flee." It was a statement and not a
question.

"Aye, I want them to leave their cloth and save their
lives. We make a bold show and frighten them to death!"

We reached the outskirts earlier than I had expected and I
organised ourselves in two lines. With the men at arms in the
fore, Dick's archers looked like a second line of mailed
horsemen for they all wore helmets. We crested the low rise
before the town and then cantered across the open ground.
The hooves of our horses made the ground shake. I heard the
church bell sounding the alarm. I kept an eye on the gate.
They did not bother to shut it and the sentries on the walls
fled. It was not cowardice. Had they tried to stand against us
they would have been slaughtered. It was a wise decision.

We galloped through the gate and I saw that doors were
swinging open showing how swiftly they had fled. My men
knew their duties. Some went to find the wagons we would
need. I had no doubt that every horse had been used in the
flight. My archers would bring those back. Others went to
find the lace and cloth which were as valuable as gold. My
archers returned with half a dozen horses. Will Red Legs
was grinning, "The men on the horses almost filled their
breeks, my lord, when we emerged from the woods."

"Did you have to hurt any?"

He shook his head, "We just pointed our bows at them
and they gave us the horses without a murmur!"

Long Tom shouted, "We have found two decent sized
wagons, lord."

Kingmaker

"Then, if you use six horses to each one, we should be able to move at a good pace. Find anything else of value. Look in their hiding places. I want to leave within the hour."

"Aye lord."

With Dick and his outriders ahead of us we made rapid progress along the main roads. If there was any opposition then it fled before us. We arrived back at Abbeville after dark. As we approached the castle we could hear great celebrations within. As we passed the first of the sentries I halted, "What is going on?"

The man grinned, "It is the Duke's son! He has had a great victory. He and Sir Richard came upon a column of men heading for Boulogne with treasure collected by the men of Flanders. He slew four men and captured great quantities of gold and silver as well as many knights who yielded to him. They talk of him as the next Warlord!"

I was pleased with Henry's success but the hairs on the back of my neck prickled. I did not know why for I could see nothing wrong in this happy turn of events but my father had always taught me to trust my instincts; would that I had.

I turned to Dick, "Have the wagons and cloth stored safely."

"Aye lord. It is good news about the young lord is it not?"

"It is, Dick. He has grown."

"And much of that is to do with you, my lord."

When we reached the king's camp I saw that everyone had been drinking heavily. Duke Geoffrey looked a little better. He tried to rise as I approached, "No, my lord, stay seated."

"Have you heard, Earl? My son has achieved a great victory! In one fell swoop, we have punished Count Thierry for his treachery!"

"And you are looking better too."

"It is nothing, Earl. The priests worry over much. Did you have success?"

"We did. We relieved the burghers of Poperinge of some cloth."

He looked disappointed, "Cloth? You are slipping, Earl! My son found gold and in great quantities too!"

160

I smiled at the insult. The cloth was a bonus. We had ridden deep into Flanders and returned unmolested. That would draw men from the border of Hainaut. I had not managed to turn Geoffrey into a great leader. I hoped I would have more success with Henry.

The young Prince bounded over to me. He was in his cups and his red cheeks showed that. I could not blame him. He had led his first independent command and been successful. Who was I to gainsay him?

"Did you hear, Earl? What a victory!" He waved over a servant who thrust some wine into my hand, "Come, celebrate with me and let me tell you all."

"Of course." As I sat I thought of my other son, William. I had missed the opportunity to hear of his success for we had been separated by the English Channel. This was a chance to make amends.

"We came upon the Flemish force. I used scouts as you had taught me." He leaned in and said in what he thought was a quiet voice, "Thiberville did not think to do so!" I glanced up and saw that the Norman had heard those words. "When we discovered them I sent riders ahead and then swept down on the column. We rode boot to boot and we scythed through them! I slew two knights and took many prisoners!"

"Well done."

"But that is not the best." I was pleased that although he had drunk he was not drunk. His eyes were still bright and his words cogent. "We found chests of coins and they were freshly minted from France. King Louis might be off to the Crusades but he still intends his allies to make mischief. We have hurt Flanders and we can now retire back to Normandy! We need to raid no more. There will be little of more value to take. Your plan was a good one." He glanced over to the Duke, "Even if my father does not recognise your true worth, I do." He raised his goblet, "Warlord!"

We spent another week making sure that the border was safe and repairing the castle. The Duke was no fool and he awarded the manor to Richard of Thiberville as a reward for helping his son. I saw the wisdom in that. Richard was a good if dull knight. He would make a good guardian of this border fort. We headed back to Rouen. I had already sent back the wagons with the cloth and other treasures. Neither the Duke nor Henry wished to share in our success. I knew that what we had was more valuable than the coins they had collected.

When we reached Rouen my wounded men greeted me. They were almost fully healed. Edgar had taken it upon himself to rent a warehouse by the river. He and the others used it as a hall and as a storage facility. I had trained my men well.

After I had seen to my horses I joined the Duke and his son in the castle. There was news from England. "The Earl of Chester has escaped captivity, Earl!"

The Duke flourished the letter as though it was a major event. I was more sceptical. The snake had shed his skin once more that was all. However I kept my voice neutral, "That is good news, my lord."

Henry said, "Perhaps it is time to renew our offensive in England, Earl."

Before I could speak his father said, "No, my son; we lost too many knights to the men of Flanders. We must use this time to build up our forces. In any event, winter will soon be upon us. Who would brave the German Sea or the English Channel in such weather?"

For once I was in total agreement with the Duke but for different reasons. The Earl of Chester's escape would not harm the Usurper. He had not been hurt since the battle of Lincoln and that was many years hence. What would hurt Stephen would be the loss of revenue. Our attack on Flanders had helped in that direction but we needed to do more. Already I had begun to plan the next phase of my offensive against Stephen. What I did not need was a botched attempt at invasion.

"Besides you can use your new-found wealth, young Henry FitzEmpress, to hire more warriors. They can augment the twenty your mother provided."

He brightened, "Thank you, Earl and I will train them so that they are the equal of yours."

I saw the briefest of frowns on his father's face before he smiled, "Just so."

A week later our two ships returned from the Holy Land. They were both heavily laden. William of Kingston stepped brightly from the cog, "We had a good voyage, my lord. After calling at Constantinople we landed your son at Antioch without incident. Your son purchased supplies and arms for his men in the markets of Constantinople. When I last saw him he and his men were preparing to head to the County of Tripoli for they heard that there was a need for Norman knights. They spent some coin buying more suitable garb for his men found it a little hotter than they had expected."

I was relieved. Inside I was joyful for I knew the dangers of the journey he had undertaken. However, I remained outwardly calm. "That is good and from your vessels, I see that you made good trades?"

He nodded, happily, "Aye we did. We shall trade some here and then the rest at Hainaut."

I pointed to the warehouses, "We also have much to trade; cloth and lace."

He frowned, "Then that might be better taken back to Stockton, lord. They produce cloth in Hainaut and our ladies cannot get enough cloth."

"You are the merchant. I will take your advice. Then when you have traded here make all speed to Hainaut. I will come with you for I wish to speak with the Count."

"And you would be welcome."

I returned to the castle where I approached Henry. "I would take my leave of you for a week or so."

He looked disappointed, "But my training is not complete."

"I know but I would visit with the Count of Hainaut. A good leader does not just take his victories without thought. I would know the effect of our raid into Flanders. Besides, you will be much occupied with hiring your new men." He nodded, "A word of advice though. I would use Dick and Edgar to examine the ones you hire first. Both are good judges of warriors, as you know."

"Thank you for the advice. I will heed it."

Two days later we were heading out to sea. I took Ralph
of Nottingham and Alan son of Alan with me as well as
Richard. We took no horses. This would be a diplomatic
visit only. As soon as we left the Seine I noticed the wintery
weather. The seas were black and rough. The skies filled
with scudding, rain-filled clouds. We wrapped our cloaks
tightly about us and huddled close together for warmth.

"This must be worse for you, William. After all, you have
just come from the warmth of the Holy Land."

"Aye lord, but we have become acclimatised to it. It grew
colder each day as we travelled north."

"Did you learn much about life in the Holy Land?"

William smiled, "There would have been a time when I
wondered at such a question but I am now a father too. You
worry about your son."

"No matter how old he is he will always be that helpless
bundle my wife held in her arms to me and I would do all in
my power to protect him from harm."

"I fear that the good days in the east are fading, lord.
Although I do not think your son has gone there to make his
fortune. He has gone to atone." I glanced at him. He smiled,
"We spent many hours talking, lord. We are of an age and
share more than a name. He does not mind the enemies he
has to fight. I met many who sought passage home. We
brought eight to Spain. They had had enough of the heat and
the Moorish horsemen have made life too hard. Your son is
made of sterner stuff."

I was happy that I had spoken with William. It did not
lessen the dangers my son would face but I respected my
captain who faced the terrors of the sea every day and he
knew courage when he saw it. My son would survive.

The winds, the waves and the tides meant it took longer
to reach Antwerpen than we had hoped. It was dusk as we
edged our way into the harbour. The cargo we carried would
be much appreciated in this busy port. William and Oswald,
Ethelred's captain, had spent their money wisely on goods
such as spices, glass, silks and the like. In Rouen, they had

both made a fortune already and now they would do the same in this northern port.

I was greeted by the harbour master as though I was a conquering hero, "My lord of Cleveland! This is an honour. Your visit is both a surprise and timely. The Count was asking, just the other day when your ships were due."

"Is there a problem?"

"It is better that my master speaks with you. I am but a simple man and I would not wish to get my facts wrong. I know tides and sailors."

I turned, "Richard, Ralph, Alan; we go ashore."

"Will we need shields, my lord?"

"No Ralph, just our swords." Turning to William I said, "Make your trades and then await my instructions."

"We cannot leave until tomorrow at the earliest, lord. The tides will not be right."

"It may be longer." I held up a purse, "Here is..."

William shook his head, "No lord, we have more than enough coins ourselves. We profit by your patronage."

The rain had sleet in it and we hurried from the port towards the town. Already I could see even more newly erected buildings. Baldwin the Builder was living up to his name. Lothair, his son, greeted us before we reached the gates. "Your visit could not have been more timely, lord. My father had begun to draft a letter to you."

"Is there a problem?"

Shaking his head he said, "Not for us. Your attack on Poperinge forced the Count of Flanders to withdraw his army. From deserters, we learned that he feared a Norman invasion. His men now wait behind walls, fearful of the wrath of the Earl of Cleveland and the young prince. No, it is you who is in danger. Come, my father will explain all."

I worried that my home was in danger. We had dealt with the danger from the Flemish mercenaries. Surely the fact that we had trounced them in the border meant that they could no longer mount a threat? I was speculating and that was always dangerous. It was better to wait for actual news rather than build a house of straw from fragments and snippets.

The Count waved us to seats inside his dining chamber. "You are more than welcome here, Earl. You shall stay the night. I have a room prepared for you." He looked at my men at arms.

"Ralph and Alan, I will not need you for a while. Is there somewhere they could find food and a bed, my lord?"

"Of course, Lothair, see to it."

My men hesitated, "I will be safe enough. Richard can be my chamberlain for the night."

After they had gone Baldwin said, "Such loyalty. The men we hired from Normandy all spoke of the bond you have with your men. It is to be admired. I am not certain my own men would do the same."

I said nothing. Whatever words I uttered would either sound insulting or patronising.

Lothair returned, "They are sharing the quarters with your bodyguards, father."

"Good." He waved a servant over, "Fetch wine and food and then see that we are not disturbed."

I took off my cloak and gauntlets for the fire had made the room hot. Richard looked relieved that I had set the precedent and he copied me. When the door closed behind the servant Lothair poured the wine. "Firstly, Earl, I am twofold in your debt. The men who came from Normandy put steel in our warriors and your attack on Flanders dampened Flanders' desire to take my land. I have no doubt that they will renew their efforts but we now have the winter to prepare our defences. I will use my skills as a builder to try to make fortresses as strong as yours and the Duke's."

"I am pleased to have been of service."

"The men you sent have been more than helpful. Richard of Angers has now been elevated to the position of Captain of the Guard and he is most useful."

I nodded, "Richard is a good man. Had he been one of my men I would have knighted him."

"Even though he is not noble-born?"

"Few of my knights are noble-born. It is not a requirement in Cleveland."

"Interesting." Baldwin sipped his wine, thoughtfully.

"Father, your news."

"Of course. There am I thinking of myself when it is you who is in danger."

"The Flemish?"

"As I said, they are behind their walls. No, it is another enemy closer to home." He placed his goblet on the table and then interlaced his fingers. He closed his eyes, briefly, as though he was weighing his words. "Three weeks since a Danish ship put into port. There was a courtier on board who brought a message from Valdemar the Great. He is on the cusp, it seems, of gaining the crown. He was testing the waters, so to speak to see if we would support him."

"And?"

Baldwin smiled, "We are a small County. It is better not to commit too soon to arrangements that might come back to haunt us. I told him that until we had ended the threat from Flanders we could not commit to an alliance but that we were not opposed to one." I smiled. Baldwin was the complete diplomat. He had avoided offending his potential neighbour without committing himself.

Lothair saw my smile, "We are not as fortunate as you, lord. We do not have an army which is the envy of all. We have to navigate a course through dangerous waters."

"I was not criticising your father, Lothair. I too have had to make compromises. All leaders do."

"You are right, Earl and that brings me to you. When the courtier was in his cups he mentioned the number of Norman and Angevin warriors we had. He let it slip that they would soon be able to earn much coin in England. I confess that I plied him with more drink and more questions for I knew that his words concerned you. It seems that the Prince of Cumberland, Prince Henry of Scotland, is flexing his muscles. He has hired men who have begun to desert King Erik the Lamb. His cause is lost and they know that Valdemar has a long memory. They are leaving like rats from a ship. Prince Henry is paying well, it seems. I could not divine their purpose but it seemed to me that they would be a threat to you."

"And you say that this was three weeks since?"

"Aye but I think you still have time. King Erik is still king, in name at least, and he still has many of his men who remain at his side. Besides, it is winter and we have heard that it has come early to your homeland. They have had snow already."

"I thank you for this information and it puts me in your debt. I shall have to get to England sooner rather than later."

"We have more news too which is also close to home."

"Yes?"

"The English king, Stephen, has overstretched his treasury. It seems he has been too generous to his friends. He has had to buy off many men. He has had to borrow from the Jews of Holland. They hold promissory notes. I fear that if Henry does become king then he will inherit debts."

I shook my head, "Those debts are Stephen's, not England's but I thank you for the news. It gives me hope."

We were feted and feasted but I did not taste any of the food. My mind was across the German Sea. The Scots had been beaten by me at every turn but if they had a contingent of Danes then that might sway the balance in their favour. I was needed at home. First, however, I would need to return to Rouen and fetch my men whilst seeking permission to leave. Henry FitzEmpress would not be happy.

Chapter 13

Ralph and Alan confirmed the king's words. Many of the soldiers they had broken bread with had spoken to the bodyguards of the Danish courtier. The gold offered by the Scottish prince was a great inducement. I was silent and Richard said, "We have some time, lord. They cannot come in winter."

I shook my head, "These are Danes. They are hardy men. They came to England and conquered it for a time. A little bad weather will not hurt them. They are also fierce fighters. They do not ride but the long axes can stop a charge of horse. My father fought alongside such men and they defeated Norman horsemen when fighting for the Emperor. I will not underestimate Danes. When we land I want everything loading aboard the two ships. I know it will take some time to navigate the Seine but we will not waste a single moment. I leave you three to see that all is done well."

"Aye lord."

As soon as we docked, four days later, I rushed to the castle. The Duke had had another relapse and was on a couch before the fire. "I am sorry to see you laid low, Duke."

"It is this wound. It makes me dizzy and sleepy. My physician says it could take until the summer for me to fully recover."

I nodded, "I have received unwelcome news which means I must return to England."

The Duke nodded but Henry said, "But why? You are still training me!"

"And I will do so but the Scottish prince is plotting. I will return home and deal with it. You could accompany me if you wish."

I could see that he was torn. His eyes flickered between me and his father. The Duke said, "It is winter, Henry, I will not be stirring. If you wish to go with the Warlord then do so. We will renew our war with Flanders in the spring."

Henry shook his head, "No. My duty is here, at the moment. I have my new men to train and I cannot abandon you while you are indisposed. Besides which this suits my purpose. I would have the Earl begin to prepare the way for my return to England. When he has defeated this new enemy, I will cross the sea and join him with my own army. With the men, I have trained and his retinue we will be an unstoppable force!"

"But not for some time I think."

His face fell. "I will work twice as hard while you are away in England. By summer you will return and then you will be the judge."

I was so worried about the Scots that I barely heard his words. "I will and I am certain that your men will be a credit to you."

We sailed early the next day. We were too far upstream for the tide to worry us and it was only the sentries who watched us slip down the Seine. I sat in William's cabin with Edgar, Dick and Richard. Edgar knew the Danes for he and Erre had trained together with the Frisians. The Frisians fought in a similar fashion.

Edgar was one of my oldest and most experienced warriors. His shaven head was covered in the scars and lumps of battle. He was also one of the biggest of my warriors. The wound he had received in Flanders might have killed a lesser man but his layers of muscle aided his armour. He rarely volunteered information. He obeyed orders and when he spoke of our enemies I knew that his words had to be heeded.

"But, lord, the Danes are the masters of the two handed axe. Some are longer than a man. A lance can get past a spear or a sword but not a Danish axe. They swing it before them as easily as Dick and his archers pull a bowstring. They move it in a rhythmic swing and in time with their fellows. Lances would be splintered before they could strike home. The horses would be slaughtered before they could reach the Danes."

I nodded. Dick said, "But they cannot hold a shield and swing at the same time can they, Edgar?"

"No, I think not. But they wear hide armour studded with plates and studs. The armour is hard to cut. That is their main defence. It takes a brave fellow to face one. Ask Erre and the Frisians."

Dick smiled, "And what about arrows?"

I nodded, "That may be the secret, Dick but how many Danes will they have and do we have enough archers?"

"I think we can muster a hundred at least, lord. There will be more trained for we left England some time ago."

"The enemy will try to get to you."

"Then we will have men holding our horses so that we can fall back and then continue our rain. They cannot both attack us and the horse, lord. There will be a risk but I know my men."

"I doubt neither you nor your men. The question now remains, where will they attack?"

We were all silent for how could you divine their intention? The border was more than ninety miles wide. Richard broke the silence, "Gilles often set the three of us tests like this, lord. He would have Henry, James and I think how we would deal with an attack from the north. We worked out that there were only a few possibilities. One would be by sea. If they had enough ships then they could land in the river. They could even go further south and invade north of Whitby. There is a long stretch of beach there and there are no castles nearby."

Edgar said, "The Scots do not have a large number of ships."

"But the Danes do. Carry on, Richard." I was learning more about my squires. Even when I was absent they were thinking as I did. It gave me hope.

"They could attack in the west by coming south from Carlisle and then south of the river."

"Piercebridge, Yarm and Gainford would have to hold them."

"And the third route is through Durham. Gilles told us that Durham now supports the Scots. They could come through Segges' Field and Thorpe."

"Good. That was clearly explained. I cannot fault your reasoning. What say you, two old campaigners?"

"He is right and it means we have only three routes that we need to watch."

"I agree, Dick. Sir Hugh and Sir Phillip can watch the western approaches. We use the two merchant ships and our fishing vessels to watch the sea. That would leave the bulk of our men to watch Durham." I leaned back. "It is a start at any rate." I folded my hands behind my head. I needed to find somewhere south of Durham where we could hold them.

As soon as I heard the lookout shout that he could see land I went on deck. I stood at the bow to watch the river as we headed upstream. It was always a long journey up the twists and turns of the Tees but it seemed so much longer this time. We reached my town in the middle of the afternoon. The further upstream we had travelled the more snow I had seen. It was not deep and would not hamper travel but it was rare for snow before Christmas. I wondered what it meant for us. I left William to see to the unloading of the ship and Richard and I raced up to my castle. John of Craven and Sir Gilles of Stockton greeted me at the inner bailey, "It is good to see you home, lord!"

I forced a smile, "Has there been any sign of danger?"

"Danger, lord? The road to York has been quiet. Sir Hugh has not reported any danger there and we have heard nothing of the Usurper since you left."

I nodded. That made sense. If the Earl of Chester had escaped then Stephen would be worrying about the west and not the north. "Good. Send for Aiden."

"Is there something wrong, my lord?"

"I am afraid there might be. I have intelligence that the Scots have risen from their slumber and planning some mischief. If you have heard nothing then we have arrived home in time." I told him how the information had reached me and what had happened in Flanders and Hainaut. "Come let us go indoors. This cold has chilled me to the bone."

Alice had had the foresight to anticipate my wishes and I heard the hiss as she plunged a hot poker into some honeyed wine. She smiled, "This will keep out the cold, lord. It would be even better with spices and lemon but..."

"This will do, Alice, but if you speak with William of Kingston you will find he has lemons and spices from the east as well as some fine cloth. We have traded more and fought less."

"This is, indeed, a time of good tidings lord!" She grinned at Sir Gilles.

"What is up with Alice? She is like a giddy girl."

"I am sorry, lord, that is my fault. Mary is with child and Alice is excited."

I embraced Sir Gilles. "And that is good news! Alice is right, these are good tidings. We must celebrate. The Christmas celebration will be even more special this year." All around me were babies and yet my own were not and my grandchildren were but a memory. I was happy for Gilles and Mary. I knew that Adela would have been happy too.

When Mary entered I saw a glow on her which reminded me of Adela. She ran in and threw her arms around me, "Now we shall have the best Christmas ever for you are here lord!"

"Your husband has told me your news and I am delighted."

She nodded, "I hope it is a boy for we shall name him Edward in honour of my father."

"And you could not have chosen a better name. If it is a boy then he could do worse than emulate that rock who stood behind me for so many years."

Aiden arrived in the middle of a toast to Mary and Sir Gilles. Dick had joined us along with John my steward. I said, "Pardon me, ladies but I must have a word with Aiden and then I shall rejoin you."

Taking a candle I led him to my solar. The sun was beginning to dip in the west.

"Trouble, lord?"

"The Scots. They are hiring Danes and I fear that Prince Henry means us harm."

Aiden never panicked or allowed himself to become angry. He was always calmness personified. Part of that was the confidence he had in his own skills and the other was the fact that he had been elevated from slave to honoured freeman. That leap had been a greater one than any since. He considered his words as he said, "Then I will need to travel their lands. I will take Edward with me. He has the look of a Scot about him. This will be a good time for they celebrate the time after Christmas like pagans. It is a time when they welcome strangers into their homes. It may take some time."

"I think it is unlikely that we will be in danger while there is snow on the ground."

"It will get worse soon."

I wondered about Aiden. I was convinced he had something of the witch in him. "How do you know?"

"The birds told me. They stripped all the berries from the bushes earlier than normal. I believe you are right, lord. They may not come immediately."

"You will miss Christmas."

He laughed, "To me, it is just another day. I have not had a challenge since you left, lord. Edward and I are happy to go. It is Edgar who has a wife. We do not. We will leave on the morrow. I think it will take fourteen days or so."

I clasped his arm, "Take care."

"I always do."

The next day I sent an invitation to the knights who lived close by. I asked them to come for Christmas. Aiden's words had made me less worried about a sudden attack but I would still be prudent. Sir Hugh and Sir Phillip would be better placed in their castles. I sent Richard, escorted by ten of my archers to deliver a letter to each of my two knights so that they knew what I did. It would just be a two-day wait to speak with them. However, I was not idle. I went to see Alf.

It was partly to give him the warning of danger and also to ask for more weapons.

He shook his head, "I thought they had been too quiet for some time. We can beat them though, eh, lord?"

"The Danes are a threat, Alf."

He nodded, "Aye, I remember the raid by those Vikings. Never fear, lord. Your people are behind you. And how are your son and his family? Are they visiting this Christmas?"

I realised that none knew of my news. I would have to tell them at the Christmas feast. It would spoil the atmosphere a little but they deserved to know. I told Alf. When I had finished, he threw his arms around me and hugged me. There are many knights who would have been offended at such familiarity but I was not one of them. We were old friends and he was comforting me. He said nothing but his mighty grip was reassuring. He was a grandfather and his grandchildren were the light of his life.

"We are men, lord, and we must bear such burdens but I feel for you and share in your sorrow."

I felt sorry for Mary and Gilles. Their good news was dampened by the loss of my son's family and his departure for the Holy Land. None of them expected to see him again and that was sad. Added to that was this veiled threat from the north. Richard had spoken with both Sir Hugh and Sir Phillip so that they knew what was expected of them. Their news was, at least, encouraging. They had seen little sign of the Scots.

I would not allow any talk of war on Christmas Day. That was wrong but on St. Stephen's Day, as we heard a blizzard whistle along the Tees, we sat in my hall with maps and wine. It would be a council of war. I had managed to drag Erre from his home in Norton. He and the Frisians would be vital to my defences. Wulfric and Sir Gilles of Normanby were also present as was Sir Tristan from Yarm. All three had left all of their men in their castles. We would not be caught napping again.

"Well Erre, you have the most experience and knowledge of these Danes what say you?"

He knuckled his white beard. His head was also bereft of hair but his had fallen out because of age and some of his teeth were lacking. He was now older than my father had been. Unlike my knights who drank wine, he was drinking honeyed ale. He took a swig and leaned back. "Dick and his archers can hurt them but not as much as they could any other enemy. They advance with their shields above them and only sling them around their back at the last minute. Your horses cannot charge them. Their axes are called horse killers for a good reason. Even your new warhorse would be in danger, Warlord."

Sir Gilles of Stockton said, "So we cannot defeat them?"

Erre smiled at my youngest knight, "I did not say that, young lord. I was merely telling you what would not work. Their hide and mail coats are heavy. Their helmets shields and axes are taxing. Give them a slope to ascend. It will sap the energy from their legs. Sow caltrops and have men to face them who know how to fight their way."

Richard, who was acting as a scribe looked up from his wax tablet, "Caltrops?"

"Metal spikes cunningly crafted so that no matter which way they fall there is always a spike sticking up. The Danes do not wear thick boots. Their leather soles are thin. The weight of the men, armour and weapons will drive them into their feet. They can still fight but their movement will be restricted."

I nodded, "Thank you. Anyone else?"

Wulfric quaffed his wine and held his goblet for a refill. His squire hurriedly poured it, "They will have gallowglasses too. We have fought them before, lord, at Northallerton. Mad buggers they are. They never know when they are defeated. If Dick and his archers are trying to kill the Danes then there is no one to stop the wild men. They are fast too."

Sir Harold said, "And we have not even mentioned their knights and men at arms."

Sir Wulfric shook his head, "They are the least of our worries. Their horses are poor and we have trounced them each time we have fought them." He pointed to me. "They

remember the Earl. He chased them all the way back to
Carlisle. Their bones marked their flight. The danger they
represent is if the Danes and the gallowglasses make a
breakthrough."

The discussion went on until Alice arrived at noon with
the cold meat left over from the previous night's feast. Along
with fresh bread, newly made cheese, smoked fish and some
pickles it was a welcome distraction.

Sir Harold said, "I see, Sir Gilles, that you have used your
coin well. You have as many men at arms as Sir Tristan
here."

"Aye, Sir Harold, but I still lack archers."

Dick laughed, "That is because you cannot buy archers
you must grow them and like the oak in the forests they take
time to mature. Train your boys. The Earl gave you one of
my best archers; James, son of Robert."

"He has but four men to command!"

Sir John shook his head, "When we fight for the Earl it
matters not for they fight under Dick here or Sir Philip. It is
our secret weapon. We do not waste our arrows piecemeal.
Dick here makes a fog of fletches through which few men
can travel."

Erre said, "Save the Danes."

We were brought back to the task and we returned to my
long table. The meal had given me time to think. "I have
come up with a plan. It is dependent upon a number of
things. Firstly, that they come down the Durham Road,
secondly that we can draw them to a slope and thirdly that
the prince wants me dead more than anything else."

I could see that I had intrigued them. "Richard, how
many men do we muster?"

"Nine knights and squires, a hundred and twenty-one men
at arms and eighty archers."

"Do not forget Aiden and his scouts." I saw him scribble
their numbers down.

"Do we take servants?"

I shook my head, "It is winter and the farmers have less
work to do on their farms. We call out some of the fyrd.
They can guard the horses and use their slings and bows to

defend our baggage." I saw that I had surprised them. "I
know I do not normally use the fyrd but I have begun to
think that is a mistake. They need the experience of war.
This way they will only be needed in the last resort but are
more likely to fight than servants. We leave the servants to
defend our castles with our old men."

Erre and Edgar looked at each other and laughed, Edgar
said, "Then we two should remain here for there are none
older."

Wulfric snorted, "I would sooner leave my horse behind
than you pair. You are both worth ten men at arms in a
battle." He looked at me, "Your plan, lord?"

I stood and elaborated. I could see from their faces that I
had surprised them and that was not easy as I had used many
weird and strange plans before but this one was new. When I
had finished I said, "I know this is an unusual plan but
Prince Henry has fought me before. I hope to surprise him
too." I paused, "One more thing; Henry FitzEmpress is
building an army. We hope that in a year or so he will be
ready to return to England and claim his birthright. He is
keen to return to England and wrest the crown from Stephen
himself. I believe the end is in sight. We have fought alone
for a long time. I hope this next battle will be the last time."

My words caused them to make such a commotion that
Alice burst in, "Fear not, Alice, my knights are just excited.
It will pass."

Chapter 14

It was the middle of January when Aiden and Edward returned. Their horses showed the journey they had endured. They were emaciated skeletons. Only my scouts could have nursed them home. I took the scouts into my hall and summoned Sir Gilles, Dick and my squires. After they had eaten and drunk honeyed warmed ale I gestured for them to speak.

"The Count of Hainaut was correct, lord. There are many Danes north of the New Castle. They are staying close by the priory of the Tyne's mouth. Prince Henry has made the New Castle his home."

"Then it will be down the Durham Road; unless of course, he has ships."

Aiden shook his head, "If the Danes came in ships then they have returned whence they came. The river had a few merchant ships, no more. There were no longships."

I felt relieved beyond words. An attack along my river would have hurt us. "What did you hear?"

"That Prince Henry is tired of his father's constrictions. He wishes vengeance for the many defeats you have inflicted upon him. In every tavern and camp, we heard the same. He has inflamed the hearts of the young warriors. Most are too young to remember the defeats. They see the land south of the Wear as ripe for the plucking." He was about to speak and then closed his mouth.

"Come, Aiden, whatever words are waiting to burst forth give them air lest they fester."

He smiled, "They say you are old and past your best. All your knights need a beard, or so they say."

It was my turn to laugh, "If Wulfric hears that it will be all that I can do to stop him from taking them on alone!"

"There was one thing. His father is displeased with this belligerence. Since the Empress returned to Normandy he has let it be known that he does not wish to risk the wrath of the English."

"Is that Stephen or me?"

"You are both held in high regard by the king."

For the first time, I spied a kind of hope. If I could get Henry to meet with King David and agree to support him under my command then we might be able to defeat Stephen. As much as it might gall me to side with my implacable enemy I now realised that I might have to bend my neck a little to achieve that which I wanted. The problem was how would King David view a battle between me and his son?

"And now the impossible question; when will they come?"

Aiden shook his head. "Not before Ash Wednesday. The roads are almost impassable. In places, the snow is as high as my horse's withers. It has been a hard winter and when the snow melts then the roads will become muddy. If the thaw begins soon then it will be Ash Wednesday. If it delays, then Lent may be over before they come."

I shook my head, "The Prince will not delay that long. He has Danes to feed and to pay. He will want his money's worth. I want you and your scouts watching the Tyne before Ash Wednesday."

"Aye lord."

After he had gone I summoned Dick, "Which four archers would you be happy to send to Chester?"

"At this time of year, lord?"

I nodded, "I need to know Ranulf's mind."

"But he is not to be trusted!"

"And that is why I need archers who can think. I have a letter I wish to send to Maud, the Earl's wife. We have but a short time before the Scots come. I would say that they will be here within the next six weeks. We are blind and know nothing of the outside world. Our ships are icebound else I would send them. Your archers are the best equipped for such a task."

"I should go."

"No, I need you to ensure that we have well-trained archers left to guard our walls."

"Then Ralph of Wales, Henry Warbow, Rafe and Long Tom; they are the best that we have and Ralph of Wales knows Chester well."

"Good. I will write the letter. Have them ready to leave on the morrow and make sure they have spare horses."

After I had written to the Countess of Chester I wrote another letter to Matilda. I had the ink and I had the goose feather. I had left Normandy without a proper goodbye. As soon as the ice had left the river I would send William of Kingston to Anjou and ask Sir Leofric to deliver the letter directly to her. I could trust my captain and my knight.

Stockton
Dearest Maud,
I am uncertain if I will ever see you again. I should have spoken before I left for England but events overtook me. It seems we are ever doomed to be parted. I know you know of your husband's indiscretions but that does nought to aid us. You just need to know that you are ever in my thoughts and that I strive to keep the oath I swore to your father.

Henry is becoming a fine leader. I believe that in a year or two he will be ready to launch an attack on Stephen. We have yet to weaken him but it may be that he does that himself. He is profligate with money and the treasury is almost empty, or so I am told. You may not become Queen but I swear that Henry will be king. I will make it so.
As ever,
Your champion and your friend,
Alfraed

Aiden's predictions were accurate. The *'Adela'* was able to sail at the end of January. The ice made the voyage possible. William, now the proud father of a daughter as well as a son promised to be swift and to bring back more men from Sir Leofric. I was not sure that they would reach us in time to go to war but they would be able to augment the defence of my lands.

182

The break in the weather also meant that Ralph of Wales and my archers had an easier task crossing the high moors. They arrived back four days after my ship had sailed. Ralph handed me the letter from the Countess and, as they drank I questioned them, "What of the land twixt Chester and here?"

"We saw no movement, lord. We could have been on the moon for all the people we met. We skirted the castles. Only Skipton is still held by Scots. We spoke with some farmers but they keep to the castle and they are few in number. We met with the Earl." He hesitated and I spread my hands to invite him to continue. He nodded, "I am sorry, lord but I do not trust the man. His voice belies his eyes. He has honeyed words but I look into his eyes and see emptiness."

"He said he would support me?"

"He did but ..."

"But you think he will not."

"No. He will not. If the odds are stacked in our favour then he might." I cocked a quizzical eye. "We spoke with his men. They told us as much. The good news is that he has many men in his castle. He will not be taken again but he is distracted by my countrymen. The Welsh see him as a weak leader."

"Thank you. You have done well."

Once alone I read the letter. It was brief and to the point.

Chester
Alfraed,
I am pleased that you, at least, still live. I did not bury my father and I will have to live with that. Your men told me of your son and his loss. I am sorry you seem fated to suffer.

My husband has returned but I fear that despite his good intentions he will not stir against Stephen. If you counted on his help then I am afraid it is a misplaced hope. Your hope lies in two things, Stephen's poor use of coin and Henry FitzEmpress.
Your friend
Maud.

It confirmed Ralph's words but at least I knew where I stood. Henry would have to wait a little longer to reclaim his throne. When time allowed, I would write a letter to him to give him the news. First I had a Scottish Prince to defeat.

I sent word to my knights to prepare their men and then I sent my scouts north. They had strong horses and plenty of supplies. We were now in their hands. I threw myself into the defence of Stockton. John my steward had laid in plenty of supplies in the autumn and my people would not go short. Alf helped me choose the men who would accompany us north. He persuaded me to take twenty of the town's boys to use as slingers. "They wish to serve you, lord. This is how they will become warriors and they are nimble enough. If you tell them to run then they will do so."

I did not like the idea of grieving mothers but I agreed. Alf made each of them a dagger to take with them. The pommel was a wolf and they were as proud of that dagger as anything. I also had a new helmet made for me. It was plainer than the one I normally used with just a nasal rather than a face mask. Alf had not questioned my request but I could see that he was curious. I smiled, "Deception, Alf, deception. This is a strong helmet is it not?"

"Aye lord, stronger than your other but it will not afford as much protection."

"I need to move quickly and for my vision to be unimpaired. This will do fine."

He also gave me new mail mittens which had double riveted mail. They were a little heavier than I was used to but I had enough time to strengthen my hands and forearms. Fighting an axeman, they might come in handy.

Two days after Ash Wednesday Hal rode in. He had grown over the winter but he still looked like a boy to me. "Lord, the Scots are gathering. They have a camp close by the village of Dunstan." I waited. I knew that Aiden would have sent more information. "Aiden says they will be ready to travel in three days. The roads mean it will take them five more to reach Durham."

"Good. Return to your master. Take a fresh horse from the stables. You have done well."

I sent riders out to summon my knights. It would only take them a day to reach me. I was tempted to send for Sir Phillip and his archers but I needed my back door guarding. William of Aumale and his Yorkshire levies had been quiet but if they got wind of my movements they might chance their arm. I was not willing to risk that.

Two days after Hal's arrival we headed north up the Durham road. The snow had all but melted making the going slippery. We had to ride carefully. I rode Rolf knowing that I had Edward with the fyrd at the rear. He was being ridden by Colm, the tanner's son. He seemed confident but I hoped that Edward would be gentle with him. He was a warhorse and his bite could be nasty. Colm seemed to like horses and that helped.

Wulfric looked at me askance as we rode together at the head of the column. "Why the new helmet, lord?"

"Remember my plan, Wulfric?"

"I had hoped that you might rethink that part of it, lord. You should not put yourself in such danger. With the Earl, Sir Miles and the others all gone you are the young prince's last hope. If you were to fall then I fear he would never gain the throne."

"The day I start to worry about dying is the day I will die. If it is my time then so be it but I go into each battle expecting to survive. Would you have me change?"

"No lord but Edgar, Dick and I are the last of those who first followed you. The others are now memories. I know that one day my time will come. Our journey is not yet over but I fear I will never see the haven."

"That is the winter talking, Wulfric. You have not had a battle for over a year. Once you draw your weapon you will feel more optimistic."

"I do not think there is a warrior out there who can defeat me but I felt that way about Roger of Lincoln and Sir Edward. They fell."

I glanced behind me but James was too far away to have heard, "Sir Edward was not himself when he died and Roger... well it was his time and he died well."

185

"That is all that a warrior can ask, is it not? To die well."
I saw him shake himself and touch the pommel of his sword.
It was a gesture many of my knights did to ward off evil.
"Do we meet them at Auckland again?"

"Aiden has not told us yet. If they came that way then I
would be happy for we fought there before and we won but I
fear it will not be that easy. Prince Henry knows me and will
try to fool us."

As we rode I tried to outthink my Scottish opponent. He
knew that I had patrols out. I guessed that he might even
know that I had mobilised my men. The movement of so
many men in an empty landscape could not be hidden. He
would not need scouts. He had those who supported him
living hard by. Word would have reached him. However, he
would not know the direction I would take. He might expect
me to head to Auckland or to anticipate him using Durham.
Durham would give him a refuge if things went ill. If he
went further west he risked Sir Hugh's patrols and the
garrison at Piercebridge. The more I thought about it then the
more I favoured a route closer to Hartness along the coast.
The boggy ground north and east of Norton would not suit
my horses. He also had Hartness to use as a refuge too.

As we passed Thorpe I pointed to the northeast. "We will
head to the road between Fissebourne and Segges field.
Dick, send two archers to watch the road from Durham to
Auckland in case he comes that way. Aiden will let us know
soon enough about his plans."

"Aye lord." After his men had ridden off my captain of
archers joined Wulfric and me as we took the greenway, now
slushy grey and muddy, towards Fissebourne. "There is a
piece of sloping ground and a stream to the south and west of
Fissebourne."

I nodded, "I remember. It is just north of Segges Field
and straddles the road to Stockton. The trees will be to our
back and can be used to hide the horses. I just pray that he
chooses that route."

"It matters little lord. We are all mounted and with Danes
afoot we can reach them even if they head towards
Piercebridge."

We reached the slope and the woods just before dark. I had the men make camp and light fires. Aiden would give us warning of the approach of the enemy. A little comfort on a cold night would raise the spirits of the men. Who knew what the morrow might bring?

Before dawn I had the men preparing stakes to be embedded on the lower slopes. They were not intended to impede an enemy but they would stop a line of horsemen charging us or prevent Danes from swinging their axes in unison. Until Aiden arrived or sent word that was all that we could do. It was late in the afternoon when he and young Osbert rode in.

"They are camped at Coxhoe. They come this way, lord. There are a thousand of them, lord. We counted thirty knights. There are two hundred Danes as well as a hundred of those gallowglasses. There are over a hundred and fifty men at arms although they are not all mailed. The rest are retainers of their mormaer."

"Horses?"

"Perhaps a hundred maybe a few more."

"Any men of Northumbria?" There had been a time when rebels had joined the Scots. Over the years we had whittled down their numbers.

"No lord. They are either Scots or Danes."

That pleased me for I never liked killing my countrymen.

Dick asked, "Do we raid their camp?"

"We have too few men to risk it. Send for your two archers. We will need every bow we can get." He detailed off a rider. "Aiden, use your scouts as you see fit. You know how to kill better than most."

He grinned, "Aye lord and I fancy some of these Danes have coins."

"Why do say that?"

"We crept close to their camp. Their necks and arms are festooned with bracelets and they all have a purse around their necks. My boys and I are faster than Dick and his men."

Dick laughed, "And you are welcome, Aiden. You do that which we do not. You go into their camps. We are grateful."

He shrugged, "They do not keep a good watch. John the steward could walk amongst them and they would not know."

My knights and squires all laughed. The thought of the cleric going amongst the Scots was a ludicrous one.

I waved them around me. "They will not be here before tomorrow. The die is cast. There is no other road they can take south save this one. If they were going to Hartness they would have turned off at Bowburn. You know the plan and we keep to it. If they try to pass us without fighting then it is up to you, Sir Gilles of Stockton, to slow them down."

It was a grave responsibility. He would have with him just twenty men at arms drawn from mainly my conroi but augmented by some of Wulfric's most experienced riders. "I will not let you down on my first command."

"Take no risks. You hit them and then pull back. I do not think they will let us sit here and not attack us." I pointed to Richard. You must make them believe that Sir Gilles is me, Richard. Keep my standard there to draw them on." He nodded. Soon he would be knighted and this was his chance to shine. Sir Gilles would be wearing my full-face helmet. I hoped that would act like a flame for a moth.

We spent the day making our position stronger. It was a gentle slope but it was slick with the melting snow. We laid the caltrops in a wide line before us. They were not hidden but the approaching Danes would have their eyes on us. In many ways, I hoped that they would look for caltrops for then they would not have their shields over their heads and our archers might make more hits. Dick's archers waited up the road and slew three scouts who approached. When they did not return Prince Henry would know where we were. We had not travelled far from home and we had plenty of supplies. We ate well. When one of Dick's archers managed to kill a deer I decided to use the kill to our advantage.

"Aiden, have your men hunt some more animals. I want a fire building and we will roast the deer. The wind is in the right direction. I want the smell of cooking meat to drift over to the Scots."

As he went to organise his men Wulfric laughed, "I bet the Scots and Danes have been on cold rations. The smell of roasting meat will make them even hungrier."

Sir Gilles of Stockton asked, "But lord, why do you tell them where we are?"

"To make sure that they come here. They want me. When they see my banner at the top of the hill, surrounded by knights, it will make Prince Henry commit his men to the attack. You must make sure that they do come. You will ride Edward. He rears well. Make him rear and wave your sword. With the helmet, it should complete the deception. Richard can wave the banner too. That will enrage them."

Aiden and his hunters managed to kill another three deer. They were skinned, gutted and jointed in the twinkling of an eye and ten fires were lit at the top of the hill. The smell of roasting meat wafted north on the southern breeze which was already accelerating the thaw. I guessed that they would soon reach us. Coxhoe was not far away. Had they been a mounted army they would have reached us already but an army made of foot was slow and the roads were not at their best. This road had not been repaired since Bishop Rufus had ruled.

Dick and his archers, along with Edgar and Hal rode in. "They are here, lord. They have passed Bishop Middleham. They stopped to search for food but we had warned the farmer and his family. They fled, yesterday, towards Gainford. We told them they would be safe there."

"You have done well." I turned, "I want just Wulfric's conroi and mine on view until dark. After dark, it does not matter."

I was doing all in my power to make them think that we were weaker than we were. A leader who thought he had won already would be overconfident. The enemy emerged from over the small rise to the north of us. There were woods on both sides and the road swept down to a hollow before rising once more to our present position. The road was lower than our hill. It was what gave us an advantage. I saw the banners emerge in the dimming light. I recognised that of the Prince but there were others I did not. The white unicorn was

a new one as was the yellow gryphon. The light was too poor
for me to assess the armour of the knights. That might have
told me more about them. I did not know them which meant
I had not fought them. More importantly, they had not
fought me. The difference was that they knew of my
reputation.

As night fell I sent for the rest of my men. They emerged
from the dark. The fires were at the top of the hill and they
just illuminated the banners of my knights which were
arrayed there. "Come let us eat! I have an appetite."

There was almost a festive atmosphere to the camp. One
man in two was on duty and he was relieved when the other
had eaten. The boy slingers were overawed by the armour
and the surcoats of the men at arms and knights. I saw their
eyes, wide with wonder. I could see that many would choose
a life as a man at arms. Alf had been right to press them on
me.

"You boys, eat! You can admire the armour after the
battle. You will need your strength tomorrow if you are to
break up the enemy attack!"

They nodded and tucked in to the food. Dick said, "That
was well done, lord. They believe that they will win the
battle for you."

"And who knows, Dick? They may. A well-thrown stone
might take out one of the leaders and break the spirit of the
enemy. We all play a part. You of all people know that."

"Aye lord. Sometimes I forget."

More than anyone I was aware that my army was made
up of many different parts. Each contributed something. The
boys were a new element. I just did not know how they
would fare in a fight. I would soon find out.

Our sentries kept a close watch on the enemy all night.
We had four men down by the road in case they tried to
outflank us that way. The land to our left was too broken and
treacherous to pose a threat. Prince Henry had two choices:
knock us from the small hill or try to get by us on the road.
When dawn broke, we saw that he had chosen the former.
He was coming up the slope. I could see how, from his point
of view, it looked a reasonable prospect. It was not as steep

as the road he had just descended and looked as though it would not slow his men down. We knew different. The muddy ground was cloying and we had sown caltrops. The higher they came the harder it would be to keep their feet.

We were arrayed in the battle lines I had outlined in my hall. The slingers were before us, crouching just in front of our shields. If the enemy decided to use archers they could shelter behind them. I had a double line of men at arms with me. I had spread out the men at arms from my conroi so that our surcoats would not stand out. I wore a cloak about mine. Edgar and Wilfred flanked me. The only other knights in the front rank were Erre on the far right and Wulfric on the far left. They were my two rocks. I could rely on them to make good decisions and to hold the line. Behind me were Dick and the collected archers. Finally, at the top of the hill were my knights by Sir Gilles of Stockton. He would play the part of the Warlord. The fyrd and the horses were hidden in the woods. If they were needed they would bring the mounts to us. I hoped they would not be necessary.

As Prince Henry marshalled his men I had the opportunity to see his battle lines. He had his gallowglasses in the fore. They would rush us while the Danes formed the second wave. The bulk of his retainers made up the third wave. They had numbers and that was all. They wielded weapons and most had shields but few had mail of any description. He had eighty knights as his final force. When we were weak they would charge us. I saw that the knights with the new livery had fine armour and war horses which were better than anything the Scots, Prince Henry excluded, rode. I wondered if they were Scottish or, perhaps, mercenaries. It mattered not. We had three battles to destroy before we could meet the horsemen.

A horn signalled the advance and his gallowglasses raced across the four hundred paces to our lines. Behind me, I heard Sir Harold, dressed in my livery shout, "Men of Cleveland we fight for God, the Empress and Henry, the rightful King of England!" Sir Gilles made Edward raise his hooves. To the enemy, it would have appeared as though it was Sir Gilles who had shouted the command. The battle was about to begin and I would be the first to come to blows.

Chapter 15

I placed my spear against my foot. It would be some time before the wild Scotsmen reached us. This would be a long battle and I did not want to tire myself out too soon. The slippery slope soon began to cause problems for the enemy even before the slings and bows of my men could take their toll. Some ran so fast that they slipped and crashed into their comrades. Although not hurt it disrupted their line. They would be more likely to strike us piecemeal.

Dick and his archers began to send their arrows over our heads. The men who attacked us were without armour. Some had helmets and one or two had leather vests but the arrows plunged into their bodies. When the slingers sent their stones into them it dampened their ardour. They did not even reach the caltrops. Leaving twenty of their number dead or wounded they headed back down the slope. Five more were slain on the way down. It heartened the boys who began to cheer. When the men behind started a cheer Wulfric shouted, "Quiet! I will tell you when to cheer." They all fell silent.

At the bottom of the slope, I saw a clan chief berating the gallowglasses. Prince Henry nudged his horse forward and leaned down to speak with the Danish leader. He wore black armour and his shield bore a white skull upon it. On his helmet, he wore a half skull. I could not see the value in it but it was obviously intended to intimidate. The Dane held his axe and used it to point to the ridge behind us. He then pointed at the Scots.

I turned to Edgar. "He means to attack along the whole front."

"Then the man is a fool."

"Perhaps not; Erre and his men will be on the flat, close by the road. Weight of numbers might turn that flank."

"Erre will stand. I would bet my life on it."

I was not convinced. I turned slightly. I could see Dick some twenty paces higher up the slope, his war bow held ready to loose. "Watch out for a flank attack on Erre and his men."

"Aye, lord, I had seen that already."

I saw the Scottish prince nod and turn to shout to his men. He spoke for some time and then there was an enormous cheer. It came not from the Danes but the Scottish foot. I saw the clan chief chivvy the gallowglasses to stand behind the Danes. It was obviously intended to be a punishment. Then a horn sounded three times and the Danes and the Scottish warriors began to ascend the slope. The Danes approached our right and holding their shields above their heads, walked purposefully towards us. They would not run and trip themselves. A mormaer walked in front of the six hundred or so Scottish warriors; he was there to hold them in check. They were the equivalent of our fyrd. They had little skill but they had numbers. This could be bloody.

The line of bodies marked the range of my archers. They also impeded the advancing Scots and Danes. Dick and his men could launch their arrows a greater distance but they wanted no wasted arrows. We had the caltrops just twenty paces before the slingers. They would slow them up. I heard Dick's voice as he shouted, "Do not bother with the Danes yet. Thin out the others. Slingers throw your stones flat. Hit the Danes! I will give a war bow to the first boy who fells a Dane!" I heard the murmurs from before us. That was incentive enough. The Danes could protect themselves from the arrows but stones thrown on a flat trajectory could strike home. The sound of their stones hitting metal and wood sounded like hail on my castle roof. There was a perceptible slowing of the Danish line as they tried to lower their shields.

On the left, my archers had an easier task and I saw Scots tumble to the ground as they fell to the arrows. Had we had Sir Phillip's archers then I am certain we would have broken the attack there and then. However, some Scots reached the line of caltrops. I heard the squeals as some of those who had come to the battle barefoot and outrun the arrows and their fellows found the deadly pointed spikes.

I glanced at the Danes. Amazingly two had fallen to the slingers' stones One looked merely dazed but the second was unmoving. The closer they came the greater the effect. More men were struck and they were forced to put the shields to the fore. That meant two things: they could not swing their axes nor could they see the caltrops. As soon as the first Dane stepped on one I knew it was time to withdraw the boys.

"Slingers! Join the archers! Open ranks!"

We turned aside and the boys squirmed between us. We swung back and prepared our shields and spears. The spikes did their job. They broke up the Danish line as they neared the stakes we had embedded before us. The Danes slung their shields and swung the axes. The difference was that instead of a solid line as Edgar had feared, it was individuals who approached us. Fate determined that I would face the first Dane. It was not the chief; he was in the third rank. It was a younger warrior who had had a red shield with a yellow cross. He had filed his teeth so that when he grinned at me I saw a black and white mess and when he roared his challenge spittle flew from it.

I did not understand Danish but I understood his meaning. The two handed axe head whirled before me. I took my spear and jabbed it forward. He was young and strong. His swings were swift and he caught the head of my spear as it headed towards his face. He was fast but the spearhead ripped across the back of his right hand. I pulled it back and watched the blood trickle down his hand. He took a step forward and I flicked my shield up as the axe came dangerously close to my cheek. A sliver of wood flew off the edge. I pulled back my hand and darted the spear forward for the shield had checked the swing of the axe and his timing was off. This time the spearhead struck his right shoulder and I leaned into the blow. Fighting on a slope is hard and his swing had unbalanced him. He slipped backwards to the ground. Even as I raised my spear I rammed the edge of my shield into his chest. He gasped for breath and then I rammed my spear through the gaping maw of his mouth.

I stepped back and looked down the line. The Danes had engaged with us. They were now as solid as they were going to be. The stakes stopped them from standing shoulder to shoulder but soon their weight of numbers would force us back from their protection. Edgar's spear had shattered but the two dead Danes before him were testament to his skill. He now had his sword in his hand. My dead Dane formed a barrier and as I watched the second rank arrive I jabbed my spear at the Dane whose axe hacked into the side of Edgar's shield. My spear entered his right eye and I twisted it as it entered his skull. His legs gave way and he slipped to the ground.

"Thank you, Warlord!"

I had no time for any words as I caught the blur of steel as an older Dane swung his axe at me. I did the only thing I could do, I dropped to one knee. The axe had been aimed at head height. I punched the haft of my spear across his knees, hard. My mail mitten connected with his kneecap. Old men have weak knees and I heard a grunt as he lurched to one side. I rose swiftly and used my shield to hit him hard. His weakened knee, the slope and my blow made him reel. A stone flew from over my shoulder and caught him squarely between the eyes. I watched life leave them.

To my left, I saw the larger part of the Scottish force begin a retreat. The arrows had done their work and the field was littered with their dead. Holding shields above their head they made their way down the hill. The Danes before us had no such thoughts and I heard their skull-topped leader shout something which elicited a cheer from his men. They came at us with renewed vigour.

I had barely stepped back into line when another Dane challenged me. Even as he swung his axe I saw that the Danes behind were busy making kindling of our stakes. As I deflected the axe I heard a grunt from next to me and was spattered with Edgar's blood. He had been hit. The blood spurred me on and I feinted with my spear. The Dane made the mistake of hesitating and I hit his hands, hard with my shield. Bare knuckled it had the effect of numbing them. I pulled back my spear and thrust it forward. There was a gap and my spear found it. It struck between two plates but the hide armour was tough. Alf made good spearheads and it made a hole and when the Dane winced I knew that I had found flesh. He brought his axe down and it severed my spear in two. As I drew my sword I punched him in the face with my shield. His head jerked back and my sword was in my hand.

I could fight with a spear but I preferred a sword. As my weapon whirled I was aware that Dick had switched his arrows to the Danes. The slingers found gaps between us and the arrows rained down. They did not fell many but it would be enough to buy us time. We needed to switch ranks so that those in the second rank bore the brunt of the attack and gave us respite but we were all too closely engaged.

The Dane who faced me grinned and spoke to me in Saxon, "I have you now, horse shagger!" His axe began to swing. It was almost mesmerizing. I forced myself to look behind the axe head at his eyes. I held my sword at shoulder height. The hide mail was effective. I needed to find flesh and find it quickly. His gaze betrayed him. I saw them flick to my right side and knew that he intended to strike there. I twisted my left hand and, as his axe came towards my right shoulder I held my shield across my body and punched it at his hand while stabbing over it with my sword. My shield stopped his axe haft and my sword slid into his screaming mouth. The Dane behind stopped in his tracks as the blade came out of the back of his head. Putting my foot against his middle I kicked the dead Dane from my sword and he fell back into his surprised clan mate. His life was ended by another stone and I had the chance to breathe.

Even as I looked to my right I saw the axe slice into Edgar's shoulder. I whipped my sword sideways and caught the victorious Dane on the side of the head. It slowed the blow. One of Sir Wulfric's men on the other side of Edgar despatched him.

I turned and said to John of Norton, "Take Edgar's place in the front rank." He grabbed Edgar by the coif and pulled him roughly from the line. I knew that those in the third rank would tend to him. It had looked a fearful blow.

Wilfred said, on the other side of me, "Dick has sent the bulk of them packing but they are reinforcing the Danes with the gallowglasses."

"Aye." This was one of those moments in a battle when both sides take a breath. The Danes had been halted. The arrows and the stones continued to rain upon them but they had their shields before and above them for protection. They had chopped down half of our stakes and I knew that their next attack would be better coordinated. They were waiting for their gallowglasses. Our slightly elevated position meant that I could see Prince Henry. He was pointing to the ridge and Sir Gilles. He obviously thought it was me and I knew that my ruse had worked. He would not commit his knights until he had eliminated the threat of me and my knights. Worryingly I saw him wave those who had retreated to head towards the road and Erre. That was our weak flank now. We needed to change things.

"Wulfric! Flank the Danes! Erre is in danger!"

"Aye, lord! Lock shields and form on me!"

"Dick, the gallowglasses!"

"Archers, change targets!"

The field was now slick not only with mud and water but also blood and entrails. The Danes changed their tactics. The second and third rank held their shields above their first and they headed towards us. Alf's wisdom in sending the boys with us made the difference. They now had their eye in. They were more accurate. They were not throwing river pebbles but well-made lead shot from Alf. A blow on a helmet would stun while one on flesh could kill. The cacophony of noise was terrifying as the Danes advanced. They were chanting as they came. I knew they did this to help the rhythm; it worked. They came slowly to avoid falls and that allowed the slingers to thin their ranks some more.

John of Norton had a spear and I could see, by glancing along the line, the ones who had stepped from the second rank for they held spears. We would be toasting our dead that night; if we survived.

My new helmet afforded me a much better view of the battlefield but I had less protection. I was now reliant on my ventail and coif more than with my masked helmet. I saw that the Danish chief was heading towards the line to my right. Wulfric's movement was forcing the Danes slightly down the slope. I said, without turning my head, "Wilfred, let us try to join Wulfric and turn their flank!"

"Aye, lord!" I heard him as he shouted, "You heard the Warlord! When we move, I want those to the left of me to take two steps forward!"

As one they shouted, "Aye!"

The Danes suddenly lurched forward, "Now Wilfred and Wulfric!"

I stepped towards the two Danes who were advancing through the stakes. I lunged at one while I ducked beneath my shield. I heard a crack and a grunt as a stone hit one and my sword came up beneath the hide armour to tear into the groin of the other. Even as I withdrew my sword I punched at the dazed Dane. He reeled and I pushed him to the ground. Kneeling on his chest I forced my sword into his throat. Wilfred and Wulfric had managed to attack the right flank of the Danes. Those who held their shields still could not swing their axes one-handed and the spears and swords of my men found undefended flesh. There was a palpable lurch as the Danes reeled from this new attack. My men were now inside the Danish shield wall. Its integrity shattered, they fought as individuals.

I was lucky to have Wilfred on my left and John of Norton on my right. They protected my sides and allowed me to advance obliquely into their line. The two Danes I had killed meant that I was striking at the right sides of the Danes. Their axes were effective as they swung before them but could easily be deflected from the side. I punched the shoulder of the first Dane I met and then brought my sword overhand as he stumbled to his left. His hide armour could give some protection but I heard the crack as his collar bone broke. His axe dropped and John of Norton speared him.

We were advancing through them quickly now but even as we killed them I saw the Danish chief take the head of Hrolf the Swede, one of Wulfric's men. We could not afford to lose men of such skill. I redoubled my efforts although I was tiring the thought of losing more men spurred me on. I used what Wulfstan had called the 'fastest hands in Christendom'. I swung my sword as rhythmically as the Danes swung their axes but it was a shorter and faster swing. It had a longer edge and I used it. The Danes did not wear a coif and there was a gap between the bottom of their helmet and the top of their armour. I was confident that Wilfred and John of Norton would guard my sides. With my shield held tightly into my chest, I slew Danes.

I saw the Danish skull banner fall as stones and arrows fell around the Danish chief. He turned and saw me advancing. He roared a challenge and headed for me. He was not coming for the Warlord of the North, he was coming for the knight who led the wedge against his flank. This would be a crucial moment in the battle. He shouted at me and spat. Spittle spattered on my shield and coif. His axe head was notched and bloody but it could still hurt me. It was a little longer than the ones I had fought hitherto. That had both dangers and advantages. He could keep me further away but there would be a longer gap between swings. Timing would be everything.

"You two watch my flanks but stay clear of that axe."

"Be careful, Lord! He has killed four of our men already!"

"Thank you, John!"

The chief was a little older than I was but he had skills and experience. He feinted with his shoulder. Had I been watching his body I might have fallen foul of him but I watched his eyes. They never left my face. My ventail covered my mouth and he could not see my expression but I saw his lips pull back into a grin as he glanced to my left. He would strike at my shield. Keeping my eyes fixed I balanced on the balls of my feet. What I was about to do was risky and

I would have chastised one of my squires had he tried it but if it came off I would have victory.

"Wilfred, move left!"

Even as the axe came towards me I swung around in a seemingly suicidal move. Wilfred stepped to his left leaving me the space in which to spin. His axe hit fresh air and I continued my swing. I brought my sword across the mail on his back. The spin added momentum and it was a mighty blow. My blade bit through the mail and through his padded gambeson. He stepped away even as I struck but I felt the sword strike flesh and, as I withdrew it, I saw blood.

He half-turned to face me. We were now standing on the side of the hill. I had stopped the upward movement of the Danes. Out of the corner of my eye, I saw Wulfric and his men as they began to surround the Danes. Arrows showered the enemy. If we could force them down towards the road we had a chance.

Suddenly I heard a horn. It was Scottish. I knew not what it meant but I could do nothing. If I was distracted then it could spell my doom. I had to defeat the Dane. If he fell then the heart might go from these mercenaries.

"Now Stockton! One last push! Are you with me?"

The roar from behind put steel into my spine and I did not wait for the Danish chief to swing again. I brought my sword overhand and he held his axe up in two hands to block it. I punched with my shield. As a second Dane tried to swing at my left side Wilfred chopped across his throat. The chief and I were spattered with his blood. Surprisingly the chief's attention was distracted and I saw his eyes flicker to the dead warrior. I lunged and my sword found the gap under his right arm. I saw my sword's tip emerge from his shoulder and he fell from my sword. There was a collective wail and my men took advantage as Danes looked at their fallen leader. They chopped and hacked at disheartened Danes.

I felt the Danish chief's hand as it tugged at my foot. He said, in Saxon, "Give me my son's hand. I would go to Valhalla with him!"

Now I understood. I knelt down and took the dead Dane's hand and placed it in the chief's. He smiled, "You are a

tricky one and I think you are the one they call the Warlord."
I nodded. "I will see you in the Otherworld!" His eyes glazed
over. I took in the cross around his next which seemed to
contradict his words. Many Danes, it seemed, apparently
embraced Christianity but hung on to their beliefs.

"Lord! The Scottish attack!"

I turned and saw where Wilfred pointed. Prince Henry
had launched an attack up the hill, not at us, but my knights.
He thought that it was I who was on the hill.

"Dick! The horses!"

"Archers, aim left!"

Even as I watched I saw the Scottish knights begin to
falter as some of their horses were struck. They had begun
the attack thinking that the Danes were about to succeed.
Now the Danes were streaming down the hill. Prince Henry
made a classic blunder. He could have retreated or continued
with the attack. Instead, he and some of his knights hesitated.
The ones who did not, rode into Sir Harold and my knights
and squires. When the Scottish standard fell Prince Henry
turned to lead a retreat back down the hill.

I could do nothing to aid my knights for we still had
enemies before us. We hacked and slashed our way down the
hill. Knots of Danes and Scots stood to fight us. Honour or
friendship made them face inevitable death together. They
fell. By the time we reached the place where the Scots had
begun, it was almost dark and we held the field. The Scots
had withdrawn to the top of the ridge close to Bishop
Middleham. There were less than five hundred left there but
they still outnumbered us.

As I stood, gasping for air, I heard the sound of hooves as
Sir Harold and Sir Gilles of Norton rode up to me. "My lord,
we have a great victory! We hold the field!"

"Aye Harold but the battle is not yet won. Have our
wounded taken back to our camp. This is not over yet!"

Chapter 16

When I reached my lines I saw Dick and some of my men at arms gathered around a cloak covered form. They parted and I saw that it was Edgar. He opened his eyes and gave me a half-smile, "A great victory, lord." He winced as pain coursed through his body. "I go now to join Sir Edward and the others who had served you. It has been an honour to fight at your side. You truly are the greatest knight of the age." He smiled and his eyes closed.

"Edgar!"

Father Robert shook his head and made the sign of the cross, "He is gone, lord. I gave him absolution. I know not how he hung on but hang on he did just to speak with you." He lifted Edgar's cloak and I saw a hole in his shoulder big enough for me to put my two hands in. The priest was right he should have been dead already.

"He was a brave man."

Dick waved his arm at the other bodies which lay covered by their cloaks. "Many were as brave."

I looked up as Sir Harold and my other knights arrived, "A timely charge, Sir Harold."

"But we did not win the day."

"There were too few of you. Keep watch on the enemy while I assess the situation. Have my horse fetched."

Sir Gilles said, "Would you have Edward?"

I shook my head, "Rolf will be adequate. Have the dead taken close to the woods and then search the bodies of our enemies."

Wulfric huffed and puffed his way up the hill. He saw Edgar's cloak and dropped to a knee. "I have lived too long, lord."

"No, you have not. He died well. I leave you in command." James trotted up with Rolf. "Dick, let us ride down to the road and see how Erre fared."

As I mounted he said, "He was hard-pressed but they did not force the road."

"I will reward him and his men well."

However, as we headed down the slope towards the road my heart sank. There was a wall of bodies, mostly Danes. They surrounded my Varangians. My Frisians were busy pulling the Danish bodies to one side. Franck of Frisia turned to look as I reined in Rolf. "They died well lord. Your Varangians obeyed your orders and none passed. They made a great slaughter but there were too many of them. We stopped them despoiling their bodies, that was all."

I looked and saw that Erre and his Varangians had fought beyond reason. They now lay dead in a circle of brothers. They had fought to the end. Erre had lost his left arm and yet his sword was still in his right. I knelt and, taking his sword from the body of the last Dane Erre had killed, laid his sword across his chest, "My father would have been proud of you as I am proud of you. You managed some peace at the end of your lives but you died as you lived, as warriors."

I took the sword from the Scot who had killed Erre and stood. "We will make a barrow for them all on the morrow. For now, take their bodies up the hill so that they may be guarded. I would not have carrion feast on their flesh."

It was a black night when I reached the ridge. We butchered the dead Scottish horses and ate. There was no joy in the food for we had all lost too many friends. It had been a hard-fought battle and it was not yet over. The light came from the slingers. Dick said, "Where is he that slew the first Dane?"

A boy of ten summers stood, "It was I lord, Tom son of Watt."

Dick handed him a war bow. "Then take this. It belonged to a fine archer. When we return home we will teach you how to use it."

I remembered the stone which had slain the Dane who was about to kill me, "And who was it saved the Warlord?"

They all pointed to a stocky boy of eleven summers. "It was Will son of Osbert."

I handed him the Scottish sword, "Then take this in thanks. It was the sword that slew Erre. He was a great warrior. Use it in remembrance of a warrior who kept his oath."

His eyes widened in joy, "Aye, lord!"

I beckoned Aiden over. He smiled, "You wish us to discover the Scottish plans, lord?"

I laughed, "Are you a seer now? Aye. I would know their intentions Do they stay or do they flee? If they flee then we will pursue."

We had lost over thirty warriors. Not all were dead but the ten who were wounded would not be able to fight again soon. Dick and the rest of my knights sensed my despair. "We had a victory, lord. The Count of Hainaut aided us with his warnings. We fought off many times our number and they have left over two hundred dead on the field."

Sir Harold nodded, "Aye and we saw many more wounded being helped from the field."

"I know but this is a battle we should not have had to fight. Regardless of the outcome when this is over I ride to speak with King David. His whelp needs curbing. If the King of Scotland is still an ally of the Empress then he should control his wild son."

Wulfric chewed on the bone before hurling it into the fire. He wiped his greasy hands on the damp grass and stood, "But what of the morrow? What do we do about the Scots?"

"That depends upon Aiden's news. If they stand then we drive them from the field. We will use our mounted horsemen. His Danes are spent."

Dick nodded, "Aye, I counted a hundred dead Danes on the field and others were wounded. Half of his horsemen were unhorsed or slain and there are only the gallowglass warriors who might be rallied."

I lay back and closed my eyes, "Then we wait for Aiden."

It was in the dark of night when he and Edgar returned. "They stand, lord. There was much debate. His Danes wished to go home. The Scottish Prince said that they could but they would not be paid. Some of his men slipped away while the prince was talking. I think he will have little more than four hundred men left by dawn."

"Then our task is simple. We dislodge them from the hill. I would have the fyrd and the slingers guard our dead and our camp. I would not risk the boys in an uphill attack. Dick, you and the archers will approach to bow range and rain arrows upon them. You have a wise enough head on your shoulders to choose the best target. I will take the horsemen to Bishop Middleham and approach from the west. It is flatter there and we will not be at such a disadvantage. If we can we will charge and dislodge them from their ridge. Aiden and Leopold of Durstein, you will stay here with the wounded and the boys. I would have you issue them spare shields and spears."

Leopold's arm was in a sling and he was in pain from his wound but he grinned, "You wish them to think we have more men than we do."

Shrugging I said, "It cannot hurt and besides it may deter the Scots from striking at our camp." I turned to Wilfred, "A word."

I took him to one side. "I would like you to be my sergeant at arms and take over from Edgar."

"It is a great honour lord but I am not certain that I am worthy. Edgar was a great warrior as was Wulfric before him."

"And I chose those; trust my judgement. You will be a worthy successor, believe me." He nodded his thanks.

James and Richard came to speak with me. Richard said, "If you give me your sword lord, I will put a decent edge upon it. It did valiant service today."

"And I will choose you a lance for the morrow." James hesitated, "Will we be riding with you, lord?"

I felt both sad and old, "I wish that you were not for it will be a hard day but needs must. I have few enough men. Aye, you will be in the second rank. I hope that you are not needed."

Richard shook his head, "I thought Edgar and Erre were made of granite and would live forever yet they were slain."

"They were both great warriors but it was their time. Never underestimate a foe. No matter how young he may be or even if he is wounded there is always a danger. The Dane I fought today discovered that and he paid with his life."

I did not sleep that night; I dozed. I feared going into a deep sleep in case I was haunted by those who had died for my cause. I went over in my mind what I might have done. Could I have sat behind my walls and waited? I knew that I could not. It would have caused more pain to my people. I had had to do what I had done and men had paid for that with their lives.

I rose before dawn. I walked around the sentries speaking to each one. I had not said goodbye to Erre and that bothered me. I did not say goodbye to the sentries but I spoke with them so that they knew I valued their service and did not take it for granted. It might not make any difference but I felt better for it. I went to the horse lines where Richard was already grooming Edward. A good warhorse was pampered. The reward was reaped each time I rode him into battle.

"He is keen to go to war, lord. He had little to do yesterday. Sir Gilles said that the horse did not take kindly to being ridden by him."

"That is his imagination. I watched as he charged. Sir Gilles did well." I turned to him, "As did you. I will knight you on midsummer's day."

"You think I am ready?"

"I know that you are ready. We will have to watch out for a squire for you. There were some likely lads amongst the slingers."

He smiled, "When I was a squire before I met you, I would have looked down my nose at someone who was not noble-born. I was a fool. I will have any that you think right."

"No, Richard, this is your choice. I chose you and trained you. I did a good job. You choose because you are preparing a knight and other men will watch him and it will reflect on you. I am proud of all my former squires and all do me honour."

As dawn broke I prepared for war again. I sheathed my newly sharpened sword and the fresh lance. Mounting Edward I surveyed my battle. I was leading a mere seven knights and seven squires. I had fifty men at arms with us but we would be facing over a hundred horsemen protected by four hundred men on foot. The odds seemed insurmountable. My men formed up in a column of four behind me as Dick waved and rode towards the bottom of the dip. Each man had a lance. Richard held mine for me. I waved my sword and led my men towards the end of the ridge above Bishop Middleham. I saw that the Scots were arrayed for battle and watched us as we went. The Prince would be happy to be able to defend against us. He had watched us do it and now thought he could do the same.

We reined in three hundred paces from the Scots and Danes. I saw that Prince Henry had angled his men so that he could face a threat from both Dick and from me. The Danes who remained with him faced my archers. I turned to Richard, "Come with me and unfurl my banner."

"Aye lord." I handed my lance to Robert, John of Elton's squire and then unloosed my wolf banner.

"Wulfric, stay here I wish to try something."

"Be careful lord. This Scottish Henry is a snake!"

"I know and I wish to play on that trait."

I spurred Edward who strode towards the Scots. I glanced to my right as I did so. Leopold of Durstein had done as I had asked. It looked as though I had a large number of men in reserve on the top of the hill. From this distance, he would not be able to tell if they were a threat or not. He would just see an armed body of men with horses behind freshly repaired stakes.

I halted a hundred paces from the Scottish line. The Scottish prince had used his better-armed men to form the front ranks. He was ready for a charge. I took off my helmet and shouted. "Prince Henry I would speak with you."

I watched as he and his standard-bearer nudged their horses and moved through their men to stand fifty paces from us. The knight with the unicorn on his surcoat and his squire came with him. He kept his face covered by his full mask helmet.

The Prince had a confident look upon his face as he said, "You wish to surrender Earl?"

"I wish to give you the opportunity to save more lives. I wish you to leave my land and pay reparation for the harm you have caused."

He laughed, "And why would I do that? I outnumber you. I count the banners of but seven knights!"

I smiled, coldly, "These seven knights have defeated Scots each time they have fought them. Do not disparage my men else it makes it worse for you."

"Then you have my answer. Go back to your men and we will settle this issue today."

He jerked on his reins and I said, "Then let us try this. You and I dispute the matter here between our armies. If you defeat me then you have won. It will save a useless slaughter of many fine men." I had spoken loudly for I wanted all of his men to hear.

He shook his head, "I am no fool! I am the Prince of Cumberland. I will not fight with an earl."

I looked at the other knight, "Then how about the knight who prefers to keep his face hidden? Perhaps he will be your champion."

The prince turned to the knight who raised his helmet to reveal a younger face than I was expecting. "This is Baron Siegfried of Trier of the County of Luxembourg."

"Well? What say you?"

The knight from Luxembourg shook his head, "There is no advantage in tilting with you, Earl. We outnumber you and when your lances are shattered on our shields I will end your life."

"Very well then." I raised my voice as I lifted Edward's head to make him rear, "I gave you the chance to save men's lives but it seems there is no honour amongst my foes this day. That is a pity. I hope, Prince Henry, that you have a good horse between your legs else I shall catch you quicker this time when you flee!" Edward snorted as his hooves crashed to the ground. In answer, Prince Henry jerked his horse's head around and galloped back to his men.

"Lord, why did you issue the challenge?"

"I hoped he would accept and then I could have defeated him once and for all but in all truth, Richard, I did not expect him to do so. I knew that his refusal would dishearten his men. Glance over your shoulder. You will see that his men are not happy. They do not cheer him then look at our men."

Even as he turned my men began to cheer me and bang their shields. It had been a still and quiet day. My words had carried and they knew better than any the import of the prince's refusal.

I faced my warriors, "I gave them the chance and I was also afforded the opportunity to view their dispositions. He has men with shields facing us but they are neither Danes nor gallowglasses. He has not put stakes there and his horses stand behind five ranks of men. We will charge. Keep a tight formation. I saw few archers and slingers. The men we face have shields but no mail. Strike true and they will break. Sir Harold, you will command the right side of our line. If we break them then take your half to attack the Danes."

"Aye, lord!"

I turned Edward and backed him between Wulfric and Wilfred. My knights were spread out evenly in our front rank but the centre was a wedge. Wulfric, Wilfred and the five men at arms there were the most experienced warriors I had. With the squires behind Wulfric and me, my plan was to make us into a wedge that would break through the centre of their line. I had sown the seeds of doubt in his men's minds.

I spurred Edward and we trotted towards the Scots. I wished to make a slower approach than normal. The tension would get to his men. I heard hooves from my right and saw that Dick was moving his archers closer. With just the Danes before him, he was safe. He halted just a hundred paces from the Danes. His horse holders held the horses and I saw my

archers prepare their bows. I made Edward go a little faster
so that we were just cantering. I watched as the Danes held
their shields above and before them. Even with the sound of
our hooves, I could hear the arrows as they soared into the
air. Dick was clever. He did not aim at the Danes. That
would be a waste of arrows. His archers loosed at the men
waiting to receive our charge. Every arrow found flesh and I
heard the screams, shouts and wails as they struck home. We
were fifty paces from the front ranks and I saw some turn to
see their comrades behind.

I lowered my lance as Dick's arrows found some in the
front three ranks. When we were thirty paces from the
Scottish shields and spears I spurred Edward and pulled back
my lance. I chose my target. He was a grizzled greybeard. I
saw fear in his eyes. The man behind him suddenly pitched
sideways as an arrow plunged into his neck and his spear
fell. I punched forward. Even as I did I saw men fleeing from
the rear ranks. My lance tore into the chest of the Scot whose
shield was too slow to rise. He was hurled backwards and
Edward was through the gap his body had made. When you
have a dam holding water back the crack, which first shows
it is breaking, is a trickle and then rapidly becomes a torrent.
The arrows and our charge had that effect. They broke. I
yelled as we burst through. "Sir Harold, take half the men to
the Danes. The rest with me!"

My lance's head had broken and so I threw the stump at
the back of a retreating Scot. It knocked him to the ground
and Wilfred's horse trampled him to death. I saw Prince
Henry and his knights. There was agitation amongst them.
His knights and mounted men at arms outnumbered us but
would that mean he would attack us? His path was barred by
his routed men. I drew my sword and began to hack a path
towards him. I held my shield loosely for no one was trying
to attack me. I swung my sword at head height and it sliced
through the shoulders of a gallowglass whose naked back
was suddenly covered in blood. I swung it to my left and
brought it down on the skull of another. Men threw away
shields and helmets to make themselves lighter as they ran
like hares across the turf. If they thought to reach the

sanctuary of their standard they were disappointed. Prince Henry turned his horse and led his men away in an inglorious retreat. This was the battle of the standards all over again.

I saw the Prince wave his arm and shout something. A line of men at arms wearing the prince's livery bravely charged us. There were just twenty of them but they rode well-spaced; they were sent to stop our pursuit. We would have to defeat them before we could pursue my prey. I reined in Edward a little so that Wulfric and Wilfred were able to join me boot to boot. They both had their lances. Our two lines were approaching rapidly. I wondered if the Scottish men at arms had had much practice at this. It is hard to control a lance at speed. It takes a steady hand and a good eye. When I saw the lancehead moving up and down then I knew that the man at arms who was hurtling towards me was not experienced. I did not watch the tip. I watched his eyes. He was coming from my right and he intended to hit me on my sword side. That suited me. I pulled my shield onto my cantle and held my sword out. I saw the triumph in his eyes as he jabbed forward with the lance. He had aimed it too high. I did not even need my shield. It caught my shoulder a glancing blow and sprang up. I saw the triumph turn to terror as he saw my sword head towards his middle. He wore mail but our combing speed meant it afforded little protection. My sword tore across his stomach. His body fell and I was through the line.

I saw that the prince had used his men's sacrifice to extend his lead. There was little point in pursuit. Our horses had charged and his were fresh. Durham was close and he would be within its walls inside an hour. I wheeled to my right and galloped towards Sir Harold. He and my men at arms were falling upon the backs of the Danes. Dick and his archers had now begun to target the Danes. Each archer was aiming at the gaps. The range was less than a hundred paces and at that distance, their arrows could pierce their hide armour. The Danes were brave and they had nowhere to go. Flight would have meant their deaths anyway and so they closed ranks ready to strike at any horse or warrior who came too close. I saw one of Sir John of Elton's men at arms go too close to them and an axe hacked through both his leg and his horse.

When he fell I shouted, "Hold! Dick, hold your arrows!" behind me I heard the sound of slaughter as Wulfric led my men at arms in pursuit of the fleeing Scots but around the island of the Danes, there was just the panting of breath and the stamping of horses. I shouted in Saxon, "Danes, you have done all that could be expected of you. If you stand we will slaughter you all. My archers have many arrows. It will not be a glorious death!"

I wondered, briefly, if they would do as King Leonidas and his Spartans had done and resist to the end. I heard their voices behind their shields. There were just forty of them left alive. Finally, a voice shouted, "What will happen to us if we surrender?"

"We will escort you to Hartness and you can take a ship. Use the coin the Scots paid you to go elsewhere and ply your trade. Miklagård still values axe men."

"You will let us go?"

"You are mercenaries. You were hired by a faithless prince who has abandoned you. I would not have you abroad in my land but you fought bravely and I respect that. Answer me quickly for my patience is worn thin."

"We accept."

"Then lower your shields." I turned to Sir Harold. "Take your conroi and Sir John's. Escort them to Hartness. Stay with them until they find a ship."

"Aye lord. Is this wise?"

I pointed to Roger of Thorpe who lay with his dead horse. "I would not lose one more warrior. We have more important matters to consider."

"Aye lord."

I saw that Sir Tristan had taken some Scots prisoner. "Sir Tristan, guard those prisoners. I have questions for them and we need more slaves."

"Aye lord."

I dismounted to rest Edward and, as I stroked him, I began to plan my next moves in this battle for a throne.

Chapter 17

We left for home the next day. We made a barrow for our dead. Erre and Edgar were laid at the two ends and the rest of our warriors and their weapons were between. Everyone who had fought helped to build the barrow and we laid turf on the top. It would stay by the road marking the place where so many had fulfilled their oaths. We had captured many horses and they took back the mail, gold and weapons we had collected. The Danes had been paid well and our men were richer. We made a pyre of the enemy dead and rode south with its black smoke billowing above our heads.

Wulfric rode with me, "What now my lord? Do we besiege Durham?"

"It would be a waste of time and men. They could laugh away a siege. No, we let the Prince lick his wounds. Those prisoners told me that King David is at Carlisle. I will go there with Sir Hugh. It is time I spoke to him directly. If he is an ally of the Empress and Henry FitzEmpress then it is time he acted like one."

"He may not be pleased with your treatment of his son."

"Equally he may not be happy with the actions of his son which do nothing for the honour of Scotland. My mind is made up. If I am to make a king of Henry then I need to act as his representative. I think my days as a warlord are numbered. You can only butt heads for so long. I need to talk. This war has gone on long enough."

The proudest in my army were the boy slingers. They strode proudly through the gate of my town. I saw their

214

anxious mothers watching for them. None had been harmed. At the head of them strode Tom, son of Watt clutching his bow and Will, son of Osbert with his captured sword on a Scottish belt. Richard had told me that they had both promised to become warriors like Edgar and Erre. They were the future.

William of Kingston had still not returned from Normandy and so I was blind. I had no information. It would not change my plans. I sent for Alice. "I need my best surcoat. I am to travel to meet with a king."

She smiled, "I had hoped you would, my lord. While Mary and her ladies were working on the tapestry I made two new ones. I also made one for Richard. A knight should have a well-dressed squire."

"Good. You are an angel. We will be leaving on the morrow."

"I will sort some clothes out for you."

"How is the tapestry, by the way? I thought that Mary's marriage would have dampened her interest."

"They work on it every day. I think, now that she is with child, she enjoys talking to Morag about impending motherhood. It will be finished by Midsummer's Day."

"And that is perfect for I have a mind to knight Richard then too."

"I will begin the plans for the celebration. We rushed it for poor Sir Gilles."

I knew I was being admonished, albeit gently. I did not mind. "What would I do without you, Alice?"

She blushed and left. John the Steward had been waiting outside. "You had a great success, my lord."

John saw things in terms of profit and loss. Men's lives seemed incidental. "Edgar and Erre do not think so."

"I am sorry, lord. I grieve for them. They were both fine men but Sir Wulfric told me that they died well. I meant no disrespect."

I softened, "I know. I am to visit Carlisle but I would have Richard knighted in June and I think that Sir Gilles can take over Norton. I need a knight there and the others are settled."

"He is a good choice, lord. I will begin the documents he will need."

I waved a hand to dismiss him, "Thank you, John."

I went to my solar and wrote a letter to Matilda. It would have to wait until William returned for me to send it but I was anxious to tell her what I had done and what I had planned. I would not tell our son yet. He still had some of the impetuous nature of his father. I would speak with King David before I spoke with him. The letter penned I stared across the river to the south. The river was still the border and the attack of the Scots had shown me how little land we actually held. We were prosperous it was true but if the Scots, or Stephen the Usurper chose to bring a huge army, then we would be defeated. There were no allies left in England. I could not win the war with the forces at my command. I would have to use other means; no matter how distasteful.

I did not take Dick with me. I needed him to train more archers. I took four of his archers and four men at arms. It would be enough until we reached Sir Hugh. I was not going to war. I was going to talk. Aelric led my archers and Ralph of Nottingham led my men at arms. I needed Wilfred to take over Edgar's duties. It would take time for him to do so and he did not need me looking over his shoulder. I knew that Dick and Sir Harold would help him. We called at Piercebridge so that I could keep Sir Phillip informed about events. He offered me his men but I wanted all of my castles to be ready for any danger. The arrival of the Danes had been a warning.

Sir Hugh's castle was a welcome sight. The weather had turned a little unpleasant and a cold wind had raced in from the east bringing a chilling rain. Sir Hugh was saddened by the loss of two such experienced warriors. My young knights had all spoken to me of the effect it had had on them. If Edgar and Erre could fall with their experience then it showed them their own mortality. He was more than pleased to be my escort. "In truth, lord, I feel that I have not served you well. While you and the others have been fighting battles I had been lodged safely behind these walls with my family."

"Your task was harder, Hugh. You have had to be alert to danger and to watch for enemies. You served me as well as any knight who drew sword."

We took twenty of his men at arms as well as his squire. They were all proud of the honour. With my four archers assisting Sir Hugh's scouts we headed towards the rugged land of the west. Filled with high crags and deep lakes it had no lords of the manor. Those who had ruled there had fled when the Scots had been given the land by Stephen. Many had gone to the Holy Land and others had been given manors in other parts of the land by Ranulf Earl of Chester. It saddened me as we rode through verdant valleys that the reward of this land went to the Scots and not to Henry FitzEmpress.

We were spied when we took the road from Brampton. There was a Scottish lord ensconced there but my banner made him keep to his walls. He did, however, send a messenger to warn his liege lord of my approach. The result was that, when we neared Carlisle, we were greeted by a cavalcade of knights and men at arms. I recognised Baron William Douglas. We had fought at Northallerton and he had fled with the King.

"Earl is this visit peaceful or shall we draw weapons?"

I smiled, "Baron if I came for war then you would have known. I bring a handful of men to protect me from brigands. I wish to speak with the King. He is an ally of the Empress, his niece, is he not? And I am her loyal follower. Is there a problem?"

My calm manner made him uncomfortable and I saw him squirm a little, "No, my lord. We will escort you."

Carlisle Castle had been built by William, Henry's great grandfather. Since then it had been improved. Why Stephen had given it away I could not understand. As we dismounted Sir William said, "Your men will be housed in the barracks."

I nodded, "They know how to fend for themselves." I nodded to Ralph who grinned as he bowed. Although this was a mission of peace they would glean as much

information as they could. I had given them strict
instructions to be frugal in their intake of ale and to keep
their eyes and ears open. If this mission failed then we might
have to take more direct action.

As Baron Douglas led us inside I said, "Is there
somewhere we could change? We have travelled far and I
would not offend the king's nose."

"Of course, my lord. We have two chambers for you in
the west tower."

"Thank you." Richard and John, our squires, carried our
chests.

Washed and changed I felt able to approach the king. We
strapped on our swords and headed down to the Great Hall.
Alice had done a good job with the surcoats. These were not
surcoats for war. They were delicate and fine. She had had
my wolf emblem embroidered on my chest. She had used
gold and silver threads which stood out well against the blue
background.

Sir William was waiting for us. He gestured towards the
wine, "Help yourself, my lord. I will fetch the King."

There were two guards in the hall but they looked to be
part of the normal routine. I did not think they had been
placed there for us. It was a goblet or two of wine later that I
heard the babble of voices as the king approached. He
entered surrounded by a gaggle of advisers. I recognised a
couple of earls but the two clerics and officials were
unknown to me.

He gave me a smile as he approached, "The infamous
Warlord of the North; what brings you from your stronghold
in the east?"

"I came to speak with you," I looked pointedly at his
advisers, "in private."

There was a murmur of disapproval from his advisers.
The king held up his hand and smiled at me, "I think they
fear you wish me harm, Earl."

I shook my head and took off my sword and dagger. I
handed them to Richard, "I come in peace, my lord."

"I know and I also know you to be an honourable man. If
you wished to kill me you would not use this as a subterfuge.

Come, we will walk in the inner bailey. There, my advisers can watch like old women twitching behind a tapestry and they will see that I am safe." He waved over a servant who handed us two furs.

He did not speak until we were out in the cold. The warm fur kept out the worst of the cold wind. "How is my niece? I was sorry to hear that Robert died. I had thought he would die with a sword in his hand."

"The Empress is now in a priory in Normandy. I am sure you knew that."

He smiled, "I did but I know that you keep in close touch with the Empress. And how is her son?"

"He will be a fine King of England." I stopped, "Unlike your son, my lord. He is the main reason I am here."

He frowned. "My son?"

"Did you know that he hired Danes and brought an army to attack me?"

I watched his eyes to see if he knew of the attack. If he did then my visit would be wasted. He shook his head, "Are you certain?" He was not lying. He did not know.

"We fought north of my castle. I spoke with him and offered a challenge. He refused. I thought, lord, that your country supported the Empress and her son's claim to the throne."

"I do."

"Then this appears to be something of a problem. I have not attacked Scotland. My men have not ventured into the land you took. I have kept my side of the bargain even though the taste was bitter."

He shook his head, "My son resents you, Earl. Northallerton was a harsh defeat made worse by the fact that you followed him here. He felt humiliated."

"Then he was a boy; now he is a man. A man behaves differently. I would know, my lord, if there is to be a war between us. If you tell me aye then so be it but if you say there will be no war then I need assurances that Prince Henry will be curbed."

He frowned again, "You make demands of a king?"

"It grieves me to do so but the actions of many lords, kings and usurpers have made me Warlord. I cannot shed that skin until Henry is crowned."

He nodded, "You are an honourable man in a world which is full of treachery. I admire you, Earl. I would have peace and I would have Henry on the throne. Is that good enough for you?"

"It is and your son..?"

He chuckled, "You are persistent are you not? I will have words with my son and my lords." He hesitated, "Was he hurt in your encounter?"

"He was not for he fled before we could come to blows but we burned the bodies of over three hundred Scots and Danes that he led."

He shook his head, "What a waste. Tell me, Earl, is Henry in England?"

"No, he is in Normandy. Why?"

"I would meet with him and offer my assurances personally."

"Then I will try to arrange that."

He looked up at the battlements. His advisers and barons were lined up. "We had best go in. Give me your arm, earl. It will be a sign to all that there is peace."

Arm in arm we walked in. "I have to say, lord, that Henry and I would have returned to England those lands which Stephen gave to you."

He laughed and it was loud and fulsome, "You care not what you say, Earl of Cleveland. It is refreshing to meet someone who speaks his mind so plainly. Let us leave that until we have helped Henry achieve the crown and then we can see if those differences might be resolved."

At the feast that evening I was questioned by many of the King's knights. This was a rare opportunity for them. The wolf of the north was someone who was used to frighten Scottish children and now they had the chance to speak to him. Many knew my life story and I was asked about my time as a Champion as well as the time I had fought for the Emperor of the Byzantine Empire. It was flattering for I could see the regard in which I was held.

The next morning I was summoned along with Sir Hugh and our squires to the Great Hall. A cleric clutched a parchment. The King stood. "Let it be known by all that there is peace between Scotland and Matilda, daughter of Henry and rightful heir to the English throne. Let it also be known that I support her son, Henry FitzEmpress', claim to the throne." He tapped the parchment which the cleric unrolled. "This document has been prepared to let posterity know of my decision. In addition, I state here and now that the Earl of Cleveland is a friend to King David and an attack on him constitutes an attack on me!" He glared around the room. His eyes met mine and he nodded. I nodded back. "Good!" The cleric melted some wax on the bottom and the King used his seal. The parchment was placed in a chest.

The cleric said, "This will be taken to St. Andrews where it can be kept safe. Let all here acknowledge the King's words."

There was a collective shout of, "Aye!" With that my war with Scotland ended. It was a war that had lasted over twenty years. It was a strange feeling.

Two days later, as we prepared to leave, the King handed me a beautiful dagger in a finely crafted scabbard. "I would have you take this token, Earl, of our newfound friendship. If you have to draw it to take Scottish blood then it means I have failed."

"I hope then that I do not need to draw it for I see hope in this new friendship, my lord."

"Farewell."

As we headed home Ralph told me all that they had discovered. I had been right in my judgement of the ruler. The king had known nothing of his son's actions. The word amongst the ordinary warriors was that Henry wished the throne for himself. I saw then that the king's actions were not entirely altruistic. I was a means of helping him to control his wayward son. However, I was pleased that we had an accord. I was silent as we headed to Barnard Castle for I wondered if I should have done it years earlier. If I had how many of my men might still be alive? I parted at Barnard and we pushed our horses to reach Stockton before dark.

My first question concerned my ship, "Has *'Adela'* docked yet?"

"No lord, nor the *'Mary'*. It is now some time since they left."

John knew the vagaries of the tides, winds and seas better than any for he fretted about the goods the ships carried. I knew from his face that I was worrying overmuch. She was not due. I went directly to my solar and began to write two letters: one was to the Empress and the other to Henry. The news they contained could change Henry's future. The Empress might not be in England but she had to know that we were, once more, close to securing the crown. This time it was I who would hold the reins and not the Earl of Gloucester. Perhaps his death had been meant to be. The darkness it had created was now lit by the light of hope.

I was full of ideas and I was restless. I woke before dawn and I sought out John of Craven. I allowed Richard to sleep. John of Craven was older. He needed to rise early if only to make water. As I had expected he was awake. He was alone for the new watch was still abed and the ones on duty would have to wait until an hour past dawn to be relieved. The air was filled with the fresh-baked bread which had been brought for the watch. He stood when I entered the guard room, "Lord is there aught amiss?"

"No, John. I would speak with you." I sat with him and broke off a piece of bread. It was still warm. I took my knife and I smeared butter upon it. We ate silently and then John poured me some ale. I had told him some of our news the previous night and now I gave him the rest.

"I believe, John, that we have an alliance with the Scots. I hope that this one brings better results than the one negotiated by the Empress." His eyes widened. "I do not criticise the Empress but it did not bring us peace did it?"

John and his men had come to me as a result of the treachery of the first peace, "No lord."

"If we have peace then we can ignite the fires of rebellion against the Usurper but we have lost many men."

He nodded, "We have enough to guard our walls and we can withstand a determined siege, lord, but I would be loath to take them south. Stephen has many more men than we do. There is a difference between holding on to what you have and retaking what you do not."

He was a wise old soldier. "Then we need to hire more soldiers and train the fyrd to a higher standard. If we go to war I would strip the whole garrison. That would include you."

"You would take old men, my lord?"

"I need experience. I wish that I did not but we both know that we have little choice in the matter."

"At least the men we will take have armour and weapons which are the equal of any in the land. Our men at arms are armed as knights."

We talked of men who might become sergeants at arms. I knew the value of leaders on the field. Men like Ralph of Nottingham led men. Giving them rank just confirmed the nature of their leadership.

Sir Gilles joined us as light seeped into the guard room. "You are risen early, my lord."

John stood, "You have given me much to think on Earl. I had best be about my duties."

I gestured to the seat and Gilles sat as John left us. Like John, I had given Gilles the bare bones the previous night and I told him all and my plans. "Young Henry will have his men trained soon, lord. This is good timing."

"The time is not right yet for Henry but if he is here then I can oversee the final preparations. We need another year to make up our numbers. I have a mind to bring Sir Leofric and his men over. Anjou is quiet."

"They would be a valuable addition."

"And I would give you Norton."

"Me lord?"

"Who else could have it? Richard?"

He looked up at the roof of the guardroom. "I had thought to stay here a little longer lord."

I smiled, "You are afraid to lead." His eyes showed surprise. "Oh I know you can lead men in battle but you fear leading people in peace." He nodded. "You have Mary. She is wise and she knows how to lead people. She watched her parents do that for years. Besides Norton needs a woman as well as a knight. Erre and his Varangians were gruff old men. Norton is a place to be defended. You need to make it a place in which to live. It may never be the fortress which Stockton is but it could be as prosperous as my burgh with the right leader."

"And I am that leader?"

"You are and we both know it."

He nodded. "Then I will accept." He smiled, "And it seems the right time. Mary and the women have finished the tapestry. She would have mentioned it last night but you seemed preoccupied. It is ready to be revealed and hung."

"Good. As my father might have said, this is *wyrd.*"

Chapter 18

The tapestry, considering it had been something created to stop Mary from feeling sad, was a magnificent piece of work. Sir Gilles was clearly St. George and the expensive silken threads with their vibrant colours had made it come alive. Alice had had servants prepare the wall in my Great Hall so that it would cover the cold north wall. It made the room brighter as soon as it was unrolled. Everyone was pleased with it. I sent for Sir John and Sir Harold and Sir Tristan. Their castles were close and I wanted them to see the work. I also wished to make my announcement.

Sir Gilles had told Mary of my decision. I think he was surprised by her reaction. She was overjoyed. I knew why. She was a wife and soon to be a mother. She wanted her own nest and she had her own ideas about her home. She had hugged me. "You are a truly good man, lord."

When my knights arrived, with their wives and young children, they were equally impressed by the tapestry. Mary's sketch had captured the movement of horse and rider. Her imagination had created a dragon so fierce that Sir Harold's young daughter hid behind her mother in fear. The young boys laughed.

"And I have more news. Sir Gilles is to be lord of the manor of Norton." They cheered and John and Harold patted him on the back. I saw an envious look on Richard's face. His eye caught mine and I nodded. Soon he would be knighted and then he, too, would have his own manor. Already I had Thorpe in mind for him. "And there is more. I have spoken with King David and I have his word that there will be peace. More than that I have his promise to use his warriors to serve under Henry FitzEmpress and retake England from the Usurper."

This was even greater tidings. Harold and John could see the implications immediately. "Then the war might be over sooner, lord?"

"I hope so, Sir Harold. We need Henry in England and he needs to meet with the King of Scotland but I am hopeful."

Sometimes the fates hear our words. I know it is not a Christian idea but I believe there is something of the pagan deep in the heart of everyone. Even as the words hung in the air I heard, from my castle walls, the cry, "Sail, ho! It is *'Adela'*!"

My captain had returned and soon I would have news. "Come let us go to the quay and greet my captain! Hopefully, he brings men and news."

I could see that both ships were laden as they tacked up the river. It seemed to take them forever to do so. I saw the heads of strangers lining both decks. Sir Leofric had sent more men and that was timely. William of Kingston stood at the rudder and, as they approached I looked for a sign of news. Ominously he had a frown upon his face. As the ship was secured he was the first ashore. He was handed a small chest by his ship's boy and he hurried across to me. He bowed, "Lord I bring grave news from Anjou and letters from the Empress and Henry FitzEmpress. I came as soon as I could."

There was something in his words that disturbed me. I turned to John my Steward, "See to the unloading. Knights and squires come with me."

I took the chest from William and we hurried through my gates and into my castle. "Richard, close the doors. Tell Leopold to admit no one."

I opened the chest and took out the two letters. "What is the grave news?"

"The letters should explain all, lord."

"And I would hear from your lips. Tell, for the delay in reading the missives will not hurt."

He sighed, "Henry FitzEmpress sailed three months since for Chester. He intends to wrest the crown from Stephen the Usurper."

Sir Harold could not contain himself, "What? Is he mad?" He saw my look and bowed, "I am sorry my lord. He is the future king and I should know better but why would he do such a thing?"

"I know not." I took the two letters which lay within the box. I laid Henry's to one side. I did not want to read his words yet. They would not bring me joy. Instead, I opened the one from the Empress. It was brief and to the point.

Rouen,
My Earl Cleveland,
My son has had a letter from Ranulf Earl of Chester.
He has advised my son that England is ripe for his return. I
tried to dissuade him but his new warriors and knights
encouraged him. I write this letter in the hope that it
reaches you in time and that you can prevent a disaster
from overtaking us. I would that his father had advised him
better but since the wound, he has not been himself. I fear
for his health.
You are our only hope. I pray to God that this reaches
you in time and that you are able to stop my son from doing
something stupid.
Your friend,
Maud

I folded it up and put it in the chest. It was with a heavy heart that I opened the second one. I recognised his large strokes.

Rouen,
Warlord,
I have received hopeful news. Ranulf the Earl of
Chester has written to me. He is gathering an army to
oppose Stephen. He has urged me to join him. I have
used the money I captured from Flanders and engaged

Kingmaker

ships and hired more men. We sail for England. I hope that you receive this in time and that you can join us.

I will wait at Chester until the start of June and then we march on Lincoln.

Henry FitzEmpress.

"What is the date?"

"What, my lord?"

"The date, Sir Gilles, what is the date?"

"Today is the last day of May!"

I closed my eyes. We would be too late. Even as despair filled my heart I resolved to do all that I could. "Richard ride to Sir Wulfric, Sir Gilles of Normanby and Sir Tristan. I need them and as many men as they can muster. They will meet me at Piercebridge. James, ride to Sir Phillip and tell him that we are to head west and I will need some of Sir Hugh's men too."

As the two squires ran off Sir John asked, "What does the Prince say, lord?"

"He intends to march on Lincoln at the beginning of June."

"Tomorrow."

"Aye, tomorrow. All that I have done could be undone by this single act of recklessness. Curse Ranulf of Chester!" I paused. Losing my temper was not going to get me anywhere. I turned to William of Kingston. "William, when you docked were others aware of the prince's intentions?"

He nodded, "Aye lord. Even before Sir Leofric told me I knew for it was gossip amongst the captains on the river. All knew that Henry FitzEmpress had left for England to reclaim his throne."

"Then Stephen will know. The sea crossing to London is shorter than that to Chester. I fear that the Usurper will be waiting before they can reach Lincoln. Send for Aiden. I need my scout this day." Sir John went to the door to summon a guard. When he returned I said, "You two must prepare your men. I will take half of the new men and leave the rest to guard my castle. John of Craven I leave you as

228

castellan. I know I ask much of you but go and choose the best of the men to come with me and then I want every horse we can muster."

He smiled, "I would come with you if you asked, lord."

I nodded, "I know but we do not go to fight the battle for England; we ride to rescue the future king."

"We are well provided with horses. Each rider can have a spare."

"We will not take our warhorses. The long ride would break them and this ill news means that there will come a time when we have to wrest the crown from Stephen's fingers. Then we shall need our horses. Tell Alf I wish to see him, John."

"Aye lord."

John, my steward, stood close by. "Will you need servants, lord?"

Shaking my head I said, "No. We ride hard and sleep by the road. Already we may be too late. We cannot leave before the morrow and it will take two days to reach them; when we know where they are."

Aiden arrived. His calm face gave me hope. Henry might be reckless but my men were not. "Aiden, Henry FitzEmpress has landed at Chester and is heading for Lincoln. I fear that Stephen will reach him and bring him to battle. I leave with my army tomorrow. We go from Piercebridge. I intend to head south down the Roman Road and then try to intercept Stephen. You must find both Henry and the Usurper."

He nodded, "I will, lord." He smiled, "Do not fear, lord; I will find them and you will defeat them."

He made it sound so simple and yet I knew that it was not. My knights and squires hurried away for they had much to do. I took out the maps I had of the land. I was heading into a country that was not as familiar to me. Much of it was empty until we reached the Mersey. There were many places an army could hide. The safest route for Henry would be through Cheshire and the lands controlled by Ranulf. How quickly could he move?

Alf's arrival brought an end to my speculative thoughts. "I have to leave the valley and the town, Alf. I shall have to take most of the men."

He nodded, "The word has spread through the town, lord. Fear not. Your new peace with the Scots makes us safer and it is time we learned to defend what we have. Ethelred and I have made sure that the fyrd practices each Sunday after church and those who went with you north have come back eager to become warriors. It will be well."

"I hope so Alf but Henry FitzEmpress might have undone all of our good work."

Alf shrugged philosophically, "You do not know, lord. This might be the making of him."

"Perhaps. I will return as soon as I can."

He turned to go and then he said, "I almost forgot. I brought one of the boy slingers with me. He begged an audience with you."

"A slinger?"

"Will, son of Osbert; the one to whom you gave the sword. He waits without."

"Bring him in then." I could do without the distraction but I knew that ignoring such requests could create resentment. Better to humour him and send him on his way.

When he entered, I was surprised. It had been less than a month but he seemed to have grown. He wore a new leather jerkin and his sword was strapped to his side. The Scottish used shorter swords but it still seemed a little too big for him. He bowed, "My lord I would beg a boon of you."

I hid my smile. He sounded so formal. "Speak. I will not bite."

"The town talks of how you go to war and I would go with you, my lord."

"I take no slingers, Will, son of Osbert."

"No, lord, I would go as a warrior. I have practised with this sword and I would use it."

I was about to shake my head and refuse when I had an idea. "Can you ride?"

I saw the lie in his eyes as he said, "Aye my lord."

I shook my head. "If you are to serve me then never tell me a lie. I ask again, can you ride?"

He hung his head, "I have never tried, my lord."

"That is better. I have a need for someone to groom my horse and to care for my second. If you can learn to ride in a day then I will take you."

His eyes lit up. "Then I will learn."

I nodded. "I will send my squire to test you at sunset. If you cannot sit astride a horse and ride around the outer bailey then you cannot come." I waved a hand to dismiss him.

"That was kindly done, lord."

"I saw something in his eyes. He deserves the chance."

Alf nodded, "I will teach him myself. I have a pony that is gentle." He laughed, "I suspect he is in for some pain. He will be sleeping on his front this night."

The day passed in a blur. Richard arrived back with the news that my knights had begun to mobilise and would be at Piercebridge at the appointed time. "Good. When you have eaten find Will, son of Osbert. He wishes to come with us. I told him he had to show you that he could ride. Be honest with him. If he cannot ride then tell him so."

"But why do you need him, lord?"

"I do not, yet, but when you are knighted I will need a squire. This will help me to see if he has skills. You, too, will need to find a squire. Keep your eyes open."

"Aye lord. I learn each day I am with you."

After he had gone I wished that Henry had learned more from me.

We had two hundred men as we headed south. I had gleaned the rough numbers of Henry's forces from William of Kingston but as it was gleaned half from gossip and half from the size of the ships which had taken them I was not certain of its accuracy. It ranged between four hundred and six hundred men. Either way, it was not enough to bring Stephen to battle. The Earl of Chester had men. I knew that he could field five hundred decently armed men and knights with a healthy sprinkling of archers. The men I would trust but their leader? We rode quickly. I did not fear any of

Stephen's forces in the north. He would have sent for the best and I had beaten them too many times to worry. We passed Arncliffe and the field looked peaceful. How many had died there and for what?

Wulfric rode next to me. Richard rode at the rear of my men at arms with Will son of Osbert. The boy had proved he could ride and now Richard was instructing him in his duties. Wulfric looked at the sky. "The weather has cleared for us, lord. We should make the Lincoln road in two days."

"Aye, but where on the Lincoln Road? Aiden has to find them and then find us."

Wulfric laughed, "I have no doubts about either of those outcomes, lord. He will find them and he is like a hound; he can find his master easy enough." He leaned forward to stroke his horse's mane. "My worry, lord, is what we do when we find Stephen. He will have more than a thousand men. We both know that."

"I would say nearer to two thousand, perhaps. If he knows that Henry is in England he can end the threat in an instant. With Henry captured we could do nothing. I just hope to use surprise and guile rather than brute force."

We camped that night by the village of Goodshaw. We had covered more than half of the journey. We had heard nothing from Aiden but I had not expected news yet. We were still well placed to either head for Chester or Lincoln. Both would be within a day's ride of us. Our horses had done well. We had all changed horses many times during the day. It had meant we could ride quickly. As we camped and ate cold rations I gathered my knights around me. I had more knights than I had had for a while for Sir Phillip and Sir Hugh were with me. It also meant that I was well endowed with archers.

"I know not what we shall meet when we find Stephen. I will rely on you all to do that which you have done before. None of you is foolish and none are reckless."

Wulfric asked, "And what is our object lord? Do we try to defeat Stephen?"

"Would that I could say yes but I cannot. Our only aim is to extricate Henry FitzEmpress from this trap. It is a harsh thing to say but I do not mind if we lose the rest of his men so long as he is safe. We head back to Stockton when that is done." I turned to Dick and Sir Phillip. "You two are my secret weapon. I know not how I will use your men so when we sight the enemy stay close to me."

"Aye lord. We have plenty of arrows."

"It may be we use other skills, Dick."

I knew that I was being enigmatic but I had an idea in my head. I knew not where it came from but I saw a way to wrest the advantage from Stephen. It all depended upon Aiden. My eyes would be burned raw seeking sight of him.

We were approaching the old Roman fort which lay to the north of Cheshire when Edward rode in. He had Hal with him. "We have found Henry FitzEmpress, lord. When we left they were camped at Rushton Spencer."

I nodded, "It was held by the Earl's man, Norman de Verdun."

Edward said, "The enemy warriors have a camp by Danebridge. Aiden said there were over fifteen hundred men."

"And Henry FitzEmpress."

"Less than six hundred but many were mounted."

"Did Aiden manage to speak with Henry and tell him that we were coming?"

"We only saw them at dusk. Aiden wanted to find out the enemy dispositions first."

"What is the ground like between them?"

"It is rough, lord. There are small copses and the ground has many rocks and dips. It will not suit horses."

"He did right. Lead on then and take us to them." I turned to Wulfric, "Have spears issued."

"You have a plan lord?"

"I have an idea. Plan is too grand for what is in my head."

Richard brought me my lance, "Have Will watch the horses when we go into battle. You will ride by Rolf's rump with my banner."

"Aye lord."

We were five miles from Danebridge when Edgar rode up to us, "Lord, they have joined battle!"

My heart sank, "Tell me the worst."

Stephen held his men on a low ridge and the Earl of
Chester and Henry FitzEmpress charged. They lost many
men and fell back. The enemy pursued them and they are
now back at Rushton Spencer."

"Has Stephen the Usurper brought a baggage train,
Edgar?"

"He has. They have wagons and guards."

I turned, "On, we have no time to lose."

Dick rode next to me, "Orders my lord?"

"Take Phillip and head east. I want you to capture their
baggage train."

"And then, lord?"

"That depends upon what we can do. We are in the hands
of God now."

The land through which we travelled was neither level
nor even. Troughs and dells gave way to low rises. Bushes
and scrub made small barriers along the rough greenway. So
it was that we only saw the battle when we were half a mile
north of Rushton Spencer. Even as we crested the rise and
saw Aiden emerge from the trees I saw that Henry and the
Earl of Chester were being hard-pressed. The manor had a
small motte and bailey castle but it was too small to hold
many. Someone had placed archers within and it was they
who were holding off the knights and men at arms who
charged the thinly held lines. The enemy were less than half
a mile from us. They would see us but not immediately.
Therein lay our opportunity.

"Form three lines!"

As I watched I saw fifty or sixty men at arms suddenly
detach themselves from Henry's right flank and gallop south.
His army was fragmenting. We were too late. Even as we
watched another group joined them.

Turning in my saddle I yelled, "We charge the right flank
of Stephen the Usurper's lines. I want us to hit him hard. We
are but a hundred mounted men but I would have us fight as
a thousand!"

They cheered. That was enough for me. I spurred Rolf
and he took off. We cantered hard towards the Usurper's

men. With the departure of so many men, I could not see
how Henry and the Earl of Chester could hope to survive. I
forced myself to rein Rolf in a little. It would do no good to
reach the enemy with blown horses and a disorganized line. I
lowered my spear when we were two hundred paces from
them. I leaned forward in my saddle as I sought an enemy.
Some of those at the rear of their lines heard us and turned.
Their shouts of alarm were lost in the hubbub of the mêlée. I
pulled back my arm as the knight with the yellow surcoat
and red diagonal tried to turn his horse to face me. It was a
race against time and he was losing. I spurred Rolf and he
leapt forward. I punched hard with my spear. The knight had
turned the wrong way and my spear struck him in his right
side. I felt it grate against bone and then he was thrown from
his saddle and we were amongst them.

The dying knight's body had pulled him from my spear
and I was able to thrust it into the unprotected back of a man
at arms. He threw his arms in the air as the head tore through
his mail, gambeson and flesh. Ahead of me, I saw that we
had closed to within thirty paces of Henry and his
bodyguards who were fighting for their lives. Our sudden
drive had taken us deep into the heart of the enemy and they
had become disorganised as men fell without seeing their
foes. We had to get to Henry soon before they could rally.

Wilfred and Leopold of Durstein were ahead of me.
They had lost their spears but their swords carved a passage
for me. I saw one of Henry's bodyguards fall and a knight
with a dark blue surcoat saw his chance. He spurred his
horse into the gap. I stood in my saddle and hurled my spear
at him. I hoped to hit his body but the knight stood to deliver
the killing blow. My spear clattered into his helmet and he
fell from his horse.

I turned, "Richard! Signal the rally! On me!"

We had the chance to form a barrier of fresh warriors
before Henry. It was all that I could think of. I drew my
sword and met the mace of an angry knight who also wore a
dark blue surcoat. A mace could be deadly but my sword
was sharper. I saw wood chipped from the mace's handle. I
whipped Rolf's head around so that I faced the knight's

shield and I stood to use the longer reach of the sword. It was
not an elegant blow but I swung it sideways at head height. I
heard it ring into the helmet. I had suffered such a blow
before and knew that it disorientated a warrior. Continuing
Rolf's turn I pulled back my arm and rammed my blade into
the left side of the knight who fell from his horse.

It was now a true mêlée. There was no order. However, I
had succeeded in placing my one hundred men between
Stephen and Henry. As I turned Rolf I saw Stephen and his
bodyguards; they were racing towards me. He could end the
war in a couple of blows. He had his greatest enemy and his
greatest threat close to hand.

"Wulfric! Sir Harold! Form on me!"

If I was to fight Stephen and his bodyguards I needed my
own men around me. The two of them hacked and slashed
their way to my side. Sir Gilles of Stockton was close behind
Harold and I saw Sir John rein in next to Wulfric. Stephen
and his men reached us at a walk. They had been fighting
since morning and our mounts were slightly fresher. Battles
turn on such things. I made for Stephen. This would be
between us two. My knights would keep the others from me.

He had brought a warhorse. It was a huge black beast. If I
had been riding Edward then they would have been well
matched. Rolf was a smaller horse but he was clever. He
would have to avoid the warhorse's teeth and hooves for it
would take all of my skill to defeat Stephen. I now knew that
was what it would take to win the day.

I had fought Stephen before and knew some of his moves
but he knew mine too. I would have to outthink him if I was
to beat him. I used Rolf's nimble hooves and the fact that he
was fresher. I spurred him as I rode at Stephen's left side. I
saw him pulling his horse's head around and, at the last
moment, I jerked Rolf to the right. Stephen tried to react but
he merely confused his horse and it stumbled slightly. I took
advantage, for the Usurper had to use his left arm to control
his horse while his right flailed around to keep his balance. I
brought my sword hard across him and struck his upper arm.
I severed his mail and I saw his head reel; I had hurt him.

After bringing his horse under control he sought to take advantage of his bigger horse and he pulled back on the reins to make it rear. His men were trying to get to his side just as mine were trying to stop them and there was a maelstrom of horses and metal as they whirled around. I saw the black stallion's hooves rear and I spurred Rolf. He leapt from beneath them and then I jerked his head around. He was tiring now and I could not keep this up much longer. My move brought me up behind his left side. He knew the danger and tried to turn his horse's head. I stood in my stirrups and brought my sword down onto his shoulder. I had been aiming at his head but he was a skilful knight and he avoided the killing blow. The one I struck, however, was effective. It hurt him. I saw his shield drop and he spurred his horse away from me. I had him!

He was saved by a brave young knight who threw his horse between me and my prey. The young knight's shield faced me but as I was already standing I was able to sweep sideways and my sword struck him in the throat. He fell over the back of his cantle and lay still on the ground. Stephen's household knights had formed ranks around their leader and were taking him to the rear and safety. The sight of the banner falling back disheartened his men and they began to fall back. Some of the Earl of Chester's men shouted and cheered. As they tried to pursue I yelled, "Hold! I command you!"

They obeyed. We had bought time; that was all.

I turned and said, "Wulfric, I want a wall of knights and men at arms here. I will go and see how Henry is."

"Aye my lord." He looked at me, "You would have had him but for that young knight."

I saw him being tended to. His hand had been hit. It did not look like a serious wound and for that I was grateful. He smiled when he saw me, "I knew you would come, even if it is a little late!"

I bit back an angry retort. Now was not the time for such words. "I came as soon as I received your missive but, in truth my prince, this was a reckless and foolish action."

I saw Ranulf heading towards us as Henry shook his head and said, "No, Warlord, for now, you are here. You have defeated Stephen and we can win!"

I let my head drop and then looked him in the eye, "We have bought time that is all! We are still in grave danger. I will take command now." The Earl of Chester looked over at me. I saw him begin to open his mouth. "That is not a matter for discussion Earl. We will talk of your part in this when I have managed to save Prince Henry here!" I was angry and my eyes showed it. The Earl nodded. "Reform your lines and I will rejoin my men."

Henry said, "Thank you for coming to my aid, Warlord."

"It is my duty, lord."

Chapter 19

Leaving the Earl and the future king I turned Rolf's head around, "Good boy. Come on; one more effort eh?" I ruffled his mane and he snorted. He was not finished yet.

I reached my men. Wulfric turned, "The Usurper is still on his horse, lord, but you have discomfited him."

"Good. Richard, bring my standard and the horn. Sir Wulfric and Sir Harold, come with me and let us go speak with them. And let us pray that Dick has done as I asked."

I took off my helmet and hung it from my cantle. It was the sign that we wished to speak. We picked our way across the field. Dead horses and warriors along with the wounded were scattered all over. I saw a debate between Stephen and his knights and then Stephen took off his helmet. He and three knights came towards us with his standard-bearer. They stopped thirty paces from us. I could see he had his arm in a sling. He smiled ruefully, "I see you have not lost your touch, Alfraed."

I cocked my head to one side, "I suspect I have had more practice of late."

He nodded, "Well what is to be done? Do you surrender?"

I shook my head, "I think not. I came to ask if you wished to surrender."

William of Ypres was next to him and he spat out, "Surrender? We outnumber you! Let us fight him lord; he is finished."

"We have been outnumbered many times, William of Ypres, but you have yet to defeat me."

"You would fight on?"

I nodded, "I would although I suspect that you may wish to break off the engagement."

Stephen looked at me curiously, "You are up to something."

William of Ypres stood in his stirrups and stared around as though looking for a sudden influx of reinforcements, "I see no reason to stop."

I nodded and turned to Richard, "If you make two blasts on the horn, Richard, I think all will become clear."

The two blasts sounded louder than I had expected. William of Ypres' horse reared a little. He shook his head, "Is that supposed to make us fear you?"

"No. It was merely to tell my archers who have just captured your baggage train that I need them."

All five of them turned and looked towards the ridge which lay a mile or so behind them. At first, there was nothing and then a line of horsemen appeared. It was some distance away but I could see that there were two women mounted on horses. I did not know who it was but I took a guess. "And that, I believe is your queen. What say you Stephen of Blois? Do I have your attention now?"

William of Ypres shouted, "You would make war on a woman?"

"I thought the whole war was about that or am I missing something? You have hounded the Empress from this land and all we have done is capture your baggage train. I did not know that the Queen would come to war."

William opened his mouth and Stephen shouted, "Enough! We have been outwitted. What are your terms, Alfraed?"

"We withdraw to Chester and you to Lincoln."

"That is all?"

"For the present it is."

He spurred his horse towards me. His right arm was hurt but he held it towards me. I clasped it. We said no words. We both knew the bargain we had made and we would keep our word. He knew nothing of the King of Scotland. As far as he was concerned this was just a minor setback. I turned to Sir Harold, "Go and fetch my archers. Have them escort the Queen to her husband."

While we waited Stephen said, "You have done a good job with Henry. He fought well and he led well. A little reckless perhaps but we were all like that when we were young."

"He is a work in progress but I should not have left him. I will not make that mistake again." I saw that Harold had reached my archers and they headed towards us. "I did not see your son today."

"He is in Bury St. Edmunds. There was a rumour of rebels and malcontents there too."

"And he will be your heir?"

William of Ypres said, "He is a good leader. He will make a fine king."

Stephen's silence was eloquent. It confirmed what I had heard about his son, that he was weak and a bully. He used terror as a weapon.

Queen Matilda's face was a mask of anger, "What is all this? Finish the battle! You have not bargained our victory away for me have you?"

"I was a prisoner in Bristol. I would not have you share the same fate."

"I was in no danger! You should have fought on!"

I looked her in the eye. She was a hard woman, "But he did not and the bargain has been made. I hope your wounds heal quickly, my lord, for I have an idea that we will fight again and soon."

Stephen gave me a wry smile, "If this is all that you have then I look forward to it for we shall trounce you."

It was my turn to give an enigmatic smile, "You know not what forces we can bring. Fear not, Stephen the Usurper, it will be a battle worth remembering."

Queen Matilda spat out, "Show him some respect! He is the King and I am the Queen!"

"Not in my eyes. Come let us go back to the prince."

We turned our backs on them. Dick rode next to me and
Wulfric. I said, quietly, "Well done Dick. I knew you would
not let me down."

He nodded. "You did just bargain for the Queen did you
not, my lord?"

"I did but why do you ask?"

He grinned, "The Queen's jewels and the pay chest were
too tempting for my men. I fear that the Queen will be less
than happy when she discovers that we have taken them."

I laughed. Dick and his men were opportunistic and I
admired them for that.

Henry looked at me in anticipation as we reined in,
"Well?"

"We can withdraw to the Earl's castle and Stephen will
withdraw to Lincoln."

"Thank you. This could have been worse, I suppose."

I waved a hand at the dead and wounded, "This is not the
place to discuss the mistakes which were made. I am tired
and I might speak out of turn. If I might suggest, Earl, that
you send a rider to your castle to warn them and we need to
do something for our dead and our wounded."

It was almost midnight when we finally reached Chester.
We had buried our dead and tended to the wounded. With
my archers as a rearguard in case William of Ypres broke his
word, we trudged back to Chester.

Maud, the daughter of the Earl of Gloucester, greeted us.
"Come I have food prepared and there is straw for beds."
She hugged and kissed her husband before embracing Henry,
"I will get the healers to look at you, cousin."

"I am fine, lady."

"As you will." Then she threw her arms around me and
kissed me, "Once again you are our saviour, Alfraed! What
would we do without you?"

Maud was a real lady. She made sure that we were all
comfortable and well fed. When all had had their fill and
gone to their beds she sought me out and took me to the
battlements. "I am sorry it came to this, Alfraed. My
husband thought it for the best. He wished to emulate your
feats in the north. He wrote to Henry and promised him

Kingmaker

much. He promised him more than we had. Ranulf thought that the young prince had more men than he brought."

"Do not make excuses for him, Maud. He always makes bad decisions. However, this is my fault. I left Henry in Normandy and I should have kept him close at hand. I will not make that mistake again." I kissed her on the cheek, "Do not worry I will not take this out on your husband's skin."

She laughed but I saw relief in her eyes, "That is kind of you."

The next morning I was up early. I went to see Henry's squire, "Have your master come and speak with me when he rises."

"Aye lord."

I sent for Aiden. "Take your scouts and make sure that the enemy has gone to Lincoln. I trust Stephen but not that witch of a wife and her lackey. Keep an eye open for the men of Flanders."

I summoned my knights. "Sir Hugh, Sir Gilles of Normanby, Sir Tristan and Sir Phillip, I would have you return home to your castles. We have more than enough here for what I intend."

Sir Tristan asked, "What is wrong, lord?"

"William of Ypres. He is cunning. Knowing that we are here he might try to take Yarm or Piercebridge."

They nodded, "Then we will see that he does not."

The clattering of their hooves as they left the castle awakened Henry and he hurriedly dressed and came to see me. "Where have your men gone, Earl?"

"Back to defend my land."

He looked disappointed, "But I thought we could build up an army and take the war to my cousin."

"Henry I have been training you for some years. Have I ever given you poor advice?"

"Never Earl."

"Then trust me now. It was an error of judgement to try what you tried. You were lucky to escape with your life. You listened to someone you should not have. Ranulf Earl of Chester is a fool at best and a plotter at worst. I have time for neither and nor should you."

"It would have been well but for those traitors who deserted me!"

"Had you spent longer training them then you would have known their true worth. Perhaps this was meant to be for now you understand why I surround myself with men I trust completely." The Earl of Chester had just entered and I looked at him, "There are others that you can never trust."

Henry said nothing but his eyes followed my gaze. Ranulf strode up to me, "You spoke alone with my wife last night!"

"I did."

"Have you no honour sir? That was my wife!"

"And your wife has more courage in her little finger than you have in your whole body."

"You insult me in my own castle?"

"Each time you open your mouth, Ranulf, you insult yourself. Be quiet or leave! I have little patience left. You put Henry in jeopardy and almost undid all the work we have done to gain him the throne."

"At least I did something."

I stood and roared, "You did nothing! This was ill-conceived and badly planned! You tried to make a name for yourself at Henry's expense. The moment you sent word then Stephen knew what you were about. You tried to take on a mighty army with a half-trained rabble! You put in jeopardy all that we had worked for. Men had died to get to this point and you, for your own purposes put the prince's life in danger. I could slay you here and now and no one would question my actions!" I desperately wanted him to draw a weapon so that I could fight with him.

"It is a little early for such loud voices, my lord." We both looked around. Maud had entered. "I have sent for food and some watered wine. Perhaps that will calm tempers." I nodded. "And you, my husband, should know that I can meet alone with the Earl of Cleveland because he is a friend and the most trustworthy knight in Christendom. I am more than capable of defending my own honour!"

I sat and said, "I am sorry, Countess, for my outburst. Put it down to tiredness. I fear we will have to impose upon you for a few more days. Henry needs to heal as do many of our men."

"Of course."

Henry asked, "Where do we go? Do we head for the south and those lands which are still loyal to my mother?"

"No, we go to see King David of Scotland. I have made peace with him and he will support your claim to the throne. When we have met with him then we will be a step closer to the crown. I will make you king yet."

Epilogue

Richard's dubbing would have to wait. Our journey north to visit with King David was far more important. We spent a week deciding which men at arms and knights Henry would retain and then, taking the Earl of Chester and his wife with us, we headed north towards Carlisle. I had wondered if I should tell Ranulf of our plans but I knew that I would have to. If I did not then he might have used that as another excuse to change sides.

Aiden had returned to give me the news that Stephen had kept his word. I was relieved. I had no desire to have my land ravaged by a vengeful William of Ypres. I had no doubt that he might still wish to seek revenge but with my castles on the border manned once more then I was confident that he would not succeed. Aiden and his scouts returned to the valley where their vigilance would give my castles warning of any danger.

We rode north through balmy blue skies and the sight of crops burgeoning in the fields. It was a sign of hope. The land was fruitful. For many years, during the anarchy, the fields had been filled with weeds. It was as though the land was cleansing itself. We had almost had a disaster but it had been averted. Perhaps God was on our side.

I rode next to Henry and continued my teaching as we headed north. I noticed that he listened more. He had thought himself ready to be king and allowed poisonous words to turn his head. Now he knew that the advice I gave was sage.

"Can we beat Stephen on the field of battle, Earl?"

"Aye, we can. You proved that at Rushton Spencer. You held off a greater force and did so with great courage."

"But men deserted me."

"Some men deserted you but reflect on this; more men stayed. We need to build an army and we need to build alliances. The one with Scotland is the second. Hainaut may

246

not have many men to send to us but their timely warning saved your kingdom. We will make more alliances and isolate Stephen. All is not well with his son."

He nodded eagerly, "I know. I heard that he has terrorised Bury St. Edmunds."

I shook my head, "Henry, do not take pleasure in the suffering of your people. If anything happened to Stephen then Eustace might be crowned King. His mother is ruthless. There is a bridge we have yet to cross. But one thing is sure. I will not now let you from my sight until you are crowned in Westminster Abbey. I will make a king of you yet."

He grinned, "Amen to that Earl!"

The End

Glossary

Al-Andalus- Spain
Aldeneby - Alston (Cumbria)
Angevin- the people of Anjou, mainly the ruling family
Arthuret -Longtown in Cumbria (This is the Brythionic name)
Battle- a formation in war (a modern battalion)
Booth Castle – Bewcastle north of Hadrian's Wall
Butts- targets for archers
Cadge- the frame upon which hunting birds are carried (by a codger- hence the phrase old codger being the old man who carries the frame)
Cadwaladr ap Gruffudd- Son of Gruffudd ap Cynan
Captain- a leader of archers
Chausses - mail leggings. (They were separate- imagine lady's stockings!)
Conroi- A group of knights fighting together. The smallest unit of the period
Demesne- estate
Destrier- war horse
Doxy- prostitute
Fess- a horizontal line in heraldry
Fissebourne- Fishburn County Durham
Galloglass- Irish mercenaries
Gambeson- a padded tunic worn underneath mail. When worn by an archer they came to the waist. It was more of a quilted jacket but I have used the term freely
Gonfanon- A standard used in Medieval times (Also known as a Gonfalon in Italy)
Gruffudd ap Cynan- King of Gwynedd until 1137
Hartness- the manor which became Hartlepool
Hautwesel- Haltwhistle
Liedeberge- Ledbury
Lusitania- Portugal
Mansio- staging houses along Roman Roads
Maredudd ap Bleddyn- King of Powys
Martinmas- 11th November

Kingmaker

Mêlée- a medieval fight between knights
Moravians- the men of Moray
Mormaer- A Scottish lord and leader
Mummer- an actor from a medieval tableau
Musselmen- Muslims
Nithing- A man without honour (Saxon)
Nomismata- a gold coin equivalent to an aureus
Outremer- the kingdoms of the Holy Land
Owain ap Gruffudd- Son of Gruffudd ap Cynan and King of
Gwynedd from 1137
Palfrey- a riding horse
Poitevin- the language of Aquitaine
Pyx- a box containing a holy relic (Shakespeare's Pax from
Henry V)
Refuge- a safe area for squires and captives (tournaments)
Sauve qui peut – Every man for himself (French)
Sergeant-a leader of a company of men at arms
Serengford- Shellingford Oxfordshire
Surcoat- a tunic worn over mail or armour
Sumpter- packhorse
Ventail – a piece of mail that covered the neck and the lower
face.
Wulfestun- Wolviston (Durham)

Maps and Illustrations

Historical note

This is a work of fiction. I have used real events as the backdrop for a story about a fictional character. I have tried to be as accurate as I can but I have made minor changes to dates and amalgamated the actions of some characters into one. I make no apologies for this. I am a storyteller.

r. For those interested, I have put the links to three sites so that you can compare them for yourself.

http://www.historic-uk.com/HistoryUK/HistoryofEngland/Empress-Maud/
https://en.wikipedia.org/wiki/Oxford_Castle
https://en.wikipedia.org/wiki/Empress_Matilda
Following 1147 and until Henry arrives in England in 1149 the war went into a quiet phase. Barons and earls consolidated what they had. The battles were smaller in nature. The Earl of Gloucester did die peacefully and the fates of her leaders are as I wrote.

The meeting with King David and Henry did take place. I have just brought it forward by a few months. The next book will be the last one to reference the anarchy and will begin with the fateful meeting with King David. The series will, however, continue for William of Stockton is now a crusader!

Books used in the research:

The Varangian Guard- 988-1453 Raffael D'Amato
Saxon Viking and Norman- Terence Wise
The Walls of Constantinople AD 324-1453-Stephen Turnbull
Byzantine Armies- 886-1118- Ian Heath
The Age of Charlemagne-David Nicolle
The Normans- David Nicolle
Norman Knight AD 950-1204- Christopher Gravett
The Norman Conquest of the North- William A Kappelle
The Knight in History- Francis Gies
The Norman Achievement- Richard F Cassady
Knights- Constance Brittain Bouchard

Knight Templar 1120-1312 -Helen Nicholson
Feudal England: Historical Studies on the Eleventh and
Twelfth Centuries- J. H. Round
Armies of the Crusades-Helen Nicholson
Knight of Outremer 1187- 1344 - David Nicholle

Griff Hosker
November 2016

Kingmaker

Other books by Griff Hosker

If you enjoyed reading this book, then why not read
another one by the author?

Ancient History

The Sword of Cartimandua Series
(Germania and Britannia 50 A.D. – 128 A.D.)
Ulpius Felix- Roman Warrior (prequel)
The Sword of Cartimandua
The Horse Warriors
Invasion Caledonia
Roman Retreat
Revolt of the Red Witch
Druid's Gold
Trajan's Hunters
The Last Frontier
Hero of Rome
Roman Hawk
Roman Treachery
Roman Wall
Roman Courage

The Wolf Warrior series
(Britain in the late 6th Century)
Saxon Dawn
Saxon Revenge
Saxon England
Saxon Blood
Saxon Slayer
Saxon Slaughter
Saxon Bane
Saxon Fall: Rise of the Warlord
Saxon Throne
Saxon Sword

Medieval History

The Dragon Heart Series
Viking Slave
Viking Warrior
Viking Jarl
Viking Kingdom
Viking Wolf
Viking War
Viking Sword
Viking Wrath
Viking Raid
Viking Legend
Viking Vengeance
Viking Dragon
Viking Treasure
Viking Enemy
Viking Witch
Viking Blood
Viking Weregeld
Viking Storm
Viking Warband
Viking Shadow
Viking Legacy
Viking Clan
Viking Bravery

The Norman Genesis Series
Hrolf the Viking
Horseman
The Battle for a Home
Revenge of the Franks
The Land of the Northmen
Ragnvald Hrolfsson
Brothers in Blood
Lord of Rouen
Drekar in the Seine
Duke of Normandy
The Duke and the King

Kingmaker

Danelaw
(England and Denmark in the 11th Century)
Dragon Sword
Oathsword

New World Series
Blood on the Blade
Across the Seas
The Savage Wilderness
The Bear and the Wolf
Erik The Navigator

The Vengeance Trail

The Reconquista Chronicles
Castilian Knight
El Campeador
The Lord of Valencia

The Aelfraed Series
(Britain and Byzantium 1050 A.D. - 1085 A.D.)
Housecarl
Outlaw
Varangian

The Anarchy Series England
1120-1180
English Knight
Knight of the Empress
Northern Knight
Baron of the North
Earl
King Henry's Champion
The King is Dead
Warlord of the North
Enemy at the Gate
The Fallen Crown
Warlord's War

Kingmaker
Henry II
Crusader
The Welsh Marches
Irish War
Poisonous Plots
The Princes' Revolt
Earl Marshal
The Perfect Knight

Border Knight
1182-1300
Sword for Hire
Return of the Knight
Baron's War
Magna Carta
Welsh Wars
Henry III
The Bloody Border
Baron's Crusade
Sentinel of the North
War in the West
Debt of Honour
The Blood of the Warlord (Feb 2022)

Sir John Hawkwood Series
France and Italy 1339- 1387
Crécy: The Age of the Archer
Man At Arms
The White Company

Lord Edward's Archer
Lord Edward's Archer
King in Waiting
An Archer's Crusade
Targets of Treachery
The Great Cause (April 2022)

Struggle for a Crown

Kingmaker

1360- 1485
Blood on the Crown
To Murder a King
The Throne
King Henry IV
The Road to Agincourt
St Crispin's Day
The Battle For France
The Last Knight
Queen's Knight

Tales from the Sword I
(Short stories from the Medieval period)

Tudor Warrior series
England and Scotland in the late 14th and early 15th
century
Tudor Warrior

Conquistador
England and America in the 16th Century
Conquistador

Modern History

The Napoleonic Horseman Series
Chasseur à Cheval
Napoleon's Guard
British Light Dragoon
Soldier Spy
1808: The Road to Coruña
Talavera
The Lines of Torres Vedras
Bloody Badajoz
The Road to France
Waterloo

The Lucky Jack American Civil War series
Rebel Raiders

Kingmaker

Confederate Rangers
The Road to Gettysburg

The British Ace Series
1914
1915 Fokker Scourge
1916 Angels over the Somme
1917 Eagles Fall
1918 We will remember them
From Arctic Snow to Desert Sand
Wings over Persia

Combined Operations series
1940-1945
Commando
Raider
Behind Enemy Lines
Dieppe
Toehold in Europe
Sword Beach
Breakout
The Battle for Antwerp
King Tiger
Beyond the Rhine
Korea
Korean Winter

Tales from the Sword II
(Short stories from the Modern period)

Other Books
Great Granny's Ghost (Aimed at 9-14-year-old young
people)

For more information on all of the books then please visit the
author's website at www.griffhosker.com where there is a
link to contact him or visit his Facebook page: GriffHosker
at Sword Books